Also by John Galligan

Red Sky, Red Dragonfly

The Nail Knot

The Blood Knot

THE CLINCH KNOT

THE CLINCH KNOT

A Fly Fishing Mystery

John Galligan

Bleak House Books
Madison, Wisconsin

Published by
BLEAK HOUSE BOOKS
a division of Big Earth Publishing
923 Williamson St.
Madison, WI 53703
www.bleakhousebooks.com

This is a work of fiction.
Any similarities to people or places, living or dead, is purely coincidental.

Library of Congress Cataloging-in-Publication Data has been applied for.

ISBN 13: 978-1-60648-003-8 (Trade Cloth)
ISBN 13: 978-1-60648-004-5 (Trade Paper)
ISBN 13: 978-1-60648-005-2 (Evidence Collection)

Printed in the United States of America

12 11 10 09 08   1 2 3 4 5 6 7 8 9 10

In memory of Leroy Aserlind,

that he might read this in the Big Sky.

Always the Question

And then my kid fishing buddy, D'Ontario Sneed, shakes his head, rotates his beer bottle. He says, "Not my mama. My mama's nothing to me. My mama went to prison."

And this drunk girl, this local girl, this white girl, Jesse, says, "Hey! Really?" She lurches closer to Sneed. She sinks her fingers into the darkness of his arm. "This is wild. You're not going to believe this. This is so wild. My *daddy's* in prison!"

As for me, the Dog, when I think back to that moment—the Stockman tavern, Livingston, Montana, in the hot shank of August—I can't determine whether to laugh or cry. I guess when two people decide to fall in love, any reason will do.

And Sneed and Jesse were in love, I guess, depending on how you define it. I still want to believe that.

But isn't that always the question?

What is love?

Is this it?

Right here?

Now?

The Radishes Clarify

"So . . . uh . . ."

The young man's mouth goes sticky-dry. He shifts the fly rod to his shoulder, like a rifle. But that doesn't feel right, so he bombs the reel to the toe of his left boot. I hear the clunk and observe that it's a steel-toed boot. As in *Earth to Dog: he's going fishing in steel-toed boots.* But I'm deep in composition—I'm writing a goodbye note to Sneed and Jesse—and I think nothing of steel-toed boots. The young man stares down toward his boots and his reel. I stare too, yet I fail to notice there's no line on the reel. His nervous throat pumps.

"So . . . uh . . . you would, I mean, if you . . . were me . . ."

"In this heat I'd go after some cutthroat."

"Cutthroat . . ."

"Sure. They're easier to catch."

He looks up. Above us is the wide Montana sky, blurred and freighted with the smoke from a half-dozen forest fires. I focus on my scrap of grocery sack. I'm thinking to start like this, *Dear Friends. It's been a great three weeks. You ran the old Dog hard . . .* But this raw kid before me stammers, "How . . . how . . . how . . ."

"Where?"

"Yeah. Where."

Distracted, I lift my gaze to the mountains around us. There are a hundred streams, a thousand. What kind of question is *where?* The kid flinches and looks behind for the truck that brought him here. It's a red Ford half-ton pickup from the 80's, faded to pink. But his partner has followed the campground track and looped the truck around the back side of my Cruise Master RV, out of sight.

You ran the old Dog hard. I had the time of my life . . .

But this sounds mealy mouthed, doesn't it? I back up. The truth is I've become a third wheel. Sneed and Jesse are going at it like jackrabbits. They hardly fish with me any more. Jesse's using the Cruise Master like her personal walk-in closet. They're calling me Uncle Dog—goddamn it—and they say they're kidding and I try to believe it, but I'm starting to drink in the mornings, starting to drink on the stream, drinking everywhere. I guess there is something about happiness, about love, and family, about time passing around me that makes me sad.

Dear Sneed and Jesse. I'm moving on. Thanks for everything. Good luck . . .

But that sounds like sour huckleberries, and this fool kid in steel-toed boots still waits on the mystery of where to fish. He is raw and ugly as a pulled-up root, pale white with sunburned ears and neck. Because I am drinking, in fact, at this very moment— a mid-morning vodka with Tang—this kid strikes me as looking very much like a radish.

This makes me laugh inside. I feel better. I point toward the Gallatins, down by Wyoming. "Go up in there, any creek. Far as you can go. Most of it's Forest Service land. No fires yet that I know of. You park and hike."

He clears his throat and squirms. As I look the radish over, wondering why he will not leave, I somehow miss the wrongness of the fly rod matched with the shaved head. I gloss right over the tight Wrangler jeans and the wife-beater tee-shirt stenciled in crossed claw hammers. I stare at all of this. My eyes connect. But I just don't see it. I am a trout bum, not a fashion critic, and a person can fish in just about anything. Hell, Jesse, bless her troubled heart, fishes in a bikini, sunscreen, and Tevas. That works. But those boots, black leather, laced almost to the knee—I'm not sure.

So I swallow v-and-T and I ask the radish, "Those boots are steel-toed?"

He gapes down at his boots, then clenches his jaw. His temples pulse.

"Is there a problem with that?"

"Heavy."

"So?"

"You won't hike very far in those. Plus, you walk in the water all day they're going to rust."

He looks for the buddy, the truck. Then his eyes skid back to me. I think he's trying to read my note to Sneed and Jesse. "I'm good," he says. "It's not a problem."

I take a warm orange sip of v-and-T from my tin cup, tasting all the vitamins.

"I'm just suggesting those aren't the best boots for fishing."

"I said I'm good."

He jerks his head around, looking for his buddy. But the pink pickup is still hidden behind the Cruise Master, its engine noise lost beneath the heavy purl of the Yellowstone River, water flowing on and on behind me, an eternal freight train of water. I wonder if the old pickup has stalled back there, behind the Cruise Master, and a stalled vehicle gets me thinking of Sneed and Jesse. Jesse's battered Oldsmobile is a compendium of maintenance failures, among them a coolant leak. Did they break down?

How about this? *Kids: Gotta go. Take care. Safe sex and all. Uncle Dog.*

Sure. Capture that jauntiness. Devil may care. But a bolt of sadness clobbers me, right there in front of the radish. My vision blurs, my chin quivers. I have to close my eyes and breathe like some verklempt old dame, and while doing this a voice asks me: *Why can't you just tell them the truth?*

The radish is still there. He raises a hand to scratch a botched tattoo on his shoulder. The tattoo is an Iron Cross. I see the Iron Cross—but I don't see it. All I say is, "So good luck to you."

Then I look at my watch. It is now one o'clock. I have been laboring for three hours on a ten-word note. Sneed and Jesse drive guide-shuttle for a local outfitter, this shady operator named Hilarious Sorgensen, and they should have been back to camp an hour ago, ready to spend their fifty bucks a day on beer and take-out, condoms, weed and fishing tackle.

The truth being this: I have come to care for them, Sneed and Jesse, and in this state of sentimentality I have lost focus and momentum. I am stuck and all too close to happy. And lately, I mis-read water. I miss takes. I fish the wrong flies, too distracted or too lazy to change. My loop collapses in the thinnest of breezes, and I wrap line, daily, around my own dizzy head. I'm hooking whitefish, chubs, huckleberry bushes, my own ears. And I am laughing about it all, like it doesn't matter, sitting in the sun and laughing while fish rise around me. This has to stop. It has to. It confuses me.

And so it will stop. I chuck the rest of my vodka-Tang down the hatch. "Good luck," I say to the kid again. I put a shove in my voice: "Have a good one."

But *still* he stands there, this scrawny, quivering, steel-toed rad-ish who wants to fly fish.

"But which . . . which . . . which . . ." the radish stammers, glancing toward the Cruise Master.

"Cutthroat don't care which fly. Here."

I pluck a Madame X from the mess-kit dish on my picnic table. This outfitter, Hilarious Sorgensen, has me groping for cash too. I've tied a hundred Madame X for the big man on spec, a buck apiece. There is even some chance, Sneed and Jesse say, that Sorgensen will live up to the deal and pay me.

So cash in, Dog. Gas up. Go.

I push the big attractor fly across the table. I glance over my shoulder to see if finally the pink pickup has emerged around the Cruise Master.

But no.

I stand.

"Tie this on for you?"

The radish tilts the rod out of my reach. Now, finally, I comprehend that his reel has no line. He says, "I'm good."

"Your reel has no line."

"I said I'm good."

I shrug. I put the Madame X in his palm. There is a different tattoo in there—under green-white skin—but he keeps his fingers bent and the tattoo crunched up.

I ask him, "You know the clinch knot?"

"Yeah." He shoves the hook point into the rod cork.

"You sure?"

"Yeah I'm sure."

I say, "That's a beautiful old rod. They don't make them like that anymore. Can I take a quick look? Thanks. Wow. Lovely."

To which the young man mutters a word that I swear sounds like *faggot*. But this can't be right. This is not possible, I think. What cause? I'm a faggot because I like his rod? Probably it is this: always, my ears are the first ones drunk. The river is loud behind me. I believe I have misheard the radish.

But now, at last, the pickup noses out from behind the Cruise Master, and I get a better look. The truck has rusted wheel pits, an oil drum in the bed, a confederate flag decal on the box window. The driver is a bigger, rounder radish. I smell smoke suddenly, acrid, like plastic burning. The driver wears a flushed and lurid grin. He hollers, "Come on, Dumbshit. We're outta here. Get in the truck."

The radishes clarify for me suddenly. The driver is the chief radish. Assistant radish jerks and twitches before me, conflicted because I now hold his rod as a hostage. "What the hell is going on?" I demand. Because something is wrong here. Something has gone down, back behind the Cruise Master.

The assistant radish lunges, reaches out that tattooed hand and snatches at the rod. He gets the tip. Fiberglass snaps, he gets half the rod, runs.

"Hey—!"

My legs are trapped between the bench and the picnic table. I have to unwind and step high. I'm a little wobbly and way too late to grab him. Assistant radish gallops around the pink Ford, kicking up dust. He chucks the ruined fly rod into the truck bed, where it cartwheels over the oil drum and disappears with a clatter.

"Hey! What the—?"

Chief radish hits the gas. The pickup spews gravel along the campground track, fishtails up the drive, and roars off down the highway in the direction opposite those easy cutthroat trout. For good measure, chief radish lets go of the wheel. Both hands out the window, flips me a double bird as the pickup thunders away.

Dog damn it.

I wobble to the Cruise Master and then around it. Skinheads. That's what they were. Skinheads. And Sneed's little tent is on fire—has already flared down to a ring of smoldering nylon around a flaming heap of clothes and blankets, ground pads melting beneath.

The galley door to my Cruise Master RV is open. My meager trout bum possessions are strewn. Jesse's things have been yanked off their hangers. Bras and tops and panties, cargo shorts and t-shirts have been slung across my gritty floor and down the portable steps. All these things are wet and smell funny, as if they have been—I sniff—sure enough, Jesse's clothes have been peed on.

Those were skinheads.

Then, kicking dirt over the fire, I see the text of their message. Against the hot rocks the skinheads have left an orange-black sign that screams NO TRESPASSING.

I flip it over.

The message continues. The reverse side, in handwritten marker, tells someone—Sneed and Jesse I presume, black boy and white girl—*Turn back now!*

The Actual Sheriff

I flag a motorist, borrow a cell phone, and wait forty minutes. During that awful patch of time, I discover that the fat skinhead, the driver, has been under my sink too, into my lock box, and has taken my last two hundred bucks and my Glock semi-automatic pistol—all while I dithered over vodka-Tang, farewell phrasings, and the other punk's now-obvious inability to feign interest in fishing.

Dog damn it.

And where, by now, are Sneed and Jesse? They should be back.

Park County sends the big hitter. At first, when he pulls that blue-on-bronze cruiser up too close to my toes and rasps at me, "Roy Chubbuck, Sheriff," I take this as a sign that this kind of thing matters in the county, that heads will roll. Hate crime, right? Under the guise of fly fishing. What could be more sordid, more wrong? Bring on the actual sheriff.

"Skinheads," I tell him. "They were skinheads."

Sheriff Roy Chubbuck wheezes at the window of his cruiser, pants faintly through thin, cracked lips. The man looks like a turkey buzzard on life support. He is skeletal and red-faced, stooped at the neck. On his back, wedged against the seat, he wears an oxygen pack. Tubes, thin and clear, lead into his nostrils.

"Well, now . . . let's start with who you are. You got a driver's license?"

"I still can't believe it," I go on. "They had the haircuts, the tattoos—"

Something in the sheriff's manner stops me, tells me we are not exchanging astonishments or pleasantries, not even for five seconds. He cocks his head, fixes me with his furthest eye, the right one, imperious blue inside its dropsied red lid. His cruiser remains in drive, engine humming, front tire not six inches from my feet.

"Driver's license?"

"Yeah. Sure. Hang on."

As I reach for my wallet, I hear gravel crunch. I look away toward the road. I am hoping to see Jesse's golden Olds. Maybe Sneed saw pronghorns and they stopped to watch. But as I hand in my license to Sheriff Chubbuck, I see instead a black SUV up where the campground road meets the highway. The vehicle is brand new. It has tinted windows, multiple antennae, themeless bland-blue plates that could be government. It turns around in the campground driveway and lingers, sun glinting off its south-facing windshield.

"You're a long way from home," the sheriff tells me.

"Fishing trip."

"Not enough fishing out East?"

I wonder how to respond to that. The sheriff keeps that sharp blue eye on me, taking oxygen through his veined and scabby nose, waiting for an answer.

"As a matter of fact," I decide to say, "no. Not for the number of people. But that's not really why—"

"Just giving you a hard time," he cuts in, with no trace of humor. "We're proud of our fishing out here."

He returns to his study of my license. Only that right eye seems to work, drawing a bead on my real name—Ned Oglivie—and below that upon assorted other claims, mostly false. I no longer reside at 223 Thurber Lane in West Newton, Massachusetts, but instead in the 1984 Cruise Master RV, strung with laundry and baking in the sun and dust just behind me. My once-brown eyes are mostly red now, and I can no longer assert myself at a healthy one-hundred and ninety pounds, not even with my waders full of water. It is also no longer true, obviously, that I wear suits and groom myself and smile for the camera.

Nope. I am the Dog now. I am a trout hound. I fish, I drive, I fish, I drive, I fish. I follow my nose. Not to wax poetic about it, but I dig holes. I scratch myself. I howl at the moon, and I know where I will go to die. I am also, for the record, a pretty decent fly fisherman.

"Well," the sheriff rasps finally, looking from me to the picture on the license and back again, "you've still got your height."

"They were skinheads," I tell him. "They got my pistol and my cash, but that's not what worries me."

No answer except to file my license between two knobby knuckles and put the Park County cruiser in reverse. He makes an adjustment of about fifteen degrees in the angle of the car's long snout and then begins to navigate at low speed along a vector between the picnic table and the Cruise Master.

I pace alongside. "See, my buddy Sneed is a black man."

"Good for him."

I squeeze ahead around the corners of the table. "And this local girl, Jesse—"

"I know Jesse."

"She—"

"Everybody knows Jesse."

He feathers the brake, pauses alongside the front end of the Cruise Master. He turns his neck to keep that right eye in play. As it happens, it's laundry day for the Dog. A ragg wool sock dries over each extended wiper. The side mirror wears my extra boxers. My spare pants hang wet by a belt loop over the radio antenna.

"Been out a while, Mister Oglivie?"

"Four years."

"Hmm," the sheriff says. "Catch anything?"

"A few."

Again he starts the cruiser rolling. I hear another crunch of gravel on the high road—but it is more false hope. It's that same black SUV, pulling ten feet ahead, keeping us in sight while the sheriff does more geometry with the car nose, cutting closely between the bug-spattered grill of the Cruise Master and a lodge pole pine grievously wounded by the hatchet of a previous camper. Now, without leaving his vehicle, the sheriff is in full view of the crime scene.

I tell him, "The truck came around here, paused for a long time, five minutes maybe, and then—"

He interrupts. "Dry season—" his nose pulls at the tubes "—no fires."

"Sure. Okay. But—"

"Looks to me like an illegal camp fire got out of control."

"But my friends didn't—"

"Aren't those marshmallows?" the sheriff rasps. That sharp right eye is on the crusts of Jesse's Jet-Puffs from last night, melted over the fire-blackened stones. My heart jumps a little. I glance about as if in search of a witness. *What's going on?* But there are only trees, stones, the Yellowstone River, that glinting black vehicle up at the road.

"Sheriff, I smelled the smoke. The tent was burning when I came around here. And what about the sign? They left a message, for God's sake."

He pulls the cruiser forward so he can look out his window directly down on the melted ruins of Sneed and Jesse's little love nest. Then he pulls farther forward and painstakingly turns around beneath the wounded pine, as if to take another angle. I realize this: he does not plan to leave the vehicle. Not for skinheads.

"Could have been roots," he says. He coughs. "They smolder underground."

"What the—?"

"Where'd you find that sign?" he wants to know.

I'm dripping sweat now, my jaw clamped tight. I show him. The sign was propped on the fire pit rocks—and this proves, doesn't it, that the fire didn't spread from there to the tent? At least over-ground? And that root theory is asinine, a fraud.

He says, "You moved the sign. Picked it up. Is that correct?"

I glare back into that beady blue eye.

"Did you witness them leave the sign there, Mister Oglivie, where you said it was?"

"No. I didn't."

"Well, then . . ."

"I was talking to the other guy. He was distracting me. Pretending he wanted to fich. Licten, Sheriff "

But his window hums up, closes tight. *Not listening.* I watch him make a call on his radio, speak back and forth for about a minute. I'm looking up at the SUV on the road, wondering, when another one pulls up, this one midnight blue and streaked with Montana's powdery dust. The two vehicles pair up opposite, like horses swatting each other's flies. The sheriff's window hums down.

"Mister Oglivie, was your pistol registered?"

"Yes."

"When was the last time you knew for certain—" he pauses, needs O_2 "—for certain that your pistol was where it was supposed to be?"

I want to lie to him. I *should* lie to him. Something is wrong here. But my mouth skids ahead of my brain and my answer comes out straight. I haven't opened my lock box, haven't needed cash or laid eyes on the Glock, for two or three days.

"So it could have been taken yesterday," says Chubbuck. "Or the day before."

He exhales through his dry, pursed lips, watching me squirm. Then he looks at my license again. He moves his head to read, scans like a bird tracking ants back and forth across the ground. He passes my license back with a trembling hand.

I blurt, "Well?" I open my arms to the crime scene, implying the concurrence of factors here, the undeniable entirety. "Are you going to do something, Sheriff?"

"Yes, I am," he says. His radio squawks and he turns it down. "Mister Oglivie, I'm going to give you a warning."

"What?"

"Your license is expired. More than a year ago. You're driving illegally."

I stare at the damn license. So *I'm* the problem here. *I'm* the lawbreaker. Suddenly I could spit on the man, strike him, but I command myself not to.

"Pretty sizable ticket in that," the sheriff says.

"Yeah. Well. I'm sorry. I didn't realize."

"But I'm gonna let you drive out of here with just a warning." The Park County Sheriff takes a sniff from his tubes. "And here is that warning: from the look of you, you got some water that needs fishing at home. So go home, Mister Oglivie. Directly. And fish your own water."

He hits the button and his window starts up.

"But what about the—"

His window fits me neatly out. At the wheel, patiently, the sheriff executes a sine, cosine, arc-tangent maneuver and somehow inches out between the injured pine and a steep scree of brush and rock that climbs to the heat-struck highway, where the SUVs have unpaired and split to flank the campground drive.

Chubbuck pulls his cruiser up between them. For a long moment he hesitates there. At last he pulls out and trails the dusty blue vehicle south, toward Yellowstone Park, while the clean black one speeds away toward Livingston.

"—what about the skinheads?" I finish.

Then I answer myself.

Sneed and Jesse. Before you leave. Warn them.

A Chump, An Old-Timer, An Uncle

"I'm looking for Sneed."

"You got my order done?"

"Count 'em."

I submit a family-size Tang can, net contents one hundred Madame X. These are large dry flies, terrestrials, Gothic grasshoppers on steroids. An outfitter like Hilarious Sorgensen gets two-fifty each from his clientele of mostly dentists and doctors and veterinarians from mostly the east and the Midwest.

"A hundred exactly?" Sorgensen, like all cheaters, is by nature suspicious. "You know I'll have Lyndzee count 'em."

I look for Lyndzee, his wasted little harpy, but today she doesn't seem to be around among the fly bins and landing nets and racks of hats and sunglasses.

"Go ahead. Count. You owe me a hundred bucks."

"End of the month," he tries.

I take the can back. "Okay. If I can't sell them to Armstrong's or Bailey's by then I'll be back."

"Sheesh! Godalmighty!" Sorgensen is an ex-rodeo clown. He goes over the top in a hurry. "I'm a businessman, not a cash machine! Crimenently, fella! Why don't you just come in here with a gun and stick me up?"

This guy makes me tired. Jesse says a speed habit causes his fat. Pain from broken bones keeps him inactive, so he eats incessantly, mostly peanuts, to knock down the amphetamine buzz. These cling to his lips now, fragments of peanut, they hang in his beard. I have to look away.

"I'll come back if the others don't want them."

"Seventy-five bucks," he offers.

"You promised a hundred."

"Sheesh. I tell you."

He opens a drawer beneath his cluttered desk and counts out my money, relieving himself of tattered ones and wrinkled fives and finishing me off with a foursome of Canadian quarters.

I push the quarters back. "Actually, it's only ninety-nine. I gave one fly to a skinhead. So where'd Sneed and Jesse go today?"

Hilarious Sorgensen swivels in his groaning desk chair, peers red-eyed over his reading glasses, then chucks a handful of Planters into his maw and struggles to stand. I step back. He wears some kind of filthy culottes made at a tent shop. He uses plastic leg braces and a burl-wood cane, his bare legs like shaky columns of cottage cheese.

"Sneed? And Jesse? Crimenently."

This morning, upright, Sorgensen looks jittery and more soiled than usual, like he's fallen down and been stepped on by a bull. Maybe Lyndzee's out of town then, as she so often seems to be. When that happens, Sorgensen has to track everything himself: match the clients with the guides, assign the shuttle drivers, confirm the drop-off points, distribute the lunches, pay out his shuttle drivers when they finish: fifty cents a mile—minus haggling, cheating, odometer disputes, all of Sorgensen's tricks.

"Didn't them two tell you what they did?" he asks me.

"Apparently not."

"I fired those kids nearly a week ago."

"What?"

"They stole a rod from a guide's vehicle. A custom-made Sweetgrass bamboo, worth a couple thou. Trust is everything in this business, what with us handling everybody's keys. I had to let them go."

"They didn't tell me."

I flounder for a moment. This hurts me. It humiliates me. Sneed and Jesse didn't say a thing. They kept "going to work" in the morning, treating me, I guess, like a chump, an old-timer, an uncle, no kidding about it. Oh well, I manage to tell myself after a moment or two, all the more reason to go, Dog, go.

I ask Sorgensen, "You tell the cops?"

"The cops?" In goes a handful of Planters. "Hah. Never."

"You got a pen and paper?"

"What for?"

"In case they come back for some reason. I want to leave a note. Let them know about the skinheads."

Sorgensen looks uncommonly reflective for a few seconds. Or maybe a peanut is stuck in his teeth. Then I realize that while he does have pen and paper, those items are on his desk, and he has just stood up. This would be akin, I guess, to arranging several hundred pounds of books on a shelf and then discovering that the shelf needed moving.

"Lyndzee's out of town?" I ask him.

"Yeah. Death in the family."

"Another one?"

"Yeah. It's tough."

I try to picture Lyndzee with a family, wearing a funeral dress, with her squinty eyes and her mad voice, her sad dry-gulch cleavage and her cloud of Parliament smoke. But the picture, like Lyndzee herself, never quite comes to focus.

"Stay put," I tell Sorgensen. "I'll grab what I need."

I find a pen and a scrap of paper on his desk. Behind me Sorgensen mutters faintly *skinheads*, then chuckles over the idea, then just waits and breathes hard and smells like sweat and grime and burped-up peanuts while I try again to write the note.

Private Water

Dear Sneed and Jesse: I decided to hit the road. It's been great. Your tent was burned by a couple of skinhead punks and the sheriff doesn't seem at all concerned, so I'd watch out. Jesse, I washed your clothes and dropped them off with Uncle Judith at the liquor store. Take care. Keep your flies on the water. Your friend, Dog.

But this doesn't feel right either. This voice feels glib, disembodied from the secret gravity of my leaving, dismissive of the sediment amassing in my gut.

I park on a side street to avoid the sheriff. I hike to the liquor store down Main Street with an unwieldy armload of Jesse's clothing. I spill a stiff burgundy bra onto the sidewalk and have to kick it along when no one is looking. *You're botching this, Dog. You're botching it.*

Old Tick Judith, clerk at the liquor store, is the Arnold Palmer of snoose. He sees me coming through the door and nails his spittoon, drops it right in the cup, from a difficult lie among the cordials. "So they broke up, huh?"

"No. I'm leaving. Jesse's stuff was in my vehicle. I don't know where they are."

"Figured they'd break up soon."

"Well," I said, "they didn't."

"Jess ain't over the last guy," says Uncle Judith. "Not by a long shot. So I figured this would happen."

"Except it didn't."

He scrapes out his lip, tees up a fresh one, wipes his fingers on his Levis. He's a Copenhagen man, fine cut, old school, takes pinches big as walnuts, and is thus a spitter not a swallower. He sets a plastic fifth of Smirnoff's vodka on the counter, drops a routine putt into the spittoon to clear his voice. "Twenty-nine bucks. Jess and that colored fella have a fight or something?"

"Not that I know of."

"Bound to happen."

I give Tick Judith a look-over, wonder about his hearing. He is not Jesse's real uncle. He is a close pal of her father's from the bull riding days, a short, wiry, hot-tempered scrapper who hung on to his bulls like a tick—trophies back among the Grand Marnier and the Galliano to prove it. Uncle Judith is like her other father, Jesse has told me. He is her guardian, provided her crash pad until she was eighteen, all that. And sure enough, the old bull rider accepts the girl's laundry like it's part of the deal.

"She's an adult now," Uncle Judith tells me, folding a tube top. "I can't do nothing but watch." He now has a bit of a dogleg from the end of the counter to the spittoon beneath the register. He spits with a slice and bangs it in. "But I assure you that I do watch. Anybody hurts Jess is gonna answer to me. I promised that to Galen."

I pay for the vodka out of Sorgensen's money. I figure I'm going to need it. I figure, also, that this is the man to ask: "You know anything about skinheads around here?"

He grins, juicy and brown, over a handful of Jesse's panties. "You mean them two dickheads with the pink truck that bought twenty-five cases of Heinekens on Tucker's account the other day?"

"I probably do."

"Tattoos?"

"Yup."

"Knee-boots like a couple of prairie whores?"

"Yeah. What do you mean, Tucker's account? Those two little Nazis work for Dane Tucker?"

Uncle Judith clears the queue with a lazy wedge shot that splats to the floor an inch or two short. He turns away, disinterested in the gimme.

"The two of them come in here to get about twenty cases of beer. Only one explanation for that. Dane's at the ranch with a bunch of his Hollywood friends, doing their drug parties or their orgies or whatever. And those punks work for him."

"Come on. Hollywood sent skinheads to get beer?"

Uncle Judith shrugs this off. Old news to him, apparently. But me, I have only recently learned that Dane Tucker owns a two-hundred-thousand-acre spread in the Paradise Valley, a new-age western empire assembled from foreclosed family ranches. I have only begun to process the fact that the star of *Epic Force, Force Factor,* and *Force Down* hoards an entire river, the storied Roam River, a public waterway and a fly fishing gem, inside his fences. But *skinheads*?

Uncle Judith handles Jesse's panties with gnarly certitude, gets them in a nicely managed bundle. Her father went to prison, I remember, when Jesse was fifteen. Her mother has never been mentioned—except that Tick Judith, she claims once in a while, basically *is* her mother.

"Word is Tucker has those Nazi punks watching his fence lines," Uncle Judith tells me, setting those panties down inside a Jack Daniels box he carries up from the back hallway. "When they're not making beer runs."

He does something Arnold Palmer never tried, a fairway shot on the move. For this he employs the gap between his front teeth, drills one low and hard with crisp *zzzt!* and a resonant *ping!* on brass.

"Lotta beer going out to that place lately. Fancy liquor too."

Uncle Judith gets a girly pink tank top spread out in front of him, getting it oriented, nipping it in under his chin to get both hands on the job, and just then a customer—a big, raw night shifter, thirsty-looking—jangles through the door.

"Hey, old man," this guy brays, "you finally got that pretty girl's clothes off her, did ya?"

Uncle Judith folds that shirt up real nice, starts a new pile. His ears are red as he sets a pint of Jim Beam on the counter. He says, "Four ninety-five."

"I hear she's running with one of them reverse Eskimos."

"There be anything else?"

"Well, gee. Lemme see." The night shifter fairly drools over Jesse's panties. "You got anything in a size four?"

These could be fighting words. Uncle Judith would like to spit in his face, I can tell. But now he becomes the Mahatma Gandhi of snoose. I see how much he loves Jesse. I see incredible restraint. Eyes down, he just swallows, and swallows, and swallows again. As he makes change, I lean across the heap of Jesse's unfolded clothes and I ask him quietly, "Hey. Do me a favor? Can I leave them a note?"

Howl

Dear Sneed and Jesse: Two skinheads burned your tent. They work for Dane Tucker and drive an old red Ford with an oil drum in the box. They left a no trespassing sign that said turn back now, so if that means anything to you, I'd do it. You never know about people like them. As for me, I've moved on, which is my sad answer to what the two of you made me feel. Love, Dog.

Yeah, well, I guess that's it. The sky looks like a dirty sock when I step out of the liquor store. The Canyon Ferry Lake fire has pushed a smutty wrinkle up beneath the jet stream, and the smoke sprawls out over Livingston, stinking and trapping heat. I feel bad leaving. I just feel bad. But here I go.

Inside the Cruise Master one block behind Main Street I get ready to ride. I decant Smirnoff into a travel cup, shake in Tang, stir with my finger, give it a healthy taste test and then lodge the cup in its holder. I rip open a pack of Swisher Sweets, find matches, and set these in readiness on the little ledge in front of the odometer. I'm ready to pull out. I'll head down Main toward the BP station on Park Street for seventy-one bucks of gas. That's how far I'll make it toward my dark deep on the Big Two-Hearted River before I'll have to stop again and do life. I'm deciding between interstate and local when a shrill whistle makes me hit the brake.

"Trying to kill me?" huffs the jogger at my window as he passes down the middle of the street.

I'm in a bit of daze as I watch this guy. He is lean to skeletal, shirtless and freckled, in scant silky yellow shorts and a red ball cap. A large fanny pack rides one hip, a holstered water bottle the other. Dust coats his ankles like a pair of raw umber socks. He kinks along like he's in pain, his left leg splaying wide, his right hand jerking up and down like a band leader's to keep things balanced. All this and he still manages to flip me my third bird of the day.

It is one of those moments, to be sure. I am a split second from a particularly nasty fit of road rage. *Try running on the sidewalk, turkey-butt.* I yearn to flatten him with the Cruise Master. But I check it and watch, thinking I've seen this guy before.

At the next storefront—law office, I think—he stops. He's done running, is ready to collapse, but this phase too must be done centrally in the public arena. He spreads his legs across the sidewalk, puts his hands on his knees and then heaves, gobs on the sidewalk, a string of saliva yo-yoing from his chin. Then he straightens up. Hands on hips, head thrown back, he staggers in gaudy circles, gulping air. Off comes the harrier's cap and next comes the water bottle, its last few ounces dumped over the top of his stiff, reddish hair. From his next gesture—he fires the empty bottle to the pavement—all of us among his audience are to understand that he is unsatisfied, that he thinks he should have done better, and we are to discover therein how driven, how heroic this man is. Or something.

Instead I'm thinking: *As a matter of fact, I have seen this lunatic before. Someone Sneed pointed out as one of Jesse's former men friends.*

And: *Can I drive on the sidewalk? Could I get up enough speed to run him down?*

The jogger enters the office and the moment passes. I'm over it. I turn the Cruise Master around and realize I've decided on a detour.

I am leaving Livingston to the south. The Big Two-Hearted can wait a bit. I'm going to drive down along the Roam River, check out this movie star Dane Tucker's place, check out his fences and his skinhead watchdogs. I am going to look, I have decided, for a little slip-through in the fence, a little recreational trespassing. Scoot in, fish the bastard's stolen water.

But instead this happens. I drive the entire length of Tucker's property, twenty-five road miles, looking for a weakness, a way in.

There is no such thing.

I double back. All the access roads are gated and chained. All the rangeland is fenced tight with four-strand barbed wire and posted NO TRESSPASSING.

I triple up, wasting precious gas now. For long stretches, the lower Roam River is a full-bodied and sinuous dream, taunting me from the road—and then it disappears entirely into upstream canyons that force the pavement several miles west. Yet still here, along glittering rhyolite cliffs and non-negotiable jack pine screes, Tucker's fences and NO TRESPASSING signs persist, driven and strung and posted all the way south to a sign on a pitted dirt road that says *National Park Boundary* and means, I believe, that I am now entering Yellowstone Park.

So I quadruple back downstream, *Dog damn it*, to what must be Dane Tucker's main gate. I take a medicinal bellyful of v-and-T as I look the structure over. Molded concrete pillars support a roll-away Tymetal gate on a remote-controlled motor. A covered box contains the key pad and the intercom. Cameras watch from the tops of the pillars, tented under sheet metal and aimed down at me.

I was in this business once, so I know. This is the whole high-security embassy gate package. This is what my company, Oglivie Secure, once installed for House Speaker Tip O'Neill in the Boston suburbs.

But why here?

Beyond the gate stretches an access road, arcing across an expanse of desiccated rangeland where a few hobby bison graze listlessly in the heat. A plank bridge bears the road over a slow stretch of the Roam where trout make lazy dimples. Then the road turns upstream and winds with the river into a deep draw out of sight.

I press the intercom button.

After a long wait the speaker crackles: "Can I help you?"

"I want to speak to Dane Tucker."

The voice comes back twangy and harsh: "What you want to do, Pedro, is get your bug-ass off this property."

Pedro? I say, "Is this Dane Tucker?"

Silence. I look at the camera on the left-hand pillar. Its eye stares back, blank and dusty.

"I'd like permission to fish the Roam."

The speaker crackles. "This is private land."

"But the river's public. I've got a right to fish it. Are you Dane Tucker?"

Silence again, like this is a hard question to answer.

"Because if you are Dane Tucker—"

I pause here to wonder if I have had too much vodka. But this cannot be clearly established, so I continue: "Because if you are Dane Tucker, I'd like to discuss my riparian rights with you. I'd like to know the basis on which you feel justified in denying me and everybody else—"

The speaker goes dead with an obvious click. For a moment I feel disoriented. I turn a full circle. The Yellowstone River is no more than a few miles west as the crow flies, but it's a rugged and forbidding few miles, with the Roam and the 'Stone separated at this point by an ancient volcanic ridge, grizzly bear country, thick with pines stands and huckleberry tangles. I think: *isn't that the ridge, near the top, where Jesse showed Sneed and me a little spring pond with big wild cutthroats? Isn't up there where she stripped down to panties and went topless into the pond, then rode around on top of Sneed's shoulders, laughing at my tighty-whities that weren't very white or tight at all?*

I turn back, jam a finger into the intercom button. Bring on the skinheads.

But nothing.

I buzz again. The speaker snaps on. I open my mouth to speak for the masses, for all of us fly fishermen denied, but the guy inside beats me to it, his voice harsh and preemptive.

"You wanna see Dane Tucker, buy a movie ticket, asshole."

And the system goes dead.

But now I'm feisty and drunk and alive with memories, and I decide that I'm going to fish that mountain pond once more, strip naked and swim, leave behind my underwear on a stick for Jesse to find, as a joke. I'm going to miss those two. I'm going to miss my buddy Sneed, especially, and I drive off from Tucker's gate knowing I will never make a friend like that again.

I was in Idaho when it happened. I was exploring the upper north fork of the Snake River. Crossing that river on a bridge, I had become entangled in the sprawling, messy efforts of a bridge-painting crew. Paint-glazed and zombie-like, the crew was moving things—barrels, cones, hoses, compressors—to the other side of the bridge. The flagman was awol and the Cruise Master was enmeshed before I realized there was no place to go.

It was hot, mid-nineties. The foreman was pissed. Assorted ethnics reeled around high on oils and thinners, their ages and races difficult to determine through all the masks and bandanas and silver dustings of paint spray. They clanked around in their safety harnesses like sloppy robots, like bizarre Christmas ornaments. This was one miserable-ass job, I remember thinking as I tried to back up. "No, no, no, goddamnit," the foreman yelled. "Just stay put. We'll get you through here."

I did get through, eventually. But from up high, waiting, I had spotted a good hole beneath the bridge, big trout feeding in it, and so I drove only as far as the end of the bridge, where I parked behind the extended-body van that transported the painting crew. I rigged up, skidded down a steep embankment, and waded chest deep into that clear, cold water.

I had worked that hole downstream for maybe fifteen minutes—long enough to cover fifty yards or so and forget the goings-on sixty feet above—when I was startled by a banshee yell and turned to look. Down from the bridge plummeted a thin silver body.

There was no time for concern or disbelief. No time to retreat out of the way. The body was streamlined, knife-straight, and screaming. About halfway down a paint-caked hardhat separated from a dark brown head—just a kid, I saw, screaming, holding his nuts—and *splash!*

This, of course, would be my buddy Sneed, tendering his resignation from the bridge painting crew.

The kid stayed under some time. Maybe he was knocked out. Guys yelled Spanish and perhaps other languages over the bridge rail. His silver shape spun toward me along the scrambled edge of a big, slow eddy. His hard hat floated ahead, past me, and out of reach. I was pinned in heavy water. Nothing I could do except to wonder how it would feel.

Then this kid corked up to the surface. He was sputtering and wild-eyed, with silver ears and neck, laughing and coughing and cussing and dogpaddling like a guy who couldn't swim ten feet to save his life but would rather die than paint another bridge.

But then the eddy let go, and he thrashed into reach, and so that kid's life, fortuitous Dog, I had the luck to save it for him.

I drive up the dusty logging road toward that mountain pond, thinking how Jesse came into our lives more-or-less like that too. It was a couple weeks of fishing lessons later, me and Sneed townside, getting a beer and a burger on Sneed's last paycheck, and this pretty girl just parachuted in, landed drunk on a bar stool next to Sneed, started touching his arm and making talk about parents and prison and who was I and how long was he going to be around town?

The ensuing three weeks, I admit, were more like an actual life than anything I had experienced in my four years of trout-bumming. I'm not sure who was the bigger rip-snorter, Sneed or Jesse, but they seemed made for each other, and I experienced the oddness of pride in the way they flaunted their racy love around town. Screw it. Life is short. Get your own excitement. That was my position, and I sheltered them. I thought.

The logging road forks about a mile up and narrows after that. It is not wise, I know, to push the Cruise Master up this far. We left my beast at the campground and took Jesse's car, that traumatized Oldsmobile sedan, dust-on-gold, a gift to Jesse from someone she always referred to as "this guy."

Somehow, though, I'm pushing up this mountain anyway. Soon enough, as these things happen, I'm a thousand feet up an eight-foot-wide dirt road in a four-ton recreational vehicle with bad brakes, and there is no good place to turn around. I'm jittery now, mashing a Swisher, spewing smoke. I wonder why, if life is short, I am doing something so obviously stupid. It seems like I'm doing it for Sneed and Jesse, like those notes just didn't get at it—but what sense does that make?

A small turn-out appears on the inside of a straight climb about two miles up. A careful Y-turn, shavings of road taken about a hundred times, might do it.

But I keep on. The road worsens. The Cruise Master bucks and shudders a full mile upgrade until at last another opening signals the little spur to the pond. I have made it. I can swim now, reminisce, leave my underwear, maybe even get the Cruise Master turned around and down the mountain.

Why am I not relieved?

Maybe it's the altitude, or my aging nerves, or all the forest fire smoke in the sky. Or maybe it's too many Swisher Sweets and too much vodka. I can't figure out the bad feeling I have. As I hike that spur along the shoulder of the mountain, I can't suck a breath down past the top half of my chest. And then my breath stops completely when I see Jesse's car.

The girl's golden Oldsmobile is parked on the piney bank above the pond, nosed into a little thicket of huckleberry brush. I see Sneed's dark head inside the car. I see a liquor bottle spun out across the pine needles, just beyond the passenger door. Then I see Jesse about thirty feet away—Jesse face down. I am running—arms and legs spread like she's getting a suntan, except with no towel under her, only a wide, dark stain.

I skid to my knees. "Jesse!" Her face is split open at the nose, stuck in a black crust of blood that has soaked into the dry ground. Her wild blond hair parts just slightly behind one ear where a bullet has entered.

I freeze. Everything—heart, breath, thought—stops.

The car, Sneed, everything else, is at my back. But I cannot turn. My whole body wants to vomit, wants to jerk itself inside out, but I am as rigid as the hard ground, eyes fixed on Jesse's lifeless body until they burn out and stray away for relief to the liquor bottle drawing ants just beyond her left foot. The bottle is empty. *Frangelico*, it says. *Premium hazelnut liqueur*, it says. *Enjoy!* it says.

Then I lose it. I stand and stumble backwards, coughing, spilling bile across my front and calling, "Sneed . . . Sneed . . ."

He is inside the car. He is naked to the waist, his jeans on but unzipped. He is slumped in a corner of the backseat, his beautiful brown skin turned ashen purple, his lips nearly white and his eyes half open.

I grab door handles but they snap back. Locked. Front and back. "Damn it! Come on, Sneed!"

I circle, tearing at the stubborn handles. Strips of silver duct tape hang from the inside door and window seams. A can of lighter fluid rests on the seat, and on the floor, between Sneed's long, splayed legs, squats the little hibachi grill that Sneed uses to cook hot dogs when he and Jesse go on their "picnics." The grill's coals have burned out.

"Sneed, God damn it!"

I stagger to the pond edge, come back with a heavy rock. I slam the rock through the driver's window and reach in. I rip the side door open. On a tide of stale air, Sneed slumps out against me, heavy and limp.

"Dog," he moans.

"Sneed . . . what the . . ."

He makes a second feeble moan as he drags down my leg, flops onto his face and lays still on the pine needles. My eyes jerk back inside the car: on the seat, beneath the sweat-damp spot where Sneed has slumped away, rest my Glock and Jesse's keys.

I turn my face to the sky and howl.

Severe Carbon Monoxide Poisoning

Murder Shocks Paradise Valley
Death Penalty Possible for Killer, Authorities Say

LIVINGSTON, Montana (News Service)   Residents of the Paradise Valley expressed shock and sadness over Wednesday's brutal slaying of a local woman, while death penalty advocates called for swift justice for her alleged killer, an Arkansas man who survived a suicide attempt and remains under guard at Livingston Memorial Hospital.

According to investigators, D'Ontario Sneed, 20, shot his victim in the back of the head with a stolen pistol. Sneed then locked himself in his vehicle and attempted to take his own life by asphyxiation, Park County Sheriff Roy Chubbuck said at a press conference yesterday.

"We are treating it as a murder, followed by a suicide attempt," Chubbuck said. The sheriff said Sneed will be arraigned today. *(continued)*

The dead woman, 22-year-old Jesse Winifred Ringer, was a former Livingston High School Homecoming Queen and Forest Service smokejumper who had been dating Sneed while the pair worked as guide-shuttle drivers in the Paradise Valley. An acquaintance discovered the body of Ringer and subsequently pulled Sneed from his vehicle in a state of severe carbon monoxide poisoning.

Ringer is survived by her father, former bull rider and Livingston fishing guide Galen Ringer, who in 2003 was convicted of murdering a fellow guide on the Yellowstone River and currently awaits appeal of his death penalty sentence.

Chubbuck told reporters in a press conference Sunday that Sneed apparently shot Ringer after a domestic dispute. Finding no more ammunition in the pistol, Sneed then sealed himself inside the vehicle and used a small charcoal grill to attempt suicide, Chubbuck said.

A spokesperson for the Livingston Memorial Hospital would not confirm reports that Sneed was in critical condition as hospital officials seek to contact next-of-kin.

Death penalty advocates in Helena, where Montana's capital punishment law is under legislative review, called for Sneed's trial and execution.

Meanwhile, in Livingston, residents mourned the death of a popular and spirited young woman who overcame a troubled life to . . .

Can Pronghorn Jump?

"Dog?"

My tax guy back in Boston, Harvey Digman, croaked his surprise into my ear.

"Is it really you?"

In my state of blinding anguish, the old man's question confused me. Was it really me? I fumbled some non-answer down at the cruddy floor tiles.

"Dog? Where are you?"

I looked up and around. I was in the back hallway of a minimart or some such location, between the doors to the toilets. I could not remember getting there, but booze and grief will take you to places like this—and beyond.

"Yeah, Harv. It's me."

"You sound like hell, buddy." Harvey turned down the volume on what was very likely a vintage Jane Fonda jazzercise tape. "Tell me you're finally coming home."

I lurched out to the end of the phone cord. "Dane Tucker," I blurted. These words turned the head of a shape-free young woman scooting into the toilet on snapping yellow flip-flops. She gave me a pinpoint glance—*What about Dane Tucker?*—before she let the door swing.

"Can you—" I lowered my voice "—Harvey, can you do me a big favor? Can you look up Dane Tucker on the internet?"

"What? You call me for the first time in a year and want me to Google a guy?"

I was thinking in pictures: Harvey Digman was at that moment sending a hurt look across the exercise mat to his personal trainer, some lovely Stephanie. With death upon me, with death squatting in my heart and lungs and gut, I was reminded that Harvey Digman planned to live forever.

"You mean the actor? *Force Factor*? That poor man's Chuck Norris? What for?"

I plugged quarters. Toilets flushed and towels hanked out. The phone was oily, slick as a chub in my palm. I tried to center on some statement I was sure about.

"I'm in Montana, Harv."

He sighed. "Well, gee, Dog. That explains everything."

"The guy has a ranch here in the Paradise Valley."

"A ranch. Well, then of course. The man must be Googled."

But instead of keyboard tappings, I heard the telltale sound of a file drawer running out and slamming the end of its track. That was all me in there, file after file, a long and complicated mess.

"I know I'm broke, Harvey. I'm not calling for money. Just Google the guy."

"You're more than broke. Last month Miss Mary Jane sued for your half of the condo at Cape Cod. You lost."

"I've already spent my equity."

"I know you have. I cooked that book already. I can't do this for you anymore, Dog. Come home. Get a job. Start over."

There passed a quarter's worth of blank time here, me seeing pictures of a suit, a train, a stream of people, a desk and an empty apartment at the end of the day.

"I just want you to Google Dane Tucker with the word *skinhead*."

Another sigh. But now he was tapping. "I'm not following this, Dog."

"Or Nazi. Or white supremacy. Anything like that."

"Don't they have libraries out there yet?"

"Come on, Harv. This is a pay phone."

"You do not sound well, Dog."

"Damn it, just—"

But Harvey always came through for me, all the way back to the founding days of Oglivie Secure, so I fixed on fingers tapping keys, and I tried to take what I believe is referred to by the lovely Stephanies among us as a deep, cleansing breath. But right then the shape-averse young woman, coming out of the toilet with her hair fluffed, pinned me with another look. "I'm Cindra. Do you, like, know Dane or something?" I looked away as Harvey intoned into my ear, "Tucker Flick *Force Factor* loses 40 million."

"Not that stuff, Harv. I want to know if he has any connections to skinheads, Nazis, Aryan Nation, white supremacy, the whole, you know . . ."

"The whole hate community?"

Harvey, an old lefty, would have the proper term. "I guess so."

"I am loathe even to ask, Dog."

"Then don't."

"I am now conducting a Boolean search."

"Only you would know a thing like that, Harvey."

He chuckled. "Librarians. Pure, simmering libido, Dog, I'm telling you."

A wave of fatigue and nausea slammed me, made me retch over a trash can, and right on schedule Cindra brought a friend in from the car to show off the man who knew—

"Nope," said Harvey. "Nothing like that. Though it says here, in *Variety* online, that because of a flap with the ACLU Tucker hasn't been able to finance his next project, *Border Force*." He clucked. "This is all sounding a little forced, wouldn't you say, Dog?"

"All right, Harvey. Thanks—"

"Hold on."

He tapped more keys. As I waited, I saw an alternate picture of myself. A healthier Dog was out there beyond the Little Debbies and the beef jerky, beyond the window on the curb outside, weeping. I was shaking, dripping, mewling into my hands, letting Cindra and everyone else in the whole world just *know* how bad it hurt what happened to Sneed and Jesse.

But I held on, gritted my unbrushed teeth while Harvey quoted from something titled "Hollywood's Tucker Addresses Citizen Group."

"'Action film star Dane Tucker addressed a group of California Minutemen volunteers in San Diego last month'—this is from a website, Dog, *Minutemen Civil Defense Corps*—'commending the volunteers for standing guard on this nation's border to do the job our government refused to do for its citizens and decrying the rampant sex trade and rapes notorious for occurring along our porous southern border.'"

Harvey paused, smacking his dentures in disapproval. "Is that the kind of rot you're looking for?"

"Hell, I don't know."

"Your voice is shaking. What happened, Dog?"

"I don't know."

"This doesn't sound like fishing. Of course this has never been a fishing trip, not as far as I've been—"

"Harvey, type in one more thing."

"If you promise to tell me what's wrong."

"Can pronghorn jump?"

"What?"

"Pronghorn antelope. Can they jump? Type it in."

My tax guy tsked and muttered as he typed. A knot in my throat stopped my air, blackened my brain around a picture of Sneed watching pronghorn graze across the slopes above the Boulder River. Pronghorn couldn't jump, Sneed claimed, kicking angrily at a brand new fence that blocked our path to the river. So how were they supposed to migrate? That a black kid from the south would know this, would care—this meant something, or nothing, or everything. He was such a tender soul. *Sneed, how could you?*

"Nope," said Harvey. "Can't jump."

He waited.

I choked and snuffled and fought with tears.

"Dog, what's going on?"

With a gargantuan effort, with a struggle and a messiness perhaps akin to giving birth, I managed to produce a single tortured sob.

"Well, that sounds like a start," Harvey managed before I hung him up.

Hell and Back

"Sir? This is restricted area. You can't just walk here. Sir!"

But I went around the woman's desk and pushed through a swinging door of reinforced glass to find myself in an inner hallway of the Park County Sheriff's Department.

"Sir, I'll call deputy!"

Buffed floor tiles, bulletin boards, inverted cask of spring water, a burnt-coffee breeze from the air conditioning—"Sir! Mister! Stop!"—and now this Asian woman with a Western twang but no articles or prepositions, this ferocious miniature, was on my heels.

"Sir, I will call deputy," she threatened as I pitched left, took a hallway toward the coffee smell. "Russell!" she hollered into the break room as we passed.

"What's up, baby girl?"

"You call me Ms. Park-Ford. You get him."

But I was around a corner and just strides from Sheriff Chubbuck's office along the west flank of the building. The office was glass-walled and I could see right in to what looked like the living room of a trailer home: wall-to-wall carpet the color of split barley soup, mis-matched tassled lampshades, a cracked leather sofa with a rumpled pillow and blanket, a collection of hunting and fishing memorabilia crowded onto the single solid wall. The sheriff himself was asleep in his desk chair, boots up on the desk, hat pulled down and a home-knit throw across his lap. Clamped to the desk in front of him was a fly-tying vice. A three-wheeled electric scooter was parked beside the desk.

"Hey." This was the deputy. "Pal. Hold on. You can't go—"

The office was soundproof inside, perfect for the fat *thump!* of the *Bozeman Daily Chronicle* onto Chubbuck's desk.

The sheriff jerked awake. His hands clenched and then let go. After a toke of oxygen, he tipped his hat back and found me with those red-rimmed, laser-blue eyes.

"You," he said.

"Me."

"You been to Massachusetts and back already?"

"I've been to hell and back, Sheriff."

Chubbuck cleared his throat. He nursed his feet off the desk, straightened his spine as the door opened. The deputy, Russell, was a young guy with a big jaw and slicked hair. Ms. Park-Ford took up a militant posture behind him. The pair of them looked ready to extract me. But Chubbuck raised a shaky hand.

"He's harmless."

The sheriff took a second gander at me as if to assure himself. "Isn't that right, Mister Oglivie?"

"Sneed was harmless." That was my answer. "He wouldn't kill her. Or himself. You must have missed something." My tone was turning. "Such as, say, Dane Tucker's pair of skinhead punks who threatened my friends and stole my pistol."

"Thank you, Russell. Thank you, Ms. Park-Ford."

When the door was closed, the sheriff looked down at his desk. He took off his hat as if to get more light. In the jaws of the fly-tying vice was a near-finished spruce moth. Strewn beneath the vice, across official-looking papers, were his elk hair pelt, his hair stacker, dubbing wax, and scissors. He blew elk hair clippings off a document, cocked that right eyeball, the one for close work, then held the paper out.

"Your statement says you were—" his voice was reedy, strug-

gling for breath and power "—last certain of your pistol's where-
abouts no later than the twentieth of this month. Do we need to
change this?"

"I pretty much forgot I had it. But—"

"And your statement says you found the car locked with the
keys and the pistol inside."

"It also says those skinheads came to the campground about
two hours earlier—"

The sheriff put up a red and flaking hand. "Now hold on."
He rummaged beneath fly trimmings to find another paper. "And
this one says that you did not see those boys with your pistol. You
only noted—" breathing now like he was climbing a damn hill
"—that the pistol was not in your box and your box had been pried
open—"

"Yes, but—"

"—pried open we are certain by Mister Sneed." Chubbuck
licked his dry lips but was unsatisfied with that. He peered into
a coffee cup and took a feeble sip. "Mister Sneed whose prints we
found on the pistol, on the box, all over your vehicle. Are you a
heavy sleeper, Mister Oglivie?"

"You could call it that. I drink."

He nodded. "Now then . . ." He shifted more papers. I waited.
I glared at the spruce moth in his vice. The fly was junk. The
dubbed yellow body was too thin. The elk hair wing was wrapped
too loosely, and the ends blocked the hook's eye. I raised my glare
to the sheriff, caught him gazing away from his documents and
out his window toward the Wineglass Range. In the next few
moments, a kind of Ronald Reagan look of bemusement found its
way onto his tortured face. He was lost in whatever pain he had,
I figured, or maybe having a morphine moment.

"Sheriff?"

Chubbuck leaned forward with a grunt. He pressed his
intercom button. "Miss Park-Ford? Would you please tell
Deputy Crowe to hang on a minute before he goes on patrol?
Thank you."

The sheriff let up on the button. He leaned up to the computer monitor at the corner of his desk, side-eyed it in his bird-like way. He tapped on the keyboard for a full minute, clicked something with his mouse. When he looked at me again, his eyes had become tiny wet stones, ferociously blue inside their raw red rims.

"Anyway, go home, Mister Oglivie. Your license has expired."

"I want to see my friend Sneed."

"He's a murder suspect."

"He didn't kill Jesse. He wouldn't do a thing like that. Those skins—"

"Your statement says you knew Mister Sneed for no more than three weeks. Do we need to change that?"

I dropped my glare. I clenched my fists and stared at that shitty spruce fly, smelling my sweat, my alcohol, my rage. "Those skins did this," I claimed. "I know they did."

"Just go home, Mister Oglivie."

I didn't move. The sheriff's hands quaked into my vision. He unclamped the spruce moth and let it fall into his palm. He sucked oxygen and sighed. Then the both of us were silent for a very long time.

"Look," he said at last. "I understand how these things are difficult to accept, Mister Oglivie. Very, very difficult." He paused, flicked the spruce fly into his waste basket. "Grief is a bitch. It's a mess. It's a process."

"Don't tell me about grief."

He shook his head as if he pitied me. He pressed his intercom. "Ms. Park-Ford?"

"Yes, Sheriff?"

"Send Deputy Crowe on back."

"Yes, Sheriff. Oh, and Mister Walters is here from federal—" she paused, seemed to catch herself "—here from Salt Lake."

Chubbuck nodded. "Tell Mister Walters ten minutes." Then to me he said, "As a matter of fact, I will tell you about grief." He pulled the throw off his lap. He arranged it over the arm of his chair.

"You're a fisherman, Mister Oglivie, so grief goes like this." His eyes watered like they stung. "There you are, just fishing along, when you hook into something big. You pull back, expecting your usual control. But within moments, the size of what you've hooked into goes beyond your comprehension. It blows your goddamn mind."

He turned his head to gaze out his window at the mountains, at wind whipping up dust and wrinkling the smoke-freighted sky. Slowly, shakily, he began to transfer himself from his desk chair to his little twelve-volt scooter.

"I mean this thing on your line is big, Mister Oglivie. I mean you hook this sonofabitch and right away large sectors of your brain just give up and shut down. You become a reptile."

He toppled into the plastic seat of the scooter. He began to fumble at the seat belt.

"And you fight it like a man, with everything you have, until you hit the wall. You have nothing left. You have no strength." He took short, fast breaths. "And that is when you understand that this thing will never break off. Nor will you ever land it. Nor will you ever see it, ever touch it, ever know exactly what it is."

Sheriff Chubbuck reached back to his desk for his campaign hat, trembled it into place over his hairless skull. "Nor, Mister Oglivie—" he fixed me with a blue stare "—will you *ever let go of the rod*. That is grief."

His deputy, Russell Crowe, stuck his head back into the doorway. "Yes, sir?"

The sheriff burped his little scooter ahead to where he could grab the open door from the deputy and hold it. A stocky young man in a black suit, waiting outside, seemed to think this was his cue. "We just heard about another one, Sheriff, an endontist in Fresno who was—"

"Walters. Come in. Sit down."

Chubbuck turned to his deputy, gave a nod in my direction.

"Russell, this gentleman is yours. Gas him up and make sure he crosses the line into Sweetgrass County. He's going home."

Black from Both Directions

"I am no relation to the actor of course."

Chubbuck's deputy discharged this complete non sequitur into my exhausted brain as he pulled his cruiser past a dusty, neatly parked black SUV and swung from the lot.

"You know, Russell Crowe? The actor?"

My silence provoked him: "Deputy Russell Crowe. It's just my name. I can't help it. I'm not, like, an actor or anything."

This not-actor deputy had glossy black hair, exactly one centimeter too long for law enforcement. He had a distinctively oversized jaw that appealed in the general direction of handsome but did not quite arrive. He grinned at me with large yellow teeth proportioned for the mouth of a small horse. "Trust me," he said. "It's weird, but I'm actually no relation to Russell Crowe the actor."

We were headed for Sacagawea Park, where I had left the Cruise

Master in the shade of cottonwoods. The deputy ran the windows down and spun the steering wheel with the palm of his right hand. He laid his left arm out the window and used that hand to designate greetings upon a sun-beaten old rancher limping across Park Street.

"What's the good word, Walt? We gonna get some rain?"

Walt scaled the curb, pushed his ten-gallon up and looked back in dismay as we rounded onto Main Street. So perhaps I spoke for Walt too. "Well, why would you be any relation? If you were related, you wouldn't have the same name. Unless you were the guy's son."

"I'm not. I swear."

"Of course you're not."

Deputy Crowe laughed. "Yeah," he said. "It's confusing." He sent greetings to an underdressed older woman leaving the flower shop with a bouquet. She smiled and waved.

"Hello, Russell."

"Hey, baby girl."

"Working hard or hardly working?"

"You know me."

"Oh, Russell." She rolled her eyes. Russell gave her a little salute and took an unnecessary left turn.

"But you'd be totally surprised how many people don't pick up on the name thing like you did. They think I'm related to the actor." He hit the brakes. "Hey, there's Ivan."

The deputy eased up wrong-side to the curb. "Ivan, my brother!" This salutation startled a young man in grungy bermudas and a goatee who looked stoned and therefore sorely undecided about approaching a sheriff's cruiser.

"Ivan's a writer," Russell Crowe told me. "Hey, Ivan, how's that novel coming along?"

Mortified, this Ivan shifted a paper sack under his arm and made some noises, possibly also some words.

"Attaboy, Ivan. Never give up. And then you gotta write the screenplay, remember? You promised me."

We took another left at the next corner, Second and Geyser, accomplishing a one-eighty now, heading back in our original direction along a street with three saloons and five art galleries. Deputy Crowe said, "My bad. Gotta make a stop."

He pulled into the angle parking in front of a craft shop. A minute later he was back, showing me the contents of a bulging plastic sack.

"Pine cones," he said, stating the obvious. "You'd be surprised how much these cost. Two bucks apiece for something you can pick up off the ground." He tossed the sack in the back seat. "But the boss lady, she's gotta have 'em."

Two more lefts and we were taking a second tour down Main Street. The deputy confused a tourist couple with his vivid salutations. Then he froze to the hot sidewalk a deeply inebriated old gentleman with one wet pant leg. This man stood as motionless as he could manage, as if he and the deputy were playing red light-green light.

"That's Elmer Sorgensen."

Russell Crowe pulled over, hopped out and opened his back door. "Come on, Elmer, get in."

The frail old man sluiced himself in across the backseat and lay down. The smell of urine filled the cruiser until Crowe put up his safety window. "Sorgensens are a clan of sheep-herding Swedes from the old days." He swung me a jaw that looked heavy with information. "There's a ton of them around here, various states of falling apart. None of them went to school at all. Elmer's brother does okay, though, runs the outfitter Jesse worked for. Hilarious Sorgensen. I bet you know him."

Yes I did, I said, and Crowe celebrated his acumen with a horse-toothed smile. Then, as he eased away from the curb, he said, "So you don't think your black friend popped Jesse? Is that it?"

"Is that what?"

"Is that the basic problem?"

"The word black in that sentence," I said, "is the basic problem."

"Huh? Oh." He gave me a falsely contrite look. "African-American. I mean, no offense."

"It doesn't belong in the equation," I said, "unless you're going to look into black from both directions."

Deputy Russell Crowe drove a half block in utter puzzlement. At last he said, "Black from both directions?"

"Meaning my friends Sneed and Jesse were threatened by skinheads the day of Jesse's murder."

That jaw extended. "I didn't know that."

"The sheriff knew it and did nothing. He came out alone, never even left his car. He has a hate crime staring him in the face, and he never even questioned the skinheads."

Crowe had slowed down to a studious five miles per hour, trying to follow. We passed by Tick Judith in the window of the liquor store. He stared out, crumpled and bereft.

I said, "So does the sheriff have something going with Dane Tucker?"

"Dane Tucker?"

"Those two punks work for Dane Tucker."

Here came even more jaw. "They do?"

"I should think the sheriff's department would know that."

"Well . . . you said they made a threat?"

"They burned Sneed's tent. They left a note that said turn back now."

"Huh," the deputy said. He scratched along the hairless run-up to his chin. "But why would the sheriff take the call himself? He never does that. He's got emphysema, bad. He's pretty weak. He saves his energy for fishing."

"Maybe someone should ask why."

"Huh," the deputy said. "Yeah. That's right. And hey, lucky, here's my man Henderson Gray."

Crowe slowed again, veered to the wrong-side curb in front of a familiar law office. So Henderson Gray was the nasty little marathon man who flipped me off a few hours before I found Sneed and Jesse. He wore a summer suit now, looked wealthy, full of purpose and importance.

"Yo, Mister Gray!"

Russell Crowe yipped this out the window. The man looked annoyed.

"Is Dane in town? I mean, is he out at the ranch?"

Gray flicked a glance through the cruiser at yours truly. He moved internally, like running in place at a stop light. "Yes. Dane is at the ranch. Is there something I can help you with, Russell?"

"The sheriff been out to, like, see Dane? Or anything? Lately?"

"Not that I know of." I could see Gray grinding his teeth.

"Why?"

"Nah. Just wondered. Hey—you run down that deer yet?"

"I'll let you know."

"Uah," the deputy laughed. "You do that. Show me the picture. I'll buy you a beer."

Henderson Gray looked like he might hurtle the cruiser in another second or two. But Russell Crowe, no relation, showed a surprising sense of timing. "Gotta scoot," he said, and he pulled away. He left Gray scowling at his watch.

"That's Dane Tucker's attorney," Crowe told me. "Great guy. Ultra-marathoner. Trying to be the first man to run down a pronghorn antelope."

I felt the bump of that—pronghorn antelope—but my brain was done and slipping into distraction.

"So Dane is at the ranch." I heard Crowe musing as he drove on toward the place where I could sleep. "So the sheriff . . ."

Elmer Sorgensen, the drunk, moaned and babbled in the back seat. The sounds reached me faintly through the safety glass. They lulled me toward my own dark deep.

"Huh. Really. Skinheads? Working for Tucker?" Deputy Russell Crowe accelerated. "And the sheriff did nothing?"

We Work for the County

Chubbuck's deputy ladled Elmer Sorgensen onto a bench in the shade at Sacagawea Park and then followed the Cruise Master east on I-90 to a point just short of the Springdale exit at the Sweetgrass County border. There he signaled me to pull over. He swaggered up in my mirror, holding his campaign hat down against the semi-trailer gusts. I figured after he signed off, I would sleep a while and then loop around, park the Cruise Master somewhere out of sight, and ask some more Dane Tucker questions.

"Mind following me for a couple of miles?" the deputy asked instead. "Something I'd like to show you."

The deputy skipped ahead and we took the Springdale exit. From there we took a local road back under the interstate, headed southwest toward the Absorakas and the mountain peak the locals call Baldy. About fifteen miles and several turns later, we passed a sign that said:

YOU ARE NOW ENTERING PARK COUNTY

NO FIRES

and then another that said:

ABSAROKA-BEARTOOTH WILDERNESS
NO FIRES.

Finally, just after Smokey the Bear concurred with ONLY YOU CAN PREVENT FOREST FIRES, we turned into a long gravel driveway that terminated at a run-down family home tucked into a slope of aging Douglas fir. At the side of the house, a frail-looking woman tended an ash-spewing bonfire of household trash. Seeing us, she dropped the rake and slipped inside.

Deputy Russell Crowe strolled back to the Cruise Master, hitching at his loaded utility belt.

"Welcome to my home," he said. He gave me his ass-jawed grin.

"You look like you could use a cup of coffee and a piece of pie."

"Here's your pine cones, Ma."

Rita Crowe, Russell's mother, was about my age, but despite a clear effort to spruce up for company, the woman was listless and spot-skinned, with injured, sunken eyes. She was good-looking once, though, and from her Russell had inherited his dark components and his ability, at a glance, to suggest handsome. That crowbar chin came from his father, Russell Sr., the subject of an official law enforcement photo portrait on the fireplace mantel. I veered closer to parse insignia. Senior was once a Park County Sheriff.

Rita Crowe saw me looking. Her voice startled me, grated like a fly reel with sand stuck in it. "Twenty-five years of service, then railroaded by the politicians."

"He's retired?"

"Rusty? Ha! He never had the chance."

"My dad's no longer with us," Russell said. "Come on, Ma. Here's your pine cones. Look if I got your order right."

As she inspected his delivery, Russell directed my eyes. "Check it out." From surfaces throughout the house, pine cones craftily done up as assorted woodland creatures peered back at me through the kind of googly eyes they fix to saltwater streamers.

"Ma is just awesome at this."

"I wanted ten, Russell. This is a dozen."

"Sorry, Ma. I got you a couple of freebies."

Her voice came out like the swing of my galley door, fricative dry aluminum. "There are no freebies, Russell. Not in this world."

Russell fought off defeat and nudged me. Look. Her cone creatures were everywhere. Owls and more owls and spiders with pipe cleaner legs and hot-glued constructions of cones and cone scales amounting to deer and moose and skunk and porcupine and squirrel. There were even grizzly bears, rearing with a fair amount of malice despite their wibble-wobble eyes.

"She does almost one a day since we lost my dad. That's over two thousand. She goes to the schools and shows the kids how to do it."

"Ha," she said. "The schools."

"He's a fly fisherman, Ma. You think you could make a pine cone trout?"

"I do not do fish."

"You could try."

Rita Crowe stiffened. She drew in a wheezy breath. "Russell, go downstairs and get me a jar of them cling peaches."

Russell shot me a little grimace. "Hey, Ma, how about instead we thaw out that huckleberry pie? You know, the one Aunt Shureen dropped off a while ago when you weren't feeling good. I know right where it's at in the freezer."

The woman deflated. Her eyes sank in her head. She rubbed her temples. She sighed as if this child of hers had just tapped the very dregs of her strength. "Russell . . . *please.*"

None too soon we were seated at the Crowe family table around Hot Pockets and pickles, rustled up by the deputy, along with the canned peach halves and a huge bowl of potato chips that Rita Crowe said were not stale.

I started with the novelty of a pickle, spearing it with a plastic fork and counting it as my first vegetable in weeks. Rita Crowe opened with a cigarette and these words: "So I hear you're not so happy with our wonderful sheriff."

Russell bit a Hot Pocket, head down. "Ow," he mouthed.

"You always do that."

"I do not."

"The man is on them cancer drugs," she continued to me. "Heavy. Not that he would step down, of course. Not with all he's got going on."

The pickle tasted like paint thinner. Or maybe I was just out of the loop, taste-wise. I put the thing down on my paper plate and tried a chip. Stale.

"Ma did EMT for twenty years." Russell supplied this around a juggled mouthful of Hot Pocket. "Now she's finally on the county board."

"Russell, get him some coffee."

I put my hands up fast. "I'm fine."

"*Russell . . .*"

"Okay, Ma."

Russell set down black coffee in a foam cup. Rita Crowe went deep into her cigarette. She filled the room with smoke. "Of course it's a pity," she said at last. "The whole thing. I don't mean to say it's not. But now there's people coming in and out of that office got nothing whatsoever to do with Park County business."

"Ma thinks Sheriff Chubbuck should step down."

"Russell."

"Sorry, Ma."

She nudged the bowl of potato chips toward me. I tried another one. "They're fine," she said.

"Ma—"

"They are absolutely fine."

I twisted, glanced toward the Russell Sr. photo over the fireplace. A hundred googly-eyed pine cone creatures turned me back around.

"I'm not popular on the county board," Rita Crowe said. She shot a plume of smoke toward a dark spot on the ceiling. "But that man should step down. And he should have someone ready to take his place, someone who deserves it. That's how it's supposed to happen."

"It's emphysema, Ma. Not cancer."

"Does it matter?"

"Probably to him."

"You want to be smart," she said, "you can go to your room and be smart."

Now this was awkward. The deputy's jaw turned red. He kept his eyes down on his plate while his mother served him a handful of chips. Russell's chair squawked as he shoved away from the table. He stormed off all of ten feet to a chest freezer beside the porch door. Out came a frozen pie. Into the microwave it went. Through the endless awful droning that ensued, I discovered that the Hot Pockets were excellent and I decided if nothing else to fill my tank.

But then—*ding!*—there *was* something else. "So I hear tell," Rita Crowe said, "that the sheriff has something going with Dane Tucker."

"I've been around three weeks. I wouldn't quite know."

Russell brought the pie to the table. He tried a knife on it. Rock hard.

"But why?" I said. "Do you have some reason to think so?"

Her stream of smoke just cleared the top of Russell's head as he probed unsuccessfully with the knife. "I've been around a long time. I have reason to think a lot of things. Lately he goes out alone. He sends his deputies off to the far corners of the county and has Ms. Park-Ford keep him appraised of the GPS readings on their cruisers. Then he takes off for hours."

Russell, defeated, dropped the knife and said sulkily, "So Ma came up with an idea."

"Put the pie on the counter, Russell. You can eat it when you come back from work."

He looked at her warily. Her smile opened like my wing window, narrow and stuck at the wrong angle, but Russell looked as though he had been baptized in the breath of life.

"Yes!" he celebrated.

"Put it on the counter, Russell."

"Which counter, Ma?'

"Left of the sink. No, Russell. *Left* of the sink."

"Got it."

Now a phone began to ring from the wall at the other side of the kitchen. You don't much see phones like that anymore, beige slimlines, hard wired. Rita Crowe said, "Excuse me" and carried the handpiece away to the end of a long and kinky cord that placed her in the living room, out of earshot.

"It was a good idea." Russell was rejuvenated. He hunkered toward me, speaking in a low voice. "It basically would have worked. My mom followed me out to Ringling where I was supposed to pull a dead horse off the road. There was no horse. There never was. So Ma stays with the cruiser like it's me on speed patrol. I drive her truck back to town. I get there in time to catch the sheriff heading south on 89 and then up by Tucker's place. He stops by the side of the road and just sits there. Then these other vehicles show up and I'm waiting to see what the sheriff does, and then—"

He stretched away to take a look at her. She had the TV on, was listening on the phone and looking for something through the channels.

"Must be a George Clooney sighting," Russell said. "Ma's fan network has been alerted." He gave me a real-looking grin. "So I'm waiting there by Tucker's place to see what the sheriff does, and then some drunk guy—"

He double-checked the living room. "Huh," he said. "There's Dane Tucker right there. That's *Force Down*. I guess it came up on dish. And Ma's watching, so there must be some early George Clooney in there somewhere."

Russell rolled his eyes a bit. "Sorry about the pie."

"It's all right."

"Some drunk guy comes along 294 at about eighty miles an hour using both lanes. And guess what she does? She turns on the siren and takes off after him. She puts the damn cruiser in the ditch at the 89 intersection. Ms. Park-Ford picks it up from her screen and radios the sheriff. The sheriff heads for the scene. Now I have to race him in my mother's pickup and get back there before he does."

Russell paused. This was thin ice, this story. In the living room, Rita Crowe murmured into the phone while a buff and sweaty Dane Tucker rappelled from a helicopter into some foreign embassy compound. The knife in Tucker's stunning teeth turning out to be just the ticket to cut the bonds from the wrists and ankles of some dark-skinned beauty who then spat in Tucker's face. No George Clooney that I could make out. Rita Crowe advanced one more channel to a talk show. White boys, ugly ones with shaved heads and jackboots, slouched in the pillowy guest chairs. Russell and I both stared at this for a minute.

"And I made it," Russell said finally. "I beat the sheriff to the scene. Just."

The TV screen went black. Rita Crowe hung up the phone and returned to the table. She said to me, "You're right. Those boys are hammerheads. I've seen them at the liquor store on Main."

"Skinheads, Ma." Russell was grinning at her. "Or hammerskins. Not hammerheads."

Rita Crowe had started another cigarette. She set it down in a Yellowstone Park ashtray. She gathered up the paper plates and plastic forks and Styrofoam cups, put them in a pile, pushed the pile toward Russell.

"We're not supposed to burn, Ma. It's too dry. There's a county ordinance against it."

"We work for the county, Russell."

"Right, so—"

She stared him down. Eventually Russell gathered the stack of trash into his hands.

"So," she said as her son rose to obey, "the question is this: if those are skinheads and they work for Tucker, and our wonderful sheriff is hands off, then why? If the man is looking the other way, what does he get out of it?"

After a pause wherein I awakened to the fact that this question was not rhetorical, I said, "Well, isn't that easy?"

Both Crowes looked at me, eager but clueless. But they were talking about a dying fly fisherman, for God's sake, and they were talking about the Roam River, pristine, lovely, trout-choked and un-fished, locked in behind Tucker's fences. In the face of that, as far as Chubbuck was concerned, what was a little corruption of justice?

I shrugged and said the obvious: "Wouldn't it be access to fish?"

The Best Thing
That Ever Happened to Jess

I fixed one for the road, torched a remnant Swisher, and I drove directly back to Livingston, to the liquor store.

Uncle Tick Judith had become the Jackson Pollack of snoose. Loosed by his grief over Jesse, the grainy brown stains went everywhere, in streaks and splats and dribbles on his shirt front, his chin, his boots, the counter, the newspaper he was reading, even on the Crown Royal gift boxes shelved behind the counter and three feet in back of his spittoon.

"I'm sorry."

"Sumbitch sorry don't get me nothin'."

There went effluent out the corner of his mouth into the stubble on his chin. He sniffed, dragged a sleeve across the general area, adding to that canvas.

"I'm responsible," he said.

"You're not."

"Ize her sumbitch guardian. That girl's daddy—" a gobby, no-look spurt in the general direction of the spittoon "—is my good friend and he asked me to watch out for her."

"Jesse was an adult," I said. "A pretty wild one, too."

The old bull rider hoisted a plastic half-gallon of Smirnoff's from beneath the counter. He addressed the register.

"That one's half gone," I pointed out.

"Thennis half price," Uncle Judith slurred. "Twenty-nine by half." I watched the math confuse him while the register beeped.

"Point of information," I said. "How do you know those skinheads work for Tucker?"

Tick Judith pulled back and stood mutely bowlegged, regarding me as if for the first time. He worked that quid beneath his lip as tears welled into eyes that looked set by a shovel and red-rimmed from an intense stretch of anguish. He didn't process the skinhead question. Instead he fixed a shattered index finger in my direction.

"Now, *you* . . ."

"Yeah," I said. "I brought Sneed around here."

"So maybe you're responsible."

"Yeah. I am. That's what I mean when I say you're not."

If this was harder than twenty-nine by two, Uncle Judith didn't show it. In fact he bunched his quid up with a grizzled face-pinch, squeezed it hard a couple times, and tried to self-talk around the precipitate. "Sumbitch owned up," he dribbled. "I am talking to a goddang man."

He knuckle-punched the register: NO SALE. Then the cap was off the Smirnoff's—"Here's to ya, friend"—and we were passing it back and forth, a pair of good slugs each, throats on fire.

"When Galen went to prison," he gasped, "that left Jesse in my care. She was coming up on fifteen. Grown men was sniffing around her like coyotes on a yearling deer. I was by myself with it. I put down some sumbitch rules."

"I hear you."

"And that girl broke every one of them."

Uncle Judith hoisted the half-gallon again. Vodka hit him in the face. "Shiticks." He mopped himself with a bandana, pried out his snoose and flicked it into a trash can, tried to get himself organized.

"I'm sure you did your best."

"You can see about how good I did."

"You did all right."

He skidded the jug across the counter. "What the sumbitch hell do you know?"

"Not that much."

"Okay then."

I swallowed a mouthful. "About those skinheads—"

"Dwayne Hood told me."

"Who's Dwayne Hood?"

"Buddy of mine. Used to be ranch boss for Tucker. Got himself fired over some fence that was too expensive."

Suddenly, Uncle Judith was the Marcel Marceau of snoose. His mouth worked convincingly, but nothing was in there. He searched pockets for his Cope can.

"Dwayne Hood said Tucker has a whole new crew now, including a couple of little dirtbags from Spokane that was supposed to watch the fences, keep out fishermen."

I nodded. Okay. So the skins did in fact work for Tucker. "Let me ask you something."

But the jangling here produced a summer person—short pants, sandals, sunglasses—who took some care in selecting a ten-dollar six-pack of beer. Uncle Judith killed the time locating his snoose can, rapping it loudly and violently with his thumb, then one-handing the lid off and letting out a smell like wet bat guano. Now he was the Julia Child of snoose, taking a deep and critical sniff, then a short corroborative nip. He wrinkled his busted nose. He pronounced the can "rotten as a goddang Monday morning," and then he foisted in a hefty pinch.

Ten-dollar six-pack paid with plastic and left us. "My question is delicate," I went on.

"I look like I'm made of sumbitch piecrust?"

"I know you loved Jesse."

We traded vodka punches. I was getting wobbly. Uncle Judith dabbed his eyes.

"So I wonder what you think about Sneed."

"The colored boy? What about him?"

"You've seen a lot of Jesse's men. I just wondered where he fit in the general outline of things."

"That sumbitch," Jesse's guardian began. He squeezed back what looked like the impulse to cry. "I don't care what anybody says. That sumbitching colored boy was the best thing that ever happened to Jess. Just the other day I said to Galen—" He broke off, squeezed harder. "I went up there. 'What's Jess up to,' he says, 'who's she running with,' and I can't never lie to him so I told it. Then Galen got going on that subject and I said he ought to shut his goddamn—" Uncle Judith's own mouth closed involuntarily. He shook some thought from his head, and his voice became scratchy and airless. "You mark my words, fella. I seen the other thing plenty of times. That colored boy loved Jess. And I suspect that's why . . ."

He broke off into full-on tears, dripping and drooling like the Salvador Dali of snoose. I bit my lip and stared away toward the beer cooler. That Frangelico didn't make sense, I was thinking suddenly. A syrupy hazelnut liqueur, on a hot summer day, between two avid beer drinkers?

As was my way, I let Uncle Judith cry out my ration too, let him honk around inside his bandana enough for both of us while I found Frangelico on the shelf behind the counter: the bottle was unmistakable, tall and shaped like a friar in a cowl, white cord around the waist, a price tag below that said *$44.95.*

When Uncle Judith recovered, I asked him, "Who was Jesse's last boyfriend? Before Sneed?"

He did not hesitate. He jerked his hat brim toward the window. "Nut case across the street. Tucker's lawyer. Had Jess on the QT, supposedly. Everybody knew except the guy's wife."

"Henderson Gray?"

Suddenly a mad gulp of vodka, a vicious near miss at the spittoon. "That dumb girl was always spreading for a lawyer. She thought a lawyer could get her dad off. Galen wrote her letters like that—*Jess, get a lawyer, tell him I'm innocent*—leading her on like that. Hell, she'd do about anything."

"Does he know she's dead? Jesse's dad?"

"Galen beat up a guy about a week ago. Colored fella. He's in the hole right now."

I waited a moment, sick and considering, and then I made a leap and hoped for luck. "You sell any Frangelico in here?"

"Winter. Ski season."

"Lately, I mean."

Uncle Judith's eyes narrowed. He jackhammered the wad in his jaw. He was weaving now, hanging onto the counter.

I filled him in. "There was an empty at the crime scene."

"The monk?"

"Yes."

Seesawing words around a mouthful: "Why the hell didn't you tell me?"

"You sell any lately?"

"Hell yes," he drooled. He jerked his hat brim toward the window again, threw himself off balance. He gunned another savage miss—the Raging Bull of snoose.

"To Henderson Gray. And I'll kill that suck-egg sumbitch."

Yes. Now. Jesse.

Gray's girl at the reception desk was heavy and homely and trying so hard to overcome these flaws she didn't notice I was drunken, ill-groomed, and hostile, the public defender type.

"Is there any particular type of legal service that you're interested in?"

"I want to see Henderson Gray."

"I'm sorry. He's, um, out running. Can I help you with anything?"

"I'm . . . actually . . ."

"If you're the carpet guy, you'll need to see Charlotte anyway. She makes all those decisions."

"Maybe I should go . . ."

"I'll give you directions and call ahead."

Charlotte Gray was thin and good-looking, with exhausted eyes and a toddler on her hip. She was barely older than the girl at Henderson's office. The house around her was grandiose in design but half-finished and obviously uncomfortable for the mother of a crawling, falling, gnawing child.

"Carpet? I haven't even thought about carpet."

She held her ground atop construction-grade plywood in the doorway, her toddler yanking her sideways as he reached and fussed for a loose screw on the floor. She looked beyond me, taking in the Cruise Master with a look of fatigue and annoyance.

"More lies," she muttered. "You're selling stolen carpet? Is that it? Magic carpet?"

I picked up the screw and dropped it in my shirt pocket. The little boy lunged at me, screeching and causing his mother to wince and widen her stance. I went through my pockets for something to pacify: matches, a crumpled pack of Swishers, the red plastic cap to a liquor bottle, the cork butt of a broken rod, a snarl of discarded leader.

She sighed, accepted my offer of the rod butt, redirected the boy. "Maggie called me and said you stopped Tick Judith from getting hit in the middle of the street, and then you took an ice pick out of his hand and shoved him back in the liquor store." She hiked the toddler up on her hip and stepped aside. "So come in," she said, "and tell me what this bullshit is about."

"Those are the Crazy Mountains over there," she announced when we had reached a much-too-spacious back porch. "The Bitterroots are there. That smoke is from the Canyon Ferry fire. It's taking a thousand acres a day, and I just don't care."

She dropped the little gnawer and his rod butt on a pile of sawdust. She sat in a wrought iron chair and crossed her legs. A half finished drink—tea with ice and lime?—awaited her on a patio table.

"Now, what's up? I'm sure it's Henderson, and if it's anything new and girl-related, he knows I'm going to divorce him."

That was too fast for me. I needed a feel first. I started sideways. "How long has your husband had the idea to run down a deer?"

"Okay. You're from PETA or something?"

I shrugged. "Sure. Why not? Is it mutual? Does he get consent from the deer?"

She regarded me with weary amusement. Her eyes were pale blue and slightly bloodshot. Her short blonde hair contained flecks of something like oatmeal.

"You're from Earth First!?"

"Don't I dress the part? And how would your husband like to be chased until he drops from exhaustion? We can arrange that."

She accepted a handful of sawdust from the little boy. "Are you some girl's father?"

"Nope. Some boy's."

"Oh, shit."

"I'm kidding."

"I know."

"But only sort of."

"I know that too."

We traded little smiles and sat in a decently relaxed silence for a long time. Her voice had changed when she spoke again.

"Well, it's boring up here alone all day, so, let's see . . . Deer running, as it's called, was supposedly done by certain Native Americans as a test of manhood." Another fistful of sawdust came her way, this one airborne. "Peter, don't throw at Mommy. According to my husband, the Tarahumarans in Mexico still do it. His goal is to prove that it can be done and be the first white man to do it." She paused, answered me before I asked. "Don't ask me why. He's competitive. He won't stop brushing his teeth until after I do."

Now I received a handful of sawdust, launched against my shins and boots.

"Peter, don't throw at . . ."

"Dog."

"Your name is Dog?"

"Dog," said Peter. "Dog-dog-dog-dog."

"You got it."

"Your parents called you Dog?"

"It's a nickname. And I always thought deer running was a myth."

"Hendy wants to prove otherwise. Anyway he's an ultra-marathoner. He can run twenty miles a day and up to fifty if he needs to. Especially if someone else ran forty-nine."

"But deer are fast. Pronghorn are the fastest North American mammal." Sneed told me that. And they were *antelope*, not deer. Horns, not antlers.

She said, "Pronghorn are what he chases. The idea is that the animal has short-term speed but not stamina. If the human can keep disrupting its rest cycle, keep it moving, eventually the poor creature will stress and overheat and finally collapse. Then you can walk right up and touch them, kill them, whatever."

"Well hell," I said, "maybe I am from PETA."

"You're not."

"No. I'm not."

Sawdust flew in the air between us. She sighed. "Peter, how about we don't throw at all?" She brushed sawdust off her bare legs. "Hendy has a bet with a scientist from somewhere. He has this little tag thing the guy gave him. If he can videotape himself clipping that tag to the animal's ear, he's good. As long as the animal gets up and runs later, healthy, he's got proof. Then there will be articles everywhere. He's already going to be featured in this month's *National Geographic* with a story about his incredible connection to nature and ancient cultures." She said this dryly and directed my gaze across that immense back porch. "There used to be a big fir over there that had grizzly scratchings on it going back almost two hundred years. The Blackfeet used it for a sign post. But Hendy needed that corner for a hot tub to keep his muscles loose." She took a reckless gulp of her drink. "He thinks he'll be famous. He thinks there would be a movie about him—the man who ran down an antelope."

I worked on that, gazing off at the smoke in the Bitterroot range. Eventually Charlotte Gray said, "That's what I did before. I was a casting agent before we moved up here and started a family."

"Well, it's pretty here."

"Pretty goes up in flames," she said. "You want something to drink while you figure out how to get to the point?"

"Sure."

"And can you watch Peter?"

Given my track record, I watched that kid with my hair on end, vigilant for screws in the sawdust, for birds of prey swooping down, for Sudden Exploding Toddler Syndrome. When Peter Gray reached into the sawdust, pinched out a caulking tube tip and aimed it toward his mouth, I dove. I grabbed his chubby hand, pried his find away, causing him to shriek first with fright and next indignation.

"You're good," his mother said, exchanging the choking hazard for something that looked like iced tea but tasted more like some whoop-ass cocktail for college kids. "Not good," I said. "Just traumatized," and she looked at me strangely, hoping for an explanation she wouldn't get.

"So Dane Tucker's one of your husband's clients?"

"There." She was decisive. "Now I know. You're after a piece of Tucker. Well, good for you, that asshole deserves it, but sorry, you're out of luck. My husband *was* Tucker's lawyer."

"I heard it in the present tense."

"Nope." She squeezed lemon over her drink, rattled her ice. "Tucker was one of Hendy's main clients. But Tucker fired him over a year ago. It was because of some forty-mile fence that the old ranch manager put up. Tucker was on location in Australia. The ranch manager claimed the fence was my husband's idea and that Hendy okayed the job. Turns out Tucker got sued by some radical group for supposedly blocking a pronghorn migration route. He bought himself some science and my husband won the case, but it cost Tucker a load of money and brought a lot of bad press, which the moron then multiplied for himself by refusing to take the fence down. It was all pointless and ugly. Tucker fired Hendy as soon as it was over."

"People don't seem to know that."

"Oh, Hendy hides it. He hides all his little failures. Like not making the Berkeley Law Review. Like Peter's delayed speech. Like me and this." She waved her empty glass at me.

I set my drink down empty, too. Wow.

"Another?"

"Sure."

"You're on day care again."

This time I was proactive. I distracted the boy by burying my hand in sawdust and wiggling my fingers like worms. He chortled and tried to clobber the worms with a Matchbox Camero. When Charlotte Gray came back, she said, "But you're not trying to extort Dane Tucker?"

"I'm not."

"Too bad. That could be fun." She sat back with a little smile and sipped. "I should have visitors more often," she said. "Especially mysterious ones."

"Nice to be appreciated," I said, and then I looped back, following something. "Is that where your husband runs deer," I asked, "on Tucker's land?"

"No. He crosses Tucker's land to get to the place where he runs them."

I pictured Henderson Gray the first time I saw him, his showy finishing kick down Livingston's Main Street, his dramatic heaving goober onto the sidewalk, the water bottle over the head.

"So what's it take to run deer? What's it about?"

Gray's wife shrugged. "We don't talk about it much any more. It's one of our issues. He trains constantly. I don't know how he finds the time or the energy to—"

She stopped herself. She lifted her glass too strongly and ice hit her in the face. "It takes open land," she said, "good visibility. And you have to understand which direction the animal doesn't want to go. You run them that way, the way they don't want to go, and the stress tires them out."

"If your husband is fired, how does he get across Tucker's land?"

She laughed. This was nothing. "Along with Hendy, Tucker fired the ranch manager and the most of the hands too. I'm sure they all just kept their keys. Tucker's only here one month out of the year. He has no idea what goes on there day to day."

She finished her drink. She looked at me pointedly, a long time, raised her eyebrows. "Well? It's Peter's nap time. Is there anything else?"

"I'm here about your husband's girlfriend."

She did not look surprised. Instead she released a weighty exhalation that made her son look up from the sawdust pile.

"You're the tramp's father?" she said. "Or the brother. The ex?"

"I'm a friend."

"That whole episode is over," said Charlotte Gray. "Hendy and I have worked it out. He has made his apologies and explanations. This girl came after him because he is a lawyer and she wanted something. That's what he said. He made a mistake and it won't happen again. That's his story, and I've elected to believe him. It's over. He's told her to stay away and she has."

She bent between her legs, beat her child to a roofing nail that had surfaced in the pile of sawdust. Once more he yowled at his loss. Charlotte Gray extended the nail. "Here," she said. "You've got pockets. Be useful. And tell me what you want."

"Do you know where your husband was last Wednesday?" I said.

"I told you. It's over."

Sure, because Jesse is dead, I was about to say.

"We saw a counselor at Park County Mental Health. Henderson promised it was over and he would never do it again."

Gray's wife opened her arms, and the boy, angry and over-tired, toddled into them, released two punitive fistfuls of sawdust into her crotch. "What could I say?" she asked me. "He said he was sorry. He said he would never see the little bitch again. He promised."

"And these last couple of days he's been just like always? Things are normal again?"

"What do you mean? I've hardly seen him," she said. "He's so busy at work. Wednesday? I think he worked all day, probably went for a long run, came home late, had a scotch and a power bar, read Peter a story and went to bed. Is there a problem?"

I waited a long time before speaking again. I watched the Canyon Ferry smoke balloon up and spread, besotting the entire easterly sky until Gray's impressive roofline cut off the view.

"Well—"

"Well what?" She gathered red-cheeked Peter into her saw-dusty lap. "What is it you want from me?"

I was confused. I said finally, "It almost sounds as if you don't realize that Jesse is dead."

She fairly dropped the kid out of her lap. She sputtered at me, "*Jesse?*"

I nodded.

Again, louder—"*Jesse?*"—the kid, still slipping, grabbed at her shirt, yanking it open to expose exhausted breasts. She didn't care. Her voice became a croak, a snarl, and a sob.

"I was talking about *last year*. I was talking about *Ally Browning*, his old receptionist." Her eyes filled fast. "All this time you were talking about *now*, with Jesse, Jesse Ringer? He was screwing Jesse? The dead girl?"

I nodded. Yes. Now. Jesse.

"He was … that dirty lying … after all that we went through …"

She grabbed her drink, seemed surprised it was empty. She began to shake. The boy fell between her legs, but I saw it coming and caught his little skull in the palm of my hand.

"Missus Gray—"

"Not for long."

"—I'm sorry."

As I let the little boy down safely, he looked at me, looked at his mother, and then he began to thrash on the fresh cedar planks between her feet, began to thrash, and thrash, and wail.

A Likely Sneed

"Ms. Park-Ford?"

"Yes, Sheriff."

"Get Russell."

"I will do that, Sheriff."

"Thank you, Ms. Park-Ford."

Sheriff Roy Chubbuck's shaky hand lifted off the intercom button and went back to the business of writing out my ticket. *Driving with an expired license.* The tab came to three hundred and twelve dollars. I had fifteen days to pay the county. "Unless I catch you again," the sheriff said, "in which case the fines double and must be paid within twenty-four hours. The third time I can put you in jail. And I will."

He handed the ticket across his desk. I ripped it in half and tossed the pieces back toward him.

He showed me his tiny gray teeth. "You must have seen that on TV somewhere." He folded the carbons into his shirt pocket. "It's my copies that count. All you've done is lost the nice little envelope to put your money in."

"I have no money."

"Not my problem. I gave you gas."

"I guess you fish the Roam River," I said. "On Dane Tucker's land."

That startled him. "Do I?"

"You and your friends. Your buddies in the SUVs."

He drew oxygen through his nose, his sore eyes narrowing. "My buddies . . ."

I said, "Those skinheads work for Dane Tucker, so given what you're going through, I can understand why you looked the other way about the campground thing. I really can. Just the sight of that river makes my hands shake. But Tucker fired Henderson Gray a year ago. You can ask Gray where he was last Wednesday without messing up your fishing."

He kept those red slits on me for a long, silent passage into what I slowly understood was a region of no return. I had picked a fight with a dead man, hooked into his grief. Behind him, his wall of treasures from the land said it all. Among the petrified wood and arrowheads and hunting and fishing photos, one treasure in particular caught my eye. It was a wren's nest, a perfectly woven cup of dried bunchgrass and bison hair, wed to the three-pronged fork of a willow sapling. Chubbuck displayed this remarkable integration of natural elements like a trophy on the shelf behind his head.

"But I guess you're not going after Gray."

"That's correct," he said. "I am not."

"I'm a nuisance here."

"Pretty much."

"Does he talk?"

"Does who talk?"

"My buddy Sneed."

"He talks."

"Did he confess?"

"Not yet."

"Is his brain damaged?"

"Seems to be."

"Does he have a lawyer?"

"Not at this point in time."

I stared at this invalid, suffering man. He had to be delusional, had to be ripped on oxy-contin if he was headed where I thought he was.

"You're going to try to take a confession from a brain damaged black man without a lawyer? What the hell do you think this is, Alabama, nineteen-fifty-five? Don't you see how that's going to work out?"

Chubbuck pushed his chair back a bit from the desk and opened a drawer. He put a fly box on the desk. "You might be surprised how things are going to work out." It took him several tries to squeeze the clasp and open the box.

"As for a lawyer, I'm waiting on next of kin," he said as the fly box separated to display neat rows of mayfly patterns. "Depending on how things develop, we may have a call to make on life support as well as legal representation. Leave me a phone number, Mister Oglivie. I'll let you know how it goes."

I snarled back. I told him Sneed had no family. I said his mother was an offender, someone he meant never to see again. Sneed ran away from his mother and his foster care at fourteen, I said, and no one followed. But Sheriff Chubbuck disinterestedly pushed papers around his desk, found a pair of tweezers. He aimed these unsteadily into the fly box. At length, he extracted a tiny baetis dun, a mayfly imitation, held it up in the light between us.

"Say what you will. But we found a likely Sneed," he said, "working in the Houston Fire Department."

He turned the fly around for inspection. "Open your hand." He dropped the baetis into my palm. It was perfect, tight and balanced, uncommonly detailed for a size 18. "I tied that," he told me. "Just a year ago."

I looked up. Chubbuck put that raw, dry squint on me, gave it to me hard, and he held it.

"That one fools them every time."

The door creaked open.

"Russell," the sheriff snapped, "take this man out of my county. And do it right this time."

A Desperate Tangle, A Wishful Mess

Outside in the lot, Deputy Russell Crowe said to me, "You want to see what Elmer Sorgensen can do?"

The skinny old drunk sat on a yellow parking cleat beside Crowe's cruiser gnashing Doritos with his bad teeth and rinsing the shards down with Red Bull. He grinned at me in such a way as would only make sense if I had just that moment goosed him.

"Not really."

"I think you do," said Russell. "Come on. Follow a little. Elmer, get in, it's show time."

So once more I pulled the Cruise Master in behind the Park County deputy's lead and tailed this son-of-a-former-sheriff who was not, as you might think, related to a famous actor, even though he had the same name.

I ground my teeth and went with it. What else did I have? This time we paraded around the block, past the fuel depot and up to the chain link gate of what looked like the county impound lot. Crowe unlocked the gate and we pulled in. There at the back of the lot, striking a shiver into me, rested Jesse's dusty golden Oldsmobile.

I closed my eyes, tried to squeeze out the memory. But Crowe was at my window. He seemed driven now, edgy.

"See," he said, "I put some thought to your idea that your buddy didn't kill Jesse. There is a way. Come on. Have a look."

I climbed down and followed. The Olds was surrounded by ant hills and localized tumbleweeds, its side mirrors spidered over. Strips of desiccated duct tape hung inside the window frames. The back-seat window I had rocked out was now sloppily sealed with black plastic sheeting. Crowe peeled that up, reached forward and unlocked the doors.

"It doesn't seem possible at first, that anyone else could have done it," he said. "Truth is, you don't look too sensible in saying so—" he flashed me his long-jawed horse grin "—seeing as you're the one who says the keys and pistol were locked in there with him."

"They were."

"Okay. Whatever you say. And all the window seams were taped tight from the inside. So nobody got out and then locked the doors after."

"No."

"But that wouldn't be necessary, would it? To tape the windows?"

"What do you mean?"

"Would you do it?" he said. "Killing yourself? In a heat? Would you bother? See what I mean? These windows are tight enough. The tape is a sell job, trying to make the point that the doors weren't locked after the fact. Window dressing."

Crowe laughed at his joke. I wondered where his idea, his words, his jitters came from. But he had explicated, somehow, my unvoiced instinct. The set-up around Sneed was too thorough, too perfect. Supposedly he had just shot his lover. Then he had meant to shoot himself, only to discover my Glock was empty. In that state, with Jesse's face in pieces on the ground, Sneed had come up with duct tape—where?—and bothered to tape the window seams?

So Russell had surprised me, making sense like that. Warily, I opened Jesse's rear door and entered Sneed's back-seat coffin. The charcoal smell was still strong. Shaggy strips of duct tape dragged against me. I twisted on the seat. I touched the roof and doors. How would someone get out?

"You ready?" Russell asked me. "I know what you're thinking. It's not possible. Right? Come on out of there. You're too big. Elmer, get in the car."

I got out. Russell held the passenger door open. Elmer Sorgensen slipped in past me on a breeze of evaporated urine. Russell locked the old man in, then sprung the trunk and left it open. "Go," he said.

Sorgensen just sat there, rumpling his lips and blinking.

"Elmer, go. Do what we practiced." Russell rapped on the window. "Go."

Now the old drunk activated. He moved aside and I began to understand. I had watched Jesse do a variation of what Sorgensen did next. The Oldsmobile's rear seat split about 70/30, and both sections unlatched and folded forward, converting the trunk into a flat space that extended all the way to the front seats. Jesse did this from the outside, with the doors open. But Sneed was too long to sleep in there, and so they bought a tent.

Elmer Sorgensen, though, was inside the car, not outside reaching in. And Sneed, by hypothesis, was in there too, crowding the space. There was only room for Sorgensen to fold down the smaller seat piece, the thirty percent.

He did so—and jumped in fright. It appeared that a huge spider had set up housekeeping on the back, where the upholstery lipped over and met the trunk carpet. Sorgensen looked out at Russell, who reassured him with a flush of horse teeth. The old man looked more closely at the spider, then disregarded it and promptly wormed out through the small opening and into the trunk.

Russell and I walked around. Elmer Sorgensen said, "Uff-da." He clambered out of the trunk and stumbled off sideways for a few steps before he fell down in the dust.

"You see it now?"

"I see it now."

"The one problem," Crowe said, "is getting that seat piece shut again."

"Shouldn't be hard."

"You want to try it?"

I did indeed. I reached through the trunk but my arm wasn't long enough. I needed a full two feet more. I hooked a leg inside, tried to fit my shoulder above the spare tire. I was too thick. The only method remaining was to go in head first, groin over the trunk latch, and flail blindly for a grip on a seat that was folded down away from me. Only when I abandoned all hope for self-preservation and lunged in completely could I grip the cushioned top of the seat section. I had to hang on and worm back out, using muscle combinations unrelated to normal human behavior—but then, when I tried to close the seat, my hand was in the way, and if I let go, the section flopped back down. I tried to throw it back, whisking my hand clear, but I could not do this with enough force to make the seat piece snap into its latch. It only bounced, flopped, gaping open.

Dog damn it.

Russell was pleased. "See?"

As I kinked back out, I felt a sense of the killer's frustration, even panic. This problem with the seat was unforeseen. And maybe a clock was ticking. Sneed was stirring. Or the charcoal was burning down, the gas dissipating. All for a quarter inch of stubborn upholstery.

Russell leaned on the open passenger door, chin on his arms like a third elbow, those teeth taking air.

"What's so funny?"

"Come here. See that?"

The spider hadn't moved through all the commotion because it wasn't a spider. It was one of my big, black Madame X flies, one I had tied especially for Sneed. The fly trailed a short length of heavy tippet, curled from the stress of snapping. I looked at Russell.

"The killer had to rig up a rod," he said with complete confidence. "Then he had to jam the rod in here and hook the back of the seat with that big fly. Then he had to yank it shut and break the line."

He paused, then answered my unvoiced question. "Because that hook is barbed. It ain't coming out."

I touched the Madame X. The foam thorax was half-shredded. A tiny tuft of wool from Sneed's vest patch still clung to the hook's barb. The fly had been fished by Sneed, clipped off and put on the patch, and then retied to a tippet.

"All you gotta do is snap the line, put the rod back where you found it," Russell explained, "shut the trunk, and you're good to go."

Just in case, I tried to work the hook free.

"It won't come. You'd have to cut it out. Am I right?"

"You're right."

"And who's got time for that? And hey, speaking of time, we'd better get going. We've been in here about long enough."

On a hunch, I bent closer to inspect the knot. Sneed was fastidious about his knots. If Sneed had tied that knot, it would have been a perfect clinch knot. But it didn't look right.

"Gotta obey orders," Russell said at my back. "Heh. Or at least I gotta look like it."

I ignored him. I went to my knees, got out of my own light. Now it was clear: this was not a clinch knot at all.

"We been in here so long Elmer's started looking for a home. Heh."

I glanced up. The scrawny old drunk was trying the door handles on a confiscated panel van. But back to the knot. I checked it from a different angle. Knots were small, sure, and line was translucent, but when you fly fished, you inspected thousands of knots, the clinch knot ten times more often than any other. Every fly fisherman knew the clinch knot, and a good clinch knot, the type Sneed tied, looked like a microscopic baby's fist, the thumb sticking up inside wrapped and fisted fingers.

Russell's shadow moved over my light. "Gonna have to go deputy on you, Mister Oglivie. Load up and let's go."

No, this was not a clinch knot at all. This was a granny knot. No, worse. It was a desperate tangle, a wishful mess. The knot had held, as some knots will, by sheer luck, and by copious looping and winding and threading and cinching.

I let the knot go and straightened up. Elmer Sorgensen's legs protruded, strained and wiggled, half out of the panel van's busted windshield.

"You fly fish much, Russell?"

His eyes widened. His teeth appeared and he began to nod.

"Oh, sure," he said. "Absolutely. All the time."

The Bozeman-Livingston Guide War

Take this man out of my county. And do it right this time.

The meaning of this, Russell decided, meant mostly that I, once out of Park County, should do whatever I felt was right while he, Deputy Crowe, should exonerate himself from blame in the event that I decided to come back.

To these ends, the son of Rita Crowe suggested that he should once more follow me across the county line, whereupon, using his training, he should inflict dramatic but minor wounds upon me—say, abrasions on the neck, which were easy, and maybe also a glancing blow to the scalp, good for blood production. In this way, we would commemorate Russell's insistence that I leave the sheriff's turf and keep on going. And in this way, if and when I returned to Livingston (which, of course, was my choice), he would not be blamed.

"That's an interesting thought, Russell. You're an interesting guy."

"Or, you can beat yourself up," he offered.

"Believe me, I know."

"Just a good hard skim," the deputy suggested, "to that ridge above the eye, bleeds like heck, makes a big mess over nothing."

"Hit myself in the eye?"

"As an option," he said.

We had only gone about one mile out of town on 89 South, however, when the deputy, behind me, seemed to upend all that careful planning. First his cherries flashed in my side mirror, then his siren whooped. I pulled onto the low shoulder only to discover that he wanted to pass. He rocketed around me. One hundred yards up the road he found himself behind another RV, Yellowstone bound. This continued—flash and *whoop!* and pass—until sight and sound of the deputy were gone.

It was dinner hour, and the highway was busy. It was a good slow while before I could wallow the Cruise Master back up out of the ditch and rejoin traffic. Volition being limited when you're on a two-lane highway in a forty-footer with an un-tuned engine, I drifted along with the southbound tourists, trying to figure what next. Was Henderson Gray thin enough to squeeze out of Jesse's car? Should I, in fact, find the tire iron and hit myself? Keep Russell on whatever track he was traveling?

But those ruminations vanished a half-mile short of Carter's Bridge, as I passed the turn-in to Hilarious Sorgensen's Fly 'n' Float Outfitters.

Russell's cruiser was in there, lights flipping and snapping, and I glimpsed a milling crowd of fancy hats and vented shirts among the rental cars and pickup trucks and SUVs. The guides and their clients were back from a day of fishing, but something had gone wrong.

I turned around at the boat landing across the bridge and came back. Hilarious Sorgensen's lot was roomy—space for all the boat trailers in high season—and I parked easily inside a windbreak row of spruce at the roadside margin.

The crowd of fishermen enclosed a bloody brawl. At the approximate center of the outfitter's lot, two vehicles towing drift boats had collided. No doubt this had ignited the shoving and punching that erupted in every direction around a desperate Deputy Russell Crowe.

I wormed in closer. Real injury had been done to a paunchy, gray-haired man who lay unconscious beneath the boat hitch of a gleaming black Dodge Durango. He bled from a gash that seemed to relocate his nose into the hollow of his left cheekbone. Someone was trying to help him and Russell was screaming, "Back! Get back!"

The other vehicle in the collision was an old Jeep Wrangler, once white, with a ratty soft-top and rusted wheel wells. The apparent driver of the Jeep was bloody as well, but he was still a player, wheeling on his back in the dust, kicking at a young guide who was livid, howling with rage, trying to make good contact with a boat oar.

"Knock it off!" Russell hollered. He was spread too thin, dancing ineffectively between clusters of combatants. "You! Get back!" As I retreated he was screeching for backup into his shoulder radio, wading toward the injured man below the hitch. "Isn't somebody here a doctor?"

In fact, this being Sorgensen's crowd, the gallery had to be brimming with doctors and dentists and vets and pharmacists from Indiana and Wisconsin and wherever else Sorgensen's marketing touched down. But the energy of these professionals seemed spastic and morally confused. "Where's Bronowski?" I heard. "I'm an allergist," came the excuse. And, "Touch one of these guys and get yourself sued. Just watch." And then: "Heh-heh. That guy's gonna need a dentist. Here's my card. I'm kidding."

I moved around the mob. Hilarious Sorgensen watched all this from the doorway of his shop. The massive ex-rodeo clown had no response except to gnash Planters peanuts from a mostly empty jar.

"You've seen this before," I guessed.

Sorgensen flicked me a glance from drug-shrunk eyes. Twenty-seven broken bones and a lacerated kidney, Jesse said, were laid up inside that envelope of fat. He had a lot of pain to kill, and then a lot of painkiller to override with speed.

"Just a cat fight," he grunted, batting peanut crumbs from his filthy beard. "My old man was a sheepherder. You know what that's like? That means he was bat-shit crazy and made exactly enough cash to stay drunk between the good grass."

These comments with respect to what, I wondered. Sorgensen lumbered to the porch's side railing to flick his Planters jar into a dumpster below. He barely made it back to me with enough breath left to continue.

"Swore I was going to have a better life. But hell, working with these goofballs, I don't know." Those empty pinpricks again, right on me. "So how's our buddy Sneed?"

"He's alive. Talking."

"Hmmm. What's he saying?"

"That I don't know."

"Confession?"

"Not if he didn't do it."

"Hmmm." At this point, Sorgensen had expended his capacity to stand. He ballooned to the rear in his huge culotte-shorts and leaned his forearms on the porch rail, making it creak. He jingled a set of keys, tapped the ring on the railing. Even at my safe distance, he smelled like the underside of a door mat, plus something close to creamed corn. "Woman!" he bellowed suddenly. "Get a move on!"

He swung his bison head toward the shop and back. Tap, jingle, tap-tap-tap. "Gonna miss her flight."

"Lyndzee's traveling again?"

"Death in the family."

"Again?"

"They come in threes, don't they?"

Out on the lot, Russell was making some progress. A fisherman had approached the wounded man and knelt beside him. Around this, most of the skirmishes had attenuated to jousting and shouting, all except the madman with the helicoptering oar.

"So what's this about?" I ventured at Sorgensen.

A snort. "A bunch of girls pissing in my parking lot, mostly."

Not the real answer, of course, so I waited. "Hell," he grumbled on eventually, jabbing a key into the wood of the railing, "with

the guide rates up so high, and the shuttle drivers nicking me—"
His head again swung suddenly. "Damn it, woman! You're gonna
miss your flight!"

Lyndzee's harried voice struggled to reply. "If you'd give me
some time to get ready . . ."

Sorgensen grumbled, "This time her uncle in Memphis." He
shook his wooly head. "Woman and her damn people are bleeding
me dry. As for this out here, this is an outbreak of the Bozeman-
Livingston guide war. Every couple of years the Bozeman guides
get the idea the fishing must be better over here and they show up
by the dozens. They clog the boat ramps, jam up the river, acting like a bunch of spoiled little prom queens. Even though they
got the Gallatin, the Madison, the Beaverhead, all that water over
there. Pisses off the Livingston guides, these two girls have a fender
bender and off we go."

Before us now, a brave pair of perhaps orthodontists or veterinary surgeons had stepped in to try to curtail the flailing oar. As for
one other remaining hot spot, a shoving match over near the Cruise
Master, Russell seemed to be getting results with a taser.

"Jesse's dad—" I began.

"You're looking at it, Pal. Galen Ringer killed a Bozeman guide
one day in a fight down at Otter Creek."

"Jesse believed he was innocent."

"Yeah." The big man ejected breath. "Loyal to the death.
Poor girl."

Lyndzee clattered onto the porch with a pair of hardshell suitcases, pre-wheel. She set them down and yanked at a leather mini
skirt, tried for bright.

"Oh, hello. I'm so sorry about your friends."

"I'm sorry about your family."

"You're okay?"

"Not really. You?"

She had a voice like a squeaky pencil sharpener. "Oh . . . I . . .
um . . . I'm . . ."

"You're late. Get in the van."

Her eyes clouded over. Now muttering, head down, she lifted her suitcases and carried them off the porch toward a battered conversion van beyond the dumpster. I repositioned myself and blocked Sorgensen before he could get moving.

"Jesse told me her dad cut the guy's anchor rope and let the client go floating away down the river. She said her dad and the Bozeman guide fought, something about a cut-off on a boat ramp, but the Bozeman guide was alive and well when her dad drove off."

"That's Galen's story." Sorgensen watched Lyndzee into the van. "It took the jury eighteen minutes. They saw pictures of that poor sonofabitch trailing like a water weed with his skull busted and that anchor rope around his neck."

"Jesse said somebody showed up just as her dad left."

Lyndzee turned on the radio. *Rush*, maybe. Guitars and voice screeching off toward the Yellowstone.

"Jesse'd believe the pope did it." Sorgensen wanted to move around me. He was not a tall man, was actually small when you looked inside the fat. He had tiny hands, tiny ears, narrow shoulders. This man had once fit inside a barrel. Thwarted, he considered me with those buzzed-up eyes. "I hear you're asking a lot of questions about Jesse's death."

"Just a few," I said.

"You got one for me? That's why you're here?"

"Actually, I do."

He nodded slowly, waiting, whistling air out through his nose.

"A couple days ago," I framed it, "when I was looking for Sneed and Jesse, you said you'd fired them. You said they'd stolen a rod. So whose rod did they steal?"

But while I asked the question, Sorgensen's face transformed. He infused a cheesy lightness into his cheeks and eyes. Now he clown-smiled at me—crinkly eyes, grotesquely and falsely jolly—as he bulled out some space toward the porch steps. Passing, he reached out in a half-successful attempt to slap me on my stiffening shoulder.

"You take care."

"Whose rod?"

"Crimenently, fella. I don't know what you're getting at. Believe me, it broke my heart—" Sorgensen gripped the rail, side-stepped off the porch "—to fire those kids."

I tried once more, uselessly, at the mute slab of his back: "Did they steal a rod or not?"

He did a flaccid little jig-step, kept walking.

Imagine Dentists

The ambulance came and went. Russell busted someone. His cruiser followed the other out the driveway and turned right toward Livingston. From the deck of the Fly 'n' Float, I watched the guides and clients split from their klatches, depleted beer cans in hand, and head for vehicles, hotels, homes. I picked out a stocky kid with an older model Chevy pickup that was in dire condition. As if to forestall the truck's collapse, he had backed his trailer to the corner of the lot. Now he got out to unhitch his boat and leave it for tomorrow.

"Lot of miles on that truck."

"Hundred and fifty-nine thou." He raised up and recovered his beer from the truck box.

"Not bad for a Chevy."

"Yeah. Well, I'm trying to get one more season out of her. Don't know if she'll make it."

"Not the best for hauling clients, is it? A pickup?"

"Naw," he said. "If I got more than one, as I usually do, we have to squeeze in like we're back in high school going to a party."

"I'm Dog," I said.

"I'm Cord. Cord Cook."

He had a good grip and a good smile, longish blond hair and a sunburned nose. He started guiding, he volunteered, right out of high school, three years now. If things went right in the summer months—weather, trout, truck—he could make enough to fund tuition and housing at U of M in Missoula. "You?" he said.

"Trout bum."

"Awesome."

"You see that RV over there? That's mine. Imagine dentists in the back of that." He grinned at the picture. I pushed the sale. "Coffee and the *New York Times* on the way to the water."

"Beverages on the way home," he said.

"It's even got a trailer hitch."

"I see that."

"Hell, on a long morning haul, to the Boulder or something, to the Smith, the dentists could go back to bed in there."

"Dentists are never tired. Vets either. But the doctors I get can be pretty burned out. And oh, yeah," the kid said, raising a sun-bleached eyebrow, "I get couples all the time."

"There's a curtain between the cab and the living space. So who knows?"

Cord Cook rubbed his stubbled chin.

"A straight up trade?" I proposed. I laid a hand on his last-gasp Chevy. "Your truck for my RV?"

"Damn. Really? Maybe."

"Or how about a trial period? You take it for a week. You try it, drive some clients around. See what you think. I'll drive yours."

"Can I test it?"

"Of course. I'll try yours."

There was a break for the Dog. But as Cord Cook pulled the Cruise Master out on 89 and headed toward Yellowstone Park, exhaustion hit me like a cartoon anvil.

I blanked out for twenty minutes in the driver's seat of that pickup, blinking at nothing and chewing the inside of my mouth, craving sleep, hoping Cook would trade me. I would grab my stuff, my vodka and Tang, my fishing gear, my sleeping bag, and I would crash at some campground in the box of the truck. It wouldn't rain. It never did. The law, such as it was, would leave me alone. And I imagined if I slept hard enough, if I traveled to my dark deep and made good at the Big Two-Hearted, then Sneed and Jesse could come back good as new.

It took all this time for me to pay attention to the rodeo medal hanging on Cord Cook's rear view mirror. Then for another bleary five minutes I figured Cook was a cowboy too—maybe on the college rodeo team. But in ten more minutes, when the kid still hadn't returned with my Cruise Master, I felt an edge beneath my exhaustion, and I began to fiddle with the medal. I looked at it more closely. I shook myself. I re-laminated. *Come on, Dog.*

The engraving said:

FIRST PLACE

BULL RIDING

BULL-A-RAMA

BUTTE, MONTANA

1998

GALEN RINGER

I let the medal fall back and swing above the dashboard as the Cruise Master appeared on the drive and skidded to a stop.

I got out.

Cord Cook got out.

We approached each other in the dusk light. The kid was frowning, scratching his head. The Cruise Master's engine ticked. It was one of the belts, maybe, that smelled a little bit like burning rubber. He handed me the keys.

"What do you think?"

"Naw," he said, moving past me. "I guess not. Thanks."

Pronghorn Are Not Deer

It wasn't so much my dark deep then—at the closest campground—
as it was an epic vodka-Tang and then the blow of another, bigger
anvil: *memory.*

I was only half-asleep when the chaos of images resolved into
one nucleus of recall that spun and bumped and then cracked wide
open. A vivid, Technicolor Dog floated out onto the black screen
of the night to perform for me, and to perform badly. *I should have
known.* This was my theme. *I should have foreseen. Of all people, me.
I should have stopped it.*

"Hey! Really?"

This drunk girl says she's Jesse Ringer, says it three or four times.
But who cares? She is meat to the Dog's hungry eye. She is young
but not too young. She is small and tan and wiry. Her hair is kinky,
long, and wild, the color of cornbread crust, and she is not overly well
groomed, which is a very nice thing in a girl, Dog-wise.

"Hey! Really?" She slugs Sneed in the arm. "You're not just
shittin' me?"

Her clothes are skimpy summer stuff. But the summer seems
like 1976 or so. She wears fraying cut-off Levis over a pair of lean

brown thighs that insinuate their way effortlessly into the hot zones of personal bar-stool space. She wears an actual halter top—when have you seen that?—and she fills it to the brim, with a knot between her shoulder blades that would be oh so easy.

She is after Sneed, of course, not this mangy old Dog. She hardly looks the Dog's direction, and in this way she implicitly assigns him to the shit-faced mumbling hag at the Dog's left elbow, the one with the white wine spritzer, the queen-size cigarette, and the stupid red cowgirl hat perched atop a frosty perm.

"Whassyername?"

The Dog goes with "Cornelius."

"Wha—?"

This drunk girl, Jesse Ringer, leans in on Sneed. Upon his dark forearm she lays an envoy to her whole flesh, this hand—strong and sun-chapped, fingernails cut short and a little dirty.

"This is wild," says Jesse Ringer to D'Ontario Sneed. "You're not going to believe this. This is *so* wild. I can't believe this connection. Your mother's in prison? Well, get this. My *daddy's* in prison!"

Sneed catches the Dog's eye. The Dog discharges a shrug of affirmation, bluntly covetous, as the next-door hag jabs him with an elbow. "Huh, Corneliush? Where'd you find your interesting friend there? He fall off a Greyhound?"

Sneed ignores this and smiles at the drunken white girl, looking a little stiff. "My mama *was* in prison."

He hoists a Budweiser to free his arm from her too-forward grip.

"Jail, actually. I don't know where she's at now."

He sets the bottle down.

"I don't care either. I'm an orphan, far as I'm concerned."

"Oh," the girls laments sloppily. "Oh, that's so sad." She hooks that arm again, gives it a squeeze. "What did she do?"

Sneed tells her exactly what he's told me: Nothing. His mama didn't do a damn thing. Not really.

"I mean to get in jail."

His face clouds. "Oh. Stole, I guess. Robbed a house in the neighborhood of my foster parents. Sold the stuff for drugs."

"'Cuz my dad," this Jesse rushes in, one-upping, "supposedly murdered a guy."

This stops everything. Jesse Ringer glugs warm beer from her plastic cup. Her breasts stir beneath the halter as she jars the cup back down and leans closer to Sneed.

"But he didn't do it," she tells him. Then her voice gets too loud. "He is *so* fucking innocent."

The bar tender, the hag, the players at the keno machines, this benumbed and negligent Dog, everybody stiffens and looks the drunk girl's way.

"That's right people," she announces. "Galen Ringer is *so fucking innocent.*"

Later, next day, this Jesse Ringer girl can fish. She can pick flies. She can handle line on big water and she can set the hook. She can play and land and show and release. She credits it all to a bull rider turned Yellowstone fishing guide turned death row inmate, her father, Galen Ringer. Who is innocent. She never lets you forget that.

She wet-wades too, and she looks very, very good.

"I don't know, Dog," Sneed says, clearly troubled. "This girl is teeing it up. But man, I just don't know."

"Hey," this slipshod friend, this careless mentor, gives back, "I would."

Which is all too goddamn true.

Later still, this rough and lovely girl, generally stoned, says she has a place to live, but her car looks slept in.

This brown and barefoot girl, this lite beer champion, has a golden Oldsmobile, about ten years old, and she has this guide-shuttle partner, this earnest and besmitten virgin man-child named Kenny she knew in high school, and when Sneed comes into her life, this fire-in-the-belly girl Jesse Ringer flicks poor unrequited Kenny like a chub back into the stream of lonely and bewildered young men.

Together then, Jesse and Sneed drive for Hilarious Sorgensen, every morning, ferrying vehicles and trailers downstream to take-out points, teaming back and forth, seven days a week. This Dog character? Sleeps late. Ties flies. Nips a little v and T. Smokes the second half of last night's Swisher. Studies maps. Makes pancakes. Misses warning signs.

In the afternoons, fishing, Sneed and Jesse bitch and joke about Sorgensen. The cheap bastard gobbles peanuts and speed while his brain works overtime, finding ways to squeeze his guides, short his drivers, bilk his suppliers, ways to hornswoggle his clientele of doctors, dentists, vets, ways to keep poor little Lyndzee hooked and hopping.

But the thing is, Jesse then suggests, if anybody needs any-thing—you know, *anything*—she can talk to Sorgensen. She can get it. No problem.

And this inattentive dumb Dog, where is he? What is he thinking?

He is thinking: *Anything? Really? Would Sorgensen have Cuban cigars? How would they taste next to a Swisher?*

I thrashed and mumbled but could not wake, could not stop this relentless indictment.

Inside a week, Jesse and Sneed have bought a tent and are "liv-ing together" within earshot of the Cruise Master. Dog's ears burn, his head spins, and he does not sleep. Every morning when the kids are gone he tells himself, *Drive away now. Right now. Go, Dog, go.*

But no. There is inertia. And there is thrall. There is Jesse's skin by firelight. There is this fascinating kid Sneed, so oddly but so pas-sionately lecturing nightly on the pronghorn antelope: physiology, habits, plight. "Pronghorn are not deer. They have gall bladders.

They have horns, not antlers. They can't jump. They come to a fence they have to crawl under. Or turn around."

"Then I," announces Jesse, "have a friend you have to meet." She pauses, tries to word this carefully. "Just a guy I know. Older guy. Lawyer. Who is into pronghorn. Really into them. He chases them."

"What?"

"On foot. He chases them."

Sneed scowls. "What? Why?"

"He says the Indians did it. He says if they can do it, a white man can do it too."

"White man?"

"He's a white man, this guy that I, um, know."

"Chase antelope?"

"And catches them. Tries to. He hasn't yet."

"Pronghorn are the fastest mammal in North America."

"This guy. Well. He says antelope are fast but they tire out. After five or ten miles they give up. You can walk right up and slit their throats."

Sneed's spine straightens, his eyes narrow, the way it happens when someone mentions his mother.

"You want to meet him?" Jesse asks.

Sneed says, "Yeah. Yeah I do."

At the campground, dew descended around the Cruise Master, smoky, low, and cold. The river muttered. Pictures flowed out through the anvil crack in my brain.

Now, on Sneed's words, I see a dark bedroom. I solve his double sounds and see his life begin. I see Sneed's mother's *mother's* man friend, drunk and tearing sheets, tearing bedclothes, tearing the girl and planting Sneed.

"Go on, Sneed. Keep talking."

"So that's her excuse for everything. Like therefore she can be a crack whore and ignore me. After about ten years of that bullshit I ended up in foster care with a white family in Little Rock. Church people that smelled funny. Lady smelled like mothballs. Dude smelled like he shit his pants. They didn't like my name so they gave me a new one. Charlie. They fucking called me Charlie."

Sneed presents this for laughter. This Dog, this moral feeb, goes along chuckling at tales of soup and crackers, made beds, clean clothes, pews and catechism, chores, haircuts, lectures, prayers—and every day at school in a sea of white kids, waves of them, rip tides and reefs, Sneed re-drowning daily, dead by noon, washing up at "home" with "family."

The Dog looks around the bar, suppresses a gargantuan sadness. Sneed orders another beer. "The dude had this weird business, mostly retired. He bred ungulates, deer and antelope and sometimes elk, for zoos. He had a big lot, a couple acres, tall fence around it, at that time just a little herd of pronghorn left in there. Seven of them. My chore was food and water. And man, every day those animals would hear me coming a mile away, come snuffling up to me and bumping me with their noses and whistling to me, stepping on my damn feet, licking me, fighting for my attention. Man, we got like a real family, me and them. Me and those animals loved each other. Up until I ran away, that's how I survived." He looks around. Jesse is *still* in the restroom. At least twenty minutes now. "That's why I just about went upside the head of her lawyer friend," Sneed says. "Greg Henderson? Henderson Greg? I forget."

"Never met him."

"Don't bother."

"He helps her with her dad's case?"

Sneed shrugs. "I dunno," he says. "But damn, she is really stuck on that. She idolizes her old man. She showed me a bunch of his stuff, you know his medals and all, for rodeo? Weird scene, Dog."

"Yeah?"

"I tried to touch one of those medals? You know? Just touch it?"

I bolted up from my theater of half-sleep, dropped in a panic from my bunk. Outside, it was broad daylight, hot already. I pissed on pine needles. Drift boats glided past on the 'Stone, telling me it was mid-morning. I was too late to catch Cord Cook at Sorgensen's.

"I don't give out that information," Sorgensen told me when I asked where Cook was fishing. Since yesterday, his tone was nasty and short. I had the sense he might be missing Lyndzee.

"Why not? It's confidential?"

"Yes it is."

"You're not a doctor. You're not a lawyer."

Sorgensen rattled a handful of peanuts into his mouth and mashed them, observing me with a sense of hidden, whirring activity. At last he said, "Friend, you look like you could use a little pick-me-up."

White Fang and Top Gum

"How'd you find me?"

Cord Cook appeared less than happy to see me hiking out to the spit where he had moored his drift boat for lunch.

"I just drove along the river with my windows open. People say you can hear dentists fly casting from a mile away."

Cook eyed me. On cue, one of his clients howled, "Argggh! Buck! Mother Tucker! Sonofabutterknife!"

Cook strode muttering off the sand spit and over heavy cobble to unwind leader from the howler's terrific hat. He cut the fly out of the fellow's cherrywood landing net. From behind, he spooned himself to the caster. He pushed one elbow, lifted another, squared the guy's hips to match his own, and in this fashion, somewhat like insects mating, Cook and his client made a few decent casts together.

When Cook disengaged, however, the howling resumed. "What the hell is going on?" the dentist demanded. He looked at his rod in disbelief, betrayed.

The guide rubbed his college-kid stubble. He looked into the sky, snatched down the eternal scapegoat. "Crosswind, Kevin. I under-rodded you. It's not your fault. You're doing awesome. Just keep working that seam out there and I'll rig another rod."

Cook disengaged, hollered to the other one, thirty yards down-stream: "Gary? Can I ask you to slow down your backcast a little? Let the rod do the work? You're not serving a tennis ball. That's it. Thanks, Gary."

The kid came back needing to talk: "Dentists from Toledo. Said they could fish. They been here all week. We've been calling these guys White Fang and Top Gum. Jim Rideup had them yes-terday. He called in sick today."

"You're doing everything you can."

"No," he said. "I could shoot them. I got a pistol in my first aid box."

He felt my eyes linger, maybe felt the bad taste of Jesse's death.

"I'm kidding," he said. "I mean, I do have a pistol, but . . ."

I smoothed it over. "People are good at different things. I mean, not to get too philosophical, but how are you at filling cavi-ties? Anyway, I figured you'd pull up for lunch about here. What's cooking? Is that elk on a skillet?"

The kid grunted, "Yup."

"Where?"

"Shot him in the Little Belts last November. Me and my dad."

The elk steaks sizzled in a pan on a little propane stove beyond Cook's Clack-a-Craft. He had set up a folding table with a wine bottle and glasses, bread, olives, a tomato half-sliced on a cutting board with yellow jackets buzzing above.

"So?" Cook said. "What do you want me for? I don't know anything. I only loaned her my boat."

Doors just open sometimes. Cord Cook puffed up like prai-rie chicken, reddened in the face, then wheeled away to tend his elk steak. I lingered, surprised, watching dentist Gary perform a root canal on a pocket of water about ten feet out. Then I followed Cook around the Clack-a-Craft to the kitchen. The elk was a touch overdone, powerful in the nose.

"Let me guess. You used to go out with Jesse."

"Look, man. I'm in college now. I declared a major. I'm keep-ing my grades up, staying clean. I don't need any trouble."

"I saw her dad's rodeo medal in your truck. She normally doesn't let anyone touch those."

He shoved his skillet off the fire. "Doesn't matter now. She's dead."

"What boat? This one?"

"My rubber boat. For small stuff, whitewater, all that."

"What for?"

Cook wiped the knife on his pants and rose sharply. "Gary! Slow down!"

The downstream dentist—knock-kneed in a foot of water—ceased casting entirely. His line convulsed in the air, then collapsed in squiggles onto the water at his feet. As Gary turned, sending a hurt look toward Cook, the Yellowstone's strong current grabbed his line and straightened it downstream into deeper water. "Top Gum, shot down again," Cook muttered.

"She must have told you where she was going with it."

"She didn't."

"You didn't ask?"

"Didn't want to know."

"Where is it now?"

He waved away yellow jackets. "Shit if I know. Gone."

"The rodeo medal was collateral?"

"Was."

"She really wanted that boat."

He twisted his corkscrew in to the hilt, ripped out the wine cork. "Look, man. I know exactly nothing." He splashed red wine into the glasses. He wasn't having any. His was a liter bottle of Mountain Dew propped in the cobble where a trickle of the 'Stone kept it cool.

"I believe you." I waited for Cook to look at me. "I believe you. But I guess you also think there's something out there beyond what's already known."

"Maybe," he said, looking away—and just then the upstream guy, White Fang, screeched, "I got one! Hah! Screw you, Gary! I got one! I got the first fish!"

White Fang clodhopped laterally through knee-high water, clutching after a chaos of slack line while a good-sized rainbow tail-walked about twenty feet out, thrashing with the burden of our collective disbelief.

"What the—" Cook said, heading out to assist.

"Drinks on you tonight!" White Fang screeched. "I got one!"

Cord Cook eased up behind his combatant, spoke like Mister Rogers to a pre-schooler. "Kevin? Right behind you. Gonna help you if you need it. Now, can I ask you to get your rod tip up? Good. Excellent. Now can I ask you one more thing? Can I ask you to—"

"Sonofabutterknife!" Top Gum howled. "I got one too!"

And it was true. It does happen sometimes. Mother Nature falls asleep at the wheel. Gaia gets bored and looks away. The Great Turtle takes a dump. Anyway, there we were, with a double, Top Gum's hook-up appearing to be a big brown, digging against the dentist into the depths beyond.

"Okay," Cord Cook soothed. "Okay—listen—guys?"

"Mother Tucking sonofabutterknife!"

"Let's take it easy, guys. Keep our rod tips up. Keep our lines tight."

But their guide was caught between them, and suddenly situations devolved badly in both directions.

"Let's just stay—Gary! What the hell! Don't horse him! Get him on the reel!"

Cook charged downstream, looking like he was going to tackle Top Gum. But then he reversed field, plodded back against the current as he implored his upstream dentist: "Kevin! Never let a fish get behind you! Not downstream *and* behind you. Jesus, Kevin—"

"What should I do? Jump?"

"Cord!" wailed Top Gum, "I lost him!"

"No you didn't!" Cook roared. "Turn around and get him on the reel!"

"Oh yeah, I guess I didn't."

"What the buck! Should I jump? Cord, he's tangled around my legs."

I was waiting. Finally Cook looked at me in bewilderment and distress. "Can you help?"

"Say please," I told him.

"Screw you," he said.

"Close enough," I said. "I'll take Top Gum."

Celebratory cigars, then, after lunch, for everyone but me.

"I only brought three," Cook said.

"Don't worry about it." I sparked a crumbly Swisher. "I only smoke the good stuff."

"Cord's a helluva guide," White Fang declared. He clapped Cook on the shoulder. "This was the spot. This was the spot where they were hitting. Bam. Bam. A double, just like that."

"Good call, Cord," Top Gum said. "You put us right on the fish."

"Shit. I put a cast *right there*," White Fang fantasized. "Perfect. Right *on* that big old bastard."

"That was a female," Cook said.

"Me too." Top Gum blew a smoke ring. "Perfect cast."

"Bam," White Fang said. "Game over."

"I stuck that bitch," Top Gum said.

"Yours was a male, bud."

"Yeah! Toledo! Toledo rocks! Toledo kicks ass, baby!"

"Gentlemen, could you excuse us for a second?"

Cook walked me upstream, out of earshot at the head of the little sand spit. "Hey," he pleaded, "it's good money. It'll get me through school."

"Sure. Maybe you'll become a dentist."

"Shoot me if that happens."

"So I believe you," I said. "You don't know why Jesse wanted a boat or where it is."

"I don't. No idea."

"But you loaned it to her."

"Yeah. I sure did."

"She must have had some leverage."

Cook rubbed the blond stubble below his right ear. He gazed across the Yellowstone at the buff-colored hills of tinder dry grass. Across a distant dry gulch stepped a pronghorn, then another pronghorn, the pair disappearing with dainty steps into stones and brush.

"Yeah, well, what else would it be?" Cook said at last. "Drugs. A bunch of us from high school were still partying pretty hard together all the way up to last year. I heard Jesse got busted by the sheriff about a month ago and was getting pressured to turn people in. I didn't want to be one of them."

"You were dealing?"

"Just staying alive," he said. "Not much for jobs around here."

"What drugs?"

He swallowed, glanced at me. "All kinds of shit. You know. Anything you wanted."

"And you're not a pharmacy. So you had a source?"

"Of course I did."

"Can you tell me?"

"I got things going now, man, I want to stay alive."

"Hey, Cord!" White Fang hollered. "Let's go stick some fish!"

"So you think someone might have killed Jesse to keep her quiet?"

"I'm not going to talk about it, man, I told you."

He tried to turn away. I grabbed his arm. "Cord." I waited for his nervous gray eyes. "If that's true, you think you might be next?" I waited. "Look, kid. The sheriff has thrown me out of town. Twice. We're not on speaking terms. Anything you tell me goes straight into figuring out what happened to Jesse. Period. And maybe toward keeping you alive too."

"I'm changing flies." Top Gum crowed this from the riverbank. "How in heck does that clinch knot happen again?"

"Sorgensen," Cook relented. I let his arm go. "He supplied me,

Jesse, some other people. I don't know where he gets the shit. But maybe Jesse did."

"Maybe she did." He was edging away, using the pull of his clients. "So, listen, Cord. I know Jesse wasn't going to forget about her dad's medal, so when was she going to give your boat back?"

Cook looked at his watch for the date. "Three days ago," he said.

"A good inflatable, that's a couple thousand bucks."

"Tell me about it."

"So what are you going to do if you can't get it back? Give up fishing small water?"

He squinted downstream at his dentists. He glanced upstream at a drift boat bobbing along the opposite bank. Then he looked at me and let go of something in a hot blast of air that ruffled his bangs. From the waterproof pouch on his lanyard he extracted his fishing license, his guide's license, some cash, and then what he wanted, a ratty-edged photograph.

"No. I had an idea. For a couple thousand dollars, maybe some punk is gonna have to ante up for this."

It's Not Montana Everywhere

Sneed's room was on the third floor of Livingston Memorial Hospital, all the way to the southwest corner where traffic could be controlled. In the freight elevator on the way up, Deputy Russell Crowe whined at me in protest.

"That was a long time ago."

"There's a date on the photo, Russell. It was last year. Cord Cook said it wasn't the first time, either."

"That's not Jesse."

I leaned on the elevator wall, tired and dizzy, sick in record time from the hospital smell. And I had just bartered away the Cruise Master. *So what now, Dog? Hitchhiking? Walking around like John Muir?* My legs felt almost too weak to stand.

"Okay," Crowe admitted. "It is Jesse. But that picture's in a bar, you know, that's nothing, like, not a private party or anything."

"Cord Cook says it was your house."

"No. No way."

"He remembers your mom was in here, in the hospital."

"Cord's a liar."

"He doesn't seem like one." The elevator pinged. Third floor. "I mean, not compared to you." I held Cook's photo in front of him.

"Look carefully. Right above your arm where it goes around Jesse's shoulder. Isn't that a pine cone grizzly bear in the background?"

Russell jammed his thumb into the DOOR CLOSE button. "We all went to high school together. That's all. Old friends."

"That's cocaine, Russell."

"It's not."

"Okay. It's what? Jesse's chopping something. Vicodin capsules? Oxy? Amphetamines? Seems like this crowd had access to just about anything. And you've got a straw, buddy, but no lemonade."

"Come on. It's a party. It's just what people do sometimes. It's normal."

"I'm not judging you, Russell. I'm playing you. And I just want into my buddy's room. Without you there."

The deputy on guard at the end of the hall was an older guy, a hypertensive baldy with sticks for arms and legs, bored to the point of sudoku and pleased to have some action.

"Hey, Russell."

"Hey. Hey, uh, Schmitty." Russell unveiled belated horse teeth. "You—you old—damn—scissorbill. How's our boy?"

The deputy tipped his gleaming head toward the door. "Talking up a storm. Sheriff ordered him ziplocked to the bed. Who's this?"

"You—" Russell faltered, glanced at me, scratched up a welt along his preternatural jaw.

"Schmitty, you heard the sheriff was trying to round up Sneed's next of kin? Heard we thought we might have a lead on a firefighter down in Houston?"

"Well, uh, sure." The deputy's tiny blue eyes twinkled with the pleasure of inclusion. All day out of the loop on his ass in a hush-hush hospital hallway, babysitting, but now he knew the score. "Right. So how's that going?"

Russell took a slow, unsteady breath. "It went," he said. "And here he is. The kid's father. Cornelius Sneed."

Deputy Schmitt's good cheer froze in mid-air. His neck went stiff and he could not look at me.

"But . . . but . . ."

I couldn't afford to blow this. I had coached Russell intensively on the next one: "Come on, Schmitty. It's not Montana everywhere. Don't be so . . . Don't be so . . . *provincial*."

"I . . . Huh? . . . I'm sorry . . . I wasn't . . ."

I handed Cord Cook's photograph to Russell. He tucked it into his breast pocket. He cleared his throat. Now came another transaction. Deputy Schmitt owed him one, Russell had told me. A big one. Bigger than letting me in. Russell had been saving that debt for something special, had whined about spending it on my needs. Now I eyed him hard. He sighed. "They're getting rid of day-old peach cobbler down in the cafeteria, Schmitty. Giving it away."

Like an Escher Print

Sneed looked ashen and diminished, like he had aged forty years in the last five days. But beyond that was a bigger shock: he didn't know me. He mistook his buddy Dog, I guess, for a nurse in a Huckleberry Finn costume.

"Gotta pee," he croaked.

He had oxygen in his nose, like Chubbuck. His ankles were zip-cuffed to one another, and the plastic cuff between them was zip-cuffed to the end rail of the bed. His wrists were zip-cuffed to the canvas strap that held down his torso.

"Pee."

His hands had just enough play to reach the call button resting on his stomach. He twisted his right arm inside the zip cuff and reached for the button. I stopped his hand.

"Sneed. It's me. Dog."

He struggled against me. He had lost some strength, but not all of it, not the raw part. I held his hand back, but his body bucked hard beneath the strap. The bed skidded. His head and shoulders rose up. His neck bulged. His eyes strained with a glassy, blank ferocity. "Gaahh!" he raged. Then abruptly he was still. A spreading wet spot appeared below his hands, and the smell of medicated urine rose in the room. The spot widened to the circumference of a dinner plate and stopped.

"I'm sorry, Sneedy. But I'm not supposed to be in here."

He mumbled, eyes closed.

"It's Dog." I poked him up and down the ribs. "Come on. It's me. Talk to me."

"She just wanted the check," he replied.

"Who? Jesse?"

"For the welfare money. For drugs."

"Sure. I hear you, Sneedy."

"So did they. The wanted the government money." Tears seeped out. "That's all it was about."

I still held his hand. I squeezed it. "Who is they? Sorgensen? Gray? The sheriff's people?"

"Kellers."

"Kellers? Who's Kellers?"

He opened his eyes. For a long moment I thought he stared emptily, tasting the salt from the tears on his lips. Then he startled me. "Dog?"

"Yeah? Right here, buddy."

"I'm all mixed up, Dog."

"You're going to be fine, Sneedy. Just hang in there."

"Did Jesse drop the boat?"

"I can check. Where should I look?"

"No. She dropped it already. I remember."

"Where?"

He shut his eyes, was quiet a long moment. "I . . . I'm all mixed up."

"We'll sort it out. Don't worry."

"But that's why I killed them."

I leaned over him, stopped his mouth, whispered into his ear. "Sneed. Don't say that. Wherever that comes from, I don't care, *don't say it*. Can you remember?"

He looked at me, his eyes teary and desperate. "Am I in trouble?"

"Yes."

"Why?"

"For something you didn't do. So don't say anything. Nothing. You got it?"

"Dog . . ." He sighed. He shook his head and nearly smiled. "Dog, I think . . . I think I been talking all day."

I squeezed his hand again. "That wouldn't surprise me, Sneedy. Not at all. But from now on you gotta shut up."

"Okay, Dog."

"I'm going to figure out how to get you a lawyer."

"Mmmm."

"And there's somebody coming from Houston. Someone from your family."

"I got no family. I remember that."

"I think it's going to be your foster family. Used to be from Little Rock. The people with the pronghorn. That's all I can figure."

"Kellers?"

"Is that the name?"

He didn't answer. His eyes closed again. More tears leaked. "Yeah. I'm mixed up in trouble."

"What is it, Sneed?"

"Did Jesse drop the boat?"

"You said she did."

He looked around his room. "Then where is she?"

"She's . . . Do you remember where you saw Jesse the last time?"

He tried. I saw the effort, saw his head come forward, his jaw clench and tremble. "In . . . in . . . at the fence?"

"What fence? Whose?"

He looked at me: "What?"

"A fence."

"No. A picnic."

"A picnic? Where? When, Sneedy?"

His head fell back. For a good while he was silent. When he spoke again, I knew the inside of his head was like an Escher print, pathways leading up and down at the same time, right and left simultaneously, his thoughts traveling in impossible, nonsensical circuits through damaged brain tissues. I saw how much he suffered.

He cleared his throat. He opened his eyes. He looked at me squarely, deceptively clear-eyed. He said, "All you wanted was the welfare check."

And then, while I squeezed Sneed's hand and touched his face, the door opened. I didn't bother to turn because I knew. I heard the hum of Sheriff Chubbuck's electric tricycle coming into the room. I heard Deputy Russell Crowe's voice.

"He's in here," Russell said. "I thought so. And gosh, Sheriff, I don't know where Deputy Schmidt might of went. I guess he just walked off."

Up in the Damn Ponderosa

My tax guy, Harvey Digman, on the phone from Boston, said, "Bail you out? Again?"

"It's only five hundred bucks, Harvey. Or a thousand property."

"How about give them the title to your whatsis?"

"I just sold it to someone else." My legs went weak again.

"Well then you've got money. That vehicle had to be worth a couple thou in vintage parts anyway. Wooden wheels and whatnot."

"I exchanged it for a photograph."

The old man sighed and smacked his lips on something. Soup. Or a cocktail. "You mean for an Ansel Adams, first printing. Yosemite. Something like that. Am I right, Dog?"

"No."

"One of Avedon's cowboy portraits then."

"A guy at a party, lining up some coke. That got me in to see my buddy in the hospital, and that got me obstructing justice."

Ice tinkling now: a cocktail. Harvey liked the Shirley Temple, et al. "Your doings are a mystery, Dog."

"Five hundred, Harvey. Come on. I'll pay you back."

This initiated the long silence it deserved.

"Harvey, please. This is different."

"It's always different, Dog. Therefore it's the same."

"I tie flies for a guy out here. It's good money."

"You can't even come home now. You don't have a vehicle. So where's my investment?"

"Where's your investment?"

"Three cherries, Doll, in the next one, please."

"Where's the love, Harvey? That's my question."

"The love is in the no."

"The what?"

"The no."

"Harv."

"Not you, Sweetheart. Yes, to you. Absolutely yes. *Ja. Oui. Hai dozo.*" Harvey had his hand imperfectly over the mouthpiece. "The no is to this former client of mine who—"

"That's it," the jailer said when I hung up. "That's your call."

He was stocky and cross-eyed, concentrating on his work, breath whistling through his nose.

"You gonna need a blanket?"

But it was for a different purpose that he returned shortly along the dim and empty hallway, looking down as if perplexed by the squeaky overkill of his shiny black boots.

"Uh—" he was reading from a printout "—Mister Og-Log . . . Vee?"

"Oglivie."

"O-glow-vivee?"

"Dog," I said.

The jailer turned around, a little startled, confronting me with a rearview of pistol and cuffs. He turned back. "This is a secure area. There are no animals allowed."

I noticed he was sweating as he revisited his printout. "Your bail," he announced, "has been posted."

In the reception area, waiting for me with unconcealed irritation, was a handsome black woman, thirty-five maybe, tallish and sturdy, dressed in tight jeans and a polo shirt that exploded pink-pink-pink off the dark brown of her skin.

The jailer clicked the door shut. I was startled. He had to shoo me out.

"How—" I began.

"I forgot his name. Some guy said he was related to an actor." She measured me with clear suspicion. "Or else he wasn't. I forget. He pulled me over coming in from the airport. I thought it was DWB, but he knew it was gonna be me and he recommended I get you out."

I glanced at the jailer. His eyes were all mixed up, looking everywhere and nowhere. This stunning woman held a cell phone in one hand and it was buzzing, blinking red through the gaps of her fingers. I don't know why, but the concept of a grenade came to mind. "He said you would need a ride," she said. "Let's go. And you owe me five hundred bucks."

I said it again: "I'll pay you back."

"That's right," she said. "You will."

Outside, sun and smoke concocted a brilliant brook trout sunset. Beneath this, mainly oblivious, this woman answered her phone.

"Yeah? Well you wouldn't come up here with me. That's the kind of support you are. What? Don't you call me that! What? I'll tell you exactly what kind of man I think you are. *What?*"

She turned her back on me, stormed off into the landscaping. Moments later, she seemed to forget herself, came pacing back.

"Yes, I saw him. They got him shackled to the bed. He has no idea who I am. Because last time he saw me I was someone else, remember? This whole thing seems like a damn dream. I don't know what I'm going to do. I just walked out the fire station. I didn't have time for paperwork. Here I am suddenly up in . . . up in the damn Ponderosa."

She glanced at me, gave a little shiver.

"I gotta go." She listened, sighed. "Yeah. Sure you do. Whatever you said and me too only more and all that. I won't. I won't let them do that. Don't worry."

A pickup rumbled past blaring honky-tonk. Her eyes followed that past the railroad depot and the grain elevator and off into fathomless rangeland toward sunset on the Crazy Mountains.

"Just like on *Bonanza*. I'm not kidding. Oh yeah? You ought to get out of your ivory tower and watch a little TV sometime. Get a picture."

She shoved the phone into her jeans pocket. Then she strode past me toward a jade-green rental car at the curb.

"Aren't you coming?"

When I was on the passenger seat beside her, engine running, she said, "Okay, listen. My name is Aretha. Aretha Sneed."

I blinked at her. Her eyes were vivid hazel. Her lip gloss had sparkle. Her accent was deep south but not warm.

"You know," she said, "his mother?"

And then, with a sigh and a quick survey through the windshield of prospects ahead, she went one further: "And you are who again? Eustace Crabb?"

Long Enough to Hang Him

"Okay. I'm sorry."

Purely, I believed, for the sake of manners, Sneed's firefighting mother forced this disclaimer out through gritted teeth as we pulled away into greater Livingston.

"I'm upset. Of course you're not Eustace Crabb. I just hoped for a little more support on the home front."

We were heading north on Park Street, past Dan Bailey's Fly Shop, past the Murray Hotel, past the rail yard and the depot and the grain elevator—and then we ran out of town.

"Oh, my Lord."

Aretha Sneed hit the brakes and turned around in the lot of a taxidermist/tanning studio/archery range.

"Oh . . . my . . . Lord in heaven. My poor baby. What was he doing here?"

We headed back into Livingston's evening lights, smoldering up against a low and smoky sky. In no time flat we had drizzled out the other end of town beneath the interstate bridge. Before she could reverse directions we were out into the skanky scatter of entrepreneurial conversions that would eventually lead to Hilarious Sorgensen's Fly 'n' Float.

"Your baby was in love."

"Don't tell me that."

She turned around again in the lot of a realtor who promised affordable farmettes in the Paradise Valley.

"Do not tell me he was in love with some cowgirl white chick."

I observed this guideline in silence as she gunned that little Geo Metro like it was a pumper truck and we streaked back in past the Pamida and Town and Country Foods, coming up fast behind a cattle truck that had strayed in off the interstate. Now it was hue and yaw, hoof-scatter and stench, Aretha Sneed trapped in it with a log truck behind us and a steady drain of tourists down the opposite lane. Blowing the horn of her rental car, she discovered, produced nothing more helpful than a stream of panicked cow shit out through the ovals of the truck's back gate.

"Oh, my Lord—"

I glanced at her. Her bottom lip was between her teeth. She gripped the wheel like she would snap it.

"He was in love not just with her," I said. "With this whole place."

A steer brayed. Hooves clattered. The truck lurched, giving hope, then stopped again.

"Do not tell me that," she said unevenly into the windshield. "I have been looking for my boy, hoping and praying for the past five years. And when I finally find him—" her voice cracked "—he's half dead in the damn territory, and the plan here in Virginia City, as I understand it, is to keep him alive long enough to hang him."

"I've been working on that."

"By the neck."

"I have some ideas."

"From the gallows."

The cattle truck jolted into motion. But the scale of it in front of us, given her city driver's habit of tailgating, obscured the fact that we had once more traveled out the north end of town into rangeland.

She cussed unbecomingly, slung the car around once more. I let her head back into Livingston a third time before I asked finally, "So who is Eustace Crabb?"

She was biting her lip again, gripping the wheel too tightly.

"He's the town drunk on *Bonanza*."

"And what are we looking for?"

"I . . ."

But she seemed short of breath, suddenly needed to think about where she was. She pulled over. We sat at the edge of a gun shop parking lot, pickups straggling past. She closed her eyes.

"I left as soon as they called me. I just walked off my shift. I have been traveling all day to get here."

She looked at me. Startled tears formed, and she began to shake, taking huge, slow breaths in the hope of pulling it all back together.

"I think . . . Oh, my Lord . . . I think I'm just hungry."

What Kind of Pie Do You Have?

"I am in fact a drunk."

I confirmed this for Sneed's mother as our waitress at the Stockman set down a screwdriver and a Diet Pepsi.

"But I am not the town drunk. I don't have a town."

"Poor you." Every eye in the place was on her. She masked herself in a scowl, hunched her muscled shoulders around her ears, chose a table with her back to the wall, too close to the jukebox for easy talk.

"Reuben and fries," she told the waitress.

"I'm a traveling drunk. Kind of like the bookmobile."

Her eyes narrowed on me, then flicked away toward the keno machines. There, a whiskery old coot was wrenched around to stare at this astonishing black woman while his machine, unattended, posted numbers. Sneed's mother lowered her gaze and fit her lips around the straw. Her brow creased as she sucked down a third of her diet Pepsi. "So who's this white chick? She blonde? Blue eyes?"

"All of it."

"So where do you fit in?"

"Camp counselor."

"Meaning what?"

"Your son and I met in Idaho a few weeks back. We fished together. Jesse came into the picture later. After that I more or less just led the singing and washed the dishes."

"Jesse." Aretha Sneed gave a mournful shake of her chiseled head. Her hair was straightened and pasted down in swoops and wing-like constructions. Small gold hoops swung from her ears. "Her name was Jesse. Big surprise that is." She stabbed ice with her straw. "Listen." She met my eyes, wincing as the jukebox kicked in with some manner of boot-stomping boogie. As she leaned closer, I caught whiffs of worry, of the sourness of anxious travel cutting through the Lady Speed Stik. "Tell me. Did he talk about me?"

Tricky. Slow, Dog, slow. "I admit I had a different image of who you might be."

I watched this cause a pain she tried to hide. But her explanation was clean and strong, unflinching: "When I lost that boy, my world changed. I'm different now."

Nothing could make more sense to the Dog. *Same here, only backwards.* Still, my nod of understanding caused her jaw to tighten.

"I mean my world changed."

"I know."

"I don't mean I was so sad I had to go shopping."

"I know you don't."

"Or go recuperate in Cancun."

"I know."

Her eyes bore into me, aflame with suspicion and possibly rage. I lifted my hands away from their busy realignments of my screwdriver glass. "Okay," I said. "Okay. Let's drop that. Let's move forward. Now you're here."

"Right." She wouldn't let my eyes go. "Here on the set of *Bonanza*. With Eustace Crabb."

"That attitude isn't going to help."

"Which attitude is?"

She sat back and tried a different one. She bulled her pretty neck, stuck her tongue into her cheek, hitched and swayed to the country music for a mocking few seconds, pulling it back just an instant before it could have been a problem with the folks along the bar. She was good. She knew where the edge was.

"Yep," she muttered in a low and stumpy drawl, squinting along her straw like it was a rifle barrel broke out for cleaning. "Put it down, 'Retha. That one's property of white folks."

Next her rueben plate cracked down in front of her, then a clatter of silverware. "That be all?" breezed our waitress, not meaning it, a big and pasty girl skimming away before Sneed's mother could answer.

"You're going to need friends here," I told her.

Aretha Sneed looked at the rueben. She looked at me, still doubting her outlay of five hundred bucks.

"True friends," I said. "And I'm a start."

She cast a glance toward the bar, but a chorus of stares chased her back to the reuben.

"I'm in this," I said. "On your side. Whether you like the looks of me or not."

She tried to stare me down. I wouldn't go. After a long and fruitless attempt she unhooked, looked down and said through her teeth, "Okay, Hoss." She set her cell phone down beside her plate and began to pick kraut off the reuben.

I said, "Hey, now I'm Hoss. I got an upgrade."

By the last bite of her reuben, Sneed's mother was filled in on Jesse's murder, on her son's supposed culpability and his alleged suicide attempt, and finally on Jesse's assorted paramours and antagonists, her party friends and any possible defenders of her racial cleanliness. She had heard the names Henderson Gray, Hilarious Sorgensen, Dane Tucker, Cord Cook, Tick Judith, Deputy Russell Crowe, and Sheriff Roy Chubbuck, and she had processed the existence of skinheads within a stone's throw of the French fries that lay in a droopy mass on her plate. And she knew about the Oldsmobile, the fold-back seat, the theory.

"So this cinch knot—"

"*Clinch* knot. It's a fly fishing knot."

"Fly fishing?"

I explained about artificial insects made from fur and feathers. I made a couple back-casting strokes, laid one down into the flow of the Stockman, outlined catch and release—all this to the effect of confusion and dismay.

"Okay." She wanted to move on. "So the one who did this was not a fly fisherman? Wouldn't that be most of the sane world as we know it?"

"Not around here."

"And you say this person is small? Skinny?"

"Had to be. At least one of them. If there were more."

"And you're sure about all this."

"I'm sure your son didn't kill Jesse. The rest of it's the best guess I have."

She was quiet a while. She flipped open the cover of her cell phone, frowned at something, flipped it shut again.

"Okay," she said at last, squirting zig-zags of ketchup over that slag heap of fries. "Now let me tell you where I'm coming from."

She had to lean close as the jukebox re-charged with Merle Haggard, "Oakie from Muskogee." A spontaneous sing-along at the bar forced me to focus on her lips, trying to read them.

"The last time D'Ontario saw his mama—" they were puffy lips, wide and active, shiny with glitter gloss and reuben grease—"I was some banger's little crack whore."

She waited, dared me to come up six inches and face this fact right in its lovely green-brown eyes. She held me there, testing. I gave her a little shrug. *Tell me something I didn't know.*

"I didn't look like this," she relented finally. "I didn't talk like this, proper and truthful, and sure as hell not to a white man."

I nodded. Fine. She pushed the plate of fries away untouched, tossed her napkin on top.

"I wanted that boy back because somebody told me I could get a hundred-and-twenty-five dollars a week from the county welfare office."

"He told me," I said. "He knew that."

"That's right. He did. He knew it. That's why he did what he did."

She had to swallow here, and then again. She pressed a napkin to her lips and held it until something relaxed inside her.

"And that's right about where I stopped lying to myself. But he was already gone." Now clicking her short French nails on the table. "And I could not, for the longest time, get myself together."

"That be all?" The waitress, retreating fast, offered us her broad, blue-jeaned ass to contact in case it wasn't.

Aretha saw me frowning.

I explained, "What kind of service is that?"

"You never ate out dinner with a black person before?"

"I guess not. Just up at the bar."

She sat up straight and raised her voice: "Ma'am?" She smiled. She had lucky teeth, like Sneed's. Our service slumped back. "I just wondered if by chance you had any pie."

That big sour Montana gal looked over her shoulder toward the kitchen. "Yeah. Maybe."

"Pecan?"

"We don't got that."

"Peach?"

"We don't got that either."

"What kind of pie do you have?"

"I could check."

"Will you do that?"

"When I get a chance."

"Thank you so much."

But the waitress went away opposite the kitchen on some other errand that turned out to be a desultory chat with a mean-looking hulk at the bar, complete with glances our way.

Sneed's mother said to me, "If that bitch comes back here at all, it'll be to tell *you* what kind of pie they have."

She picked up her cell phone again, flipped it open and shut, set it back down.

"But eventually I got myself together. I completed a program. I got a waiver to enter public service. I passed that damn firefighters' course. Then I looked for my baby, but that didn't work out. There was no record of him anywhere. He must have been working illegally the whole time. He never paid a tax or got a license or even got arrested, nowhere that I could find. I gave up two years ago. Then when this happened—" her voice cracked "—and they, these people up here, they got his name and all from you. They checked it out, found my name on his birth certificate. When the phone rang I was changing wiper blades on a ladder truck."

She picked the phone up a third time, set it down, picked it up and opened it, closed it and set it down and looked at me with angry, tear-slick eyes.

"His brain is damaged."

"Yes."

"Do you know what this means?"

"I—"

She didn't give me a chance. "You heard of Ricky Ray Rector? Walter McMillian?"

"No."

"Barry Lee Fairchild? Earl Washington?"

"No. Sorry."

She sniffed, erased her tears with a quick swipe of a finger. "Of course not. But you know it's a tradition in southern law enforcement. Catching a retard black man is like hitting the jackpot on one of those gambling machines over there. They can make him say anything. They can clean off the books of any unsolved crimes. They can—"

"We got apple." The waitress interrupted Sneed's mother, and sure enough that big gal aimed her eyes and her order pad at me. "Or cherry."

"No thanks."

Aretha's eyes followed ornery hindquarters back to the bar before she returned her attention to me.

"This state is like Texas, isn't it? They have the death penalty?"

"Yes. But let's focus on this: he didn't do it."

She shook her head like I was crazy. "Listen, Hoss. The doctor tells me D'Ontario could have heart trouble," she said, "and/or kidney failure, blindness, skin lesions, balance problems, dementia, sudden death. Any of that. So let's say he doesn't talk at all. Or he talks but won't confess. He says what they don't want to hear. You know what then?"

I shook my head, not sure.

"He just dies in the hospital, snap, just like that, and nobody ever wonders. Do you see?"

"Well—"

"I don't really care, I'm saying, whether he's innocent or not. I don't have time for that. That's not going to matter."

I watched her, wondering where she might go with an end game like that. I said, "Give me a couple days."

"I owe that boy my life."

I nodded.

"I would do anything to keep him alive."

"I understand."

"I don't mean writing a check to some foundation."

"I know what you mean."

Once more her eyes narrowed on me in suspicion. "You may have a bad habit," she said, "of agreeing with people you know nothing about."

"Try me."

She kept her gaze on me for a long moment. Then she rolled her eyes as her phone began to warble. She snapped it open. Instantly her brow creased.

"Am I with someone? What kind of question is that?"

As she listened, she pressed her eyes shut and shook her head, no-no-no-no. When she had an opening, her voice was tight and cold: "That's how you support me? Getting jealous? Even when I'm up here doing what I'm doing for why I'm doing it and all it means to me? Lord in heaven, what kind of bullshit is that?"

Willie Nelson started up on the juke box. Another patch of listening made her squint at me and mutter something. Her finger-nails began to tick-tick her annoyance on the table top.

"Yeah," she said finally. "As a matter of fact I am with someone. Mmm? Hoss. Yeah. Hoss. Hoss Cartwright. He's helping me with D'Ontay. Mm-hmm. Yes, as a matter of fact he is white. Oh, maybe that demonstrates an issue with me? Does it now? Mm-hmm, cuz I'm disassociated from my anger? Oh really? What I really want is a chance to boss the man around? Cuz I come from slavery? Well, Cornell, go ahead and believe whatever you want to believe, cuz you gonna believe it anyway. All right then. You find one too. White girl. Little bitty chicken butt. You do that."

She pinched a button on the phone and snapped it shut. She slipped it away through a tight breach in the hip of her jeans. Then she cleared the air.

"My latest mistake is a goddamn professor. Needs me home to change his emotional diapers."

I was already standing, turning away to hide a grin.

"Where you going, Hoss?"

"Come on," I said. "Let's get busy on your issues. Start bossing me around."

God Knocked Backwards

"Okay, Hoss," she said. "Here is what we do. We find those people who might have done this. We get them alone. We ask them to tie this clinch knot. We go vigilante on their cowboy butts."

Her room at the Geyser Motel was cramped around a sway-backed queen bed, crowded by a hulking TV set and an ancient air conditioner rammed through the front wall like the grill of a car. Sneed's mother had stretched out on the bed, her shoulders against the studded vinyl headboard, her sandals off, her arms crossed beneath a faulty depiction of the Crazy Mountains. As for me, having demonstrated the clinch knot with a bootlace through the flip-top of a beer can, I now reclined in a dank and swampy arm chair that swallowed my hind end and left me looking up and through the cute pink bottoms of her largish, Sneed-like feet.

"First off, those skinheads," she said, dangling the clinch knot. "Then the fat man this chick was buying drugs from, and his little girlfriend. Then that skinny lawyer boyfriend freak that chases deer. See how they react."

The idea left me gripping the frayed and greasy elbows of the chair. It was a good idea, then an appalling idea, then a joke, a corny *Bonanza* plot, and then, cautiously, possibly, a good idea again—maybe even brilliant. Show you can tie the clinch knot, you're off the list. It was that simple. Just tie the knot. That's all we ask. Whereas if you were guilty . . .

"If you're the one that did this," Sneed's mother said, "and you thought you got away with it, you're gonna shit your drawers. And we're gonna smell it."

I struggled from the chair. Aretha eyed me like I might try a belly flop onto the bed with her, like I might need a mule kick in the privates. I guessed her firehouse defenses were up.

"But how?"

"How what?"

"How do we make them tie the knot?"

She smiled a little. She shifted her legs, crossed her feet to rest beside a large and well-stuffed Louis Vuitton handbag tipped onto its side at the far corner of the bed. Now I saw hot-pink toenails, detailed with glittery silver shooting stars and blue-and-yellow dabbed-on flowers—firefighters, of course, having a fair amount of down time. She burrowed a big toe inside the mouth of the bag, ran it back and forth along the zipper edge, pulled the toe back.

She said, "I used to have an uncle went by the name of Dog. You know why?"

"I do not."

"It's God knocked backwards," she said. She waited for that to sink in. "We Sneeds come from a pretty rough place."

"I see."

"No, you don't see," she said. "Not yet."

Back beneath the hand bag flaps burrowed that pink-bottomed big toe. "I got out of the airport, over there in Bozeman, before I went to deal with my baby in the hospital, I did a little shopping. And oh my Lord, there were so many choices and so few laws— even if you look like me."

With a simple hinge of her ankle she flipped the hand bag lid open, let me look in at the big damn pearl-handled Smith and Wesson.

"We get that knot going," she said, "with this."

Hell on Trespassers

Aretha Sneed had that pistol to the temple of the chief radish skin-head before I could even form intelligible notions toward talking her out of it. So instead I said to the scrawny one, trembling with his back against the blaze of his own truck lights, "A couple days ago you told me you knew the clinch knot."

I handed him a hook and a length of tippet.

"So tie me one."

"F-f-fuck you."

"Watch your language, Hochstetter." This was Aretha. Now she had the fat senior skinhead on his face in the ditch.

"That's all you have to do," I said. "Tie the knot and she doesn't shoot Sergeant Schultz over there."

"It-it's dark."

"Turn around. There. Now it's light."

"What's this?" Aretha jammed the barrel against some tattoo on the back of the fat one's neck. "A target?"

"He can't do it," that skin blurted into gravel and dust. "Denny can't do shit. But I can tie one. I tied a million of them."

I couldn't help myself. "Denny? A Nazi named Denny?"

"I guess it's Nazi Lite," Aretha said.

I grabbed the little shit, spun him around so Aretha and the .38 could switch necks. I stood up the chief radish, gave him the hook and tippet. "Tie," I said.

As his fingers fumbled at the job, I prayed for no traffic. It had been simple to summon the faded pink pickup to that spot along Tucker's fence. I had simply pounded on the intercom button, screeched some angry truths about my right to fish all that water that Dane Tucker had fenced off. After that we waited beside a NO TRESPASSING sign a half mile down until the pickup arrived. It took five minutes.

"There," said the chief Nazi Lite radish skinhead.

His hand trembled toward me through the headlights. Aretha pressed the barrel into Denny and Denny whimpered.

But his buddy had it right, a perfect clinch knot. "Whu . . . whu . . . what's this about?"

"History," I told him. "You heard of that?"

Aretha scowled, let Denny go, said, "Auf Wiedersehen, punks." And then, grimly, driving us away, she added, "Shit."

"*Hogan's Heroes* too?" I said as we came to a quiet stop beside a trailered drift boat in the Fly 'n' Float parking lot.

"Just a little. Mostly *Bonanza*. That's my speciality."

"Let me guess. You and the professor? Re-runs late at night?"

"Hell no."

"Fire house?"

"I read."

"I'm way off?"

"Mm-hm. Miles away."

Hilarious Sorgensen was buzzed on something supplemental. He was extra bloated, glassy-eyed and uncertain on his feet. We had gone behind the shop to the attached house. Sorgensen had not answered his door right away. The zeppelin shadow of the man had lunged about the walls inside until it became evident he was arming himself against the hazards of the drug trade.

Now, dangerously short of breath, he filled his doorway, fumbling an over-under shotgun in his fat fingers and whistling like an elk through his nose. He didn't recognize me at first. He was agitated and very dangerous until Aretha darted out of his desiccated shrubbery and stripped his weapon. Accordingly, the big man's first ten words were impairments of "Huh?" And all of this was backlit by a porn movie flickering into noisy culmination on a plasma screen behind him.

"Just an informational visit," I assured him.

"What's she got a gun for?"

"Same reason you did. Personal safety."

I cannot bring myself to share openly the most precise analogy for the sight of Sorgensen's clotted purple lips, straining inside the hair circle of his dirty beard to produce the foulness that came out.

"Get the motherfuck off my property."

"I'm not seeing why you'd react that way."

"I'll call the sheriff."

"I'll bet not."

He changed tack. "Well, Godalmighty. I still got a few good things in stock," he wheezed back at me. "You don't have to rob me. You can have it."

"Calm down," I said. "It's none of that."

He stepped back into the light of his cluttered foyer. Sorgensen's eyes were knife slashes through cushions of flesh. He wore boxer shorts. Below these, he was held up by jellied-leg molds inside white vinyl braces under Velcro straps. A tent of a shirt—Denver Broncos, home jersey, 00—covered the rest. He looked from me to Sneed's mother and back, got his bearings, and I saw the switch take place: *clown mode.*

"Hoo-wee," he blared. "Good to see you folks. You just startled me. That's all."

He pawed the wall, hit a light switch. Behind him rodeo figurines pitched and bucked from every surface, plaques clogged the walls, trophies and ribbons stood in for books on the shelves. "You about gave old 'Larious a heart attack." I could have sworn those were Lyndzee's bruisy legs spanning the plasma before he zig-zagged across the carpet and snapped it off.

"Why don't you folks come on in. Have some drinks. See how I can help you."

I took the shotgun from Aretha, cracked it, dropped the shells in my pocket. I tossed the weapon onto a sprung old velvet settee.

"That's all we wanted in the first place," I said.

Sorgensen yammered out colorful distractions about Lyndzee's dying uncle in Memphis as he served something sweet and yellow and potent-smelling over a chalky ice cube in a jelly glass. Aretha and I sat like chess rooks at opposite ends of a complex and sym-metrical living room set that was thirty years old and all in pow-der-blue velour. I caught her with a look: *no. Don't drink that.* She rolled her eyes: *as if.* But where to take it from there, with Sorgensen blowing smoke, clowning from inside a barrel, was an open question.

"The guy's got three kidneys or something. Christ, her family's weird. The guy's got goddamned ovarian cancer for all I know. Do I have pants on?" He did a pirouette—or more of a Y-turn. "No, I do not. I'm sorry, little lady. Avert your gaze. Whooee, I swear to old Jim Bridger you're a lovely one. Say—would you folks care for something stronger? I wasn't kidding earlier. I got some good stuff around here."

"No thanks."

"Anything?"

"No."

He toppled back into a recliner. He popped his feet a few inches into the air as if he had bounced, comic-like, which he hadn't. One of his dirty slippers fell off.

"You wanna watch a film?"

Hell, just dive in, I decided. Sorgensen was ripped, and in fanta-sia, you never knew. Plus, we were the party with the loaded weapon.

"We just want you do us one simple favor." I held up the hook and tippet for him to squint at. "Tie a clinch knot if you can."

"Huh?"

"A clinch knot. Can you demonstrate it?"

"You're a fisherman," he countered. "Don't you know?"

"I . . . I'm blocked. It happens. You know? Sometimes I start thinking too much."

His eyes darted from me to Aretha, trying to figure us out. Aretha smiled at him, the Smith and Wesson primly across her lap, pointing benignly off toward a certificate of appreciation from the Wyoming Rodeo Authority.

"Hell," said Sorgensen at last, "I can't even tie my own shoes." He wiggled his sausage fingers. "Gotta wear slip-ons." He grunted as if trying to rise. "Now the girly, if she was here . . ."

I felt Aretha's look. *Here it is.* "Oh," I said, like casual. "Can Lyndzee tie knots?"

Sorgensen grunted, bared his teeth. "You think I let that girly sit around and watch shows all day?"

He tried to get up. What I didn't see coming was the electronic tilt function that activated the chair and finished the job. He lumbered straight through the path of Aretha's pistol to a closed door at the end of the living room. He opened the door. He flicked on stark white lighting and backed out of the way, revealing a fly tier's bench under a carefully organized mountain of material.

"Girly ties for the shop," he grunted, swinging his girth sideways to squeeze in, "eight hours a day. She's got real good fingers. She can whip finish one-handed. She wraps rods. She braids lanyards. Hell. Lemme show you . . ."

As he maneuvered inside, I looked at Aretha, ready to shake my head, *no.* As in *Not them. Lyndzee wouldn't tie that knot.* But Sneed's mother already had her *shit* scowl on, was up with her pistol and angling like a chess bishop for the door.

"Let's go," she hissed at me.

I looked back through a window from outside. Sorgensen was

spinning slowly in the middle of his living room set, looking for us, meaning to show us, apparently, the entire panoply of knots.

"Now Henderson Gray," I advised Sneed's mother as she drove us back into town, "is a lawyer and more-or-less a normal citizen. He's not a Nazi or a drug dealer."

"Meaning what?"

"Meaning the pistol in that fancy bag of yours. We can't just barge in and wave a gun in his face. We don't have that kind of leverage."

"Then how about this pronghorn thing?"

"What about it?"

She was getting smarter, in vehicular terms, staying back from a truckload of sheep that lurched off the freeway and rumbled away in a cloud of exhaust toward some dark ranch to the north.

"You said he chases them up to twenty miles," she said. "Across Dane Tucker's land. But he doesn't work for Tucker any more. He got fired. So does he have permission?"

"I don't know."

"Early *Bonanza* episodes," she said, "Pa is hell on trespassers. He's always sending Hoss and Adam and Little Joe out to chase some poor goober off the Ponderosa. Guy shot a rabbit one time. One rabbit. Pa chewed his butt and ran him off. The guy came back. Pa had Sheriff Roy Coffee come out and arrest him. The guy did jail time. It wasn't for laughs, either. Pa hated anybody on his land unless they asked permission."

I glanced at her sleek profile against the lights of outer Livingston. "This *Bonanza* thing has gone too far to be ignored."

But ignore it she did. She went on, "When you told me about Henderson Gray, you said he used to be Tucker's lawyer. You said he got fired. You also said Dane Tucker is hell on trespassers. So how come those skinheads are all over us, but they don't stop Henderson Gray?"

"That's it," I told her. "You nailed it."

Thirty minutes later Gray sat at our table at the back of the Stockman, flushed and shaky. Charlotte Gray, I assumed, had informed him of my visit.

"I know why we're here," he said. He could not quite meet Aretha's eyes. "You don't work for Tucker. This is not about my gate key."

"No," I said. "But it could be. We could let Tucker know you're still using his property."

He gulped red-faced at a beer I had pre-ordered for him. He was dressed in neither running togs nor a suit but rather in a country-clubber's leisure ensemble, his spindly, freckled arms and legs sticking out of white crew cuffs. He wore his running hat though, salt-stained, sun-bleached red, pulled down as if it would hide him.

"Listen," he said. "I haven't laid eyes on Jesse for months."

He chased that lie with a slick little laugh that bared his small, even teeth.

"Except for that night right here in the Stockman," I corrected. "About two weeks ago."

Gray's whole face pinched into a frown. He didn't know me back then, wouldn't have seen me apart from the hundred other drunks in the place. Jumpy and talkative, Jesse had disappeared "to the restroom" for a while that night. When she returned, she had attached herself to Sneed more than usual, had worked that poor kid over like a cat on a scratching tree.

I told Gray, "You came in. Just like tonight. Home still clinging to you. Angry wife left behind." I pointed. "There you stood, over at the keno machines, that same hat pulled down. Jesse was with Sneed up at the bar."

As I spoke, Gray tried to smile and nod like now he had this thing under control.

"Sure. Now I remember. She called my cell in tears. She said she had to see me."

"In a bar?"

Aretha's words startled him. Gray took another gulp of beer. Aretha said, "And you got a baby, too?" She kept a cool gaze on him until Gray lunged across the table at me, fairly spat. "Jesus

Christ—You bastard—That's why Charlotte—Do you know what I do for a living—I can't believe you—I'm a goddamn attorney— I'm gonna—"

I put my hands up. "You're gonna sue me? I have nothing but what I'm wearing. Plus a little fly fishing tackle. Do you fly fish?"

"No."

"I didn't think so. So you went to meet Jesse? At midnight? In a bar? A week before she died?"

"Because she—because I—*shit!*"

Gray's eyes now burned with a plea as they met mine. "Look. That girl was crazy. Period. Sure, I got involved with her when I shouldn't have. But she came after me. She knew I was a lawyer, okay? She thought I could do something to help her father, Galen Ringer. He's on death row for—"

"We know."

"I tried to end the relationship. She wouldn't let it go. She claimed I promised to help her, promised to draw up some kind of bullshit appeal for a stay of execution. I did not promise. We discussed it. Jesse always heard what she wanted hear. But I did not promise."

He rocked back, gripped the grimy wooden arms of his chair. He clamped his jaw together. He closed his eyes and groaned a choked obscenity at the ceiling. Aretha and I traded glances. I laid the clinch knot components on the table.

"I know you don't fish, but anyway—"

Gray could not turn himself off. He raged through his teeth. "She would not leave me alone. She called me, she stalked me, she tried to make me jealous—anything to get me back—and that's what that time here was about. She called me from a toilet stall. She set that all up to make me jealous. She was crawling all over that black kid."

I recalled the moment again. Now I saw Jesse casting Sneed in an act of bar room theater. But still, she loved him. Right? "Why did you agree to meet her at all?"

"She said—*shit!*"

Gray fought to contain himself, finally conscious of the eyes on our table. A lot of bar talk could be confirmed right here. He lowered his voice.

"Jesse told me she was pregnant. Okay? What was I going to do? I was supposed to walk through here, just through, without looking at her, and she would meet me in back. Instead she was up there at the bar dry humping this black kid. I was supposed to get mad, I guess, and come back to her."

"Okay, but—"

He dropped to a strangled, airless rasp: "And when that didn't work, she brought that kid to my office, trying to make us enemies. That kid really hated the idea of me chasing pronghorn. He had some hang up about them. Thought he was the defender of pronghorn or something. He said I was stressing them out or something, driving them toward extinction. I told them both to fuck off." He seethed his way through a messy gulp of beer. "And that is the last time I saw Jesse."

I pushed the hook and a curl of tippet toward him. "If you can tie a clinch knot on that, we'd be inclined to believe you."

"And you—" he glared at both of us "—you fuck off too."

"You'd better have an alibi, Gray."

His eyes stung, then closed. Soon, very faintly, he began to nod, as if massaging a thought. Then he scraped his chair back, stood to his full skeletal height. "You know what, asshole? I do. I do have an alibi."

He punched a key on his cell phone. Here came a different voice, like sugar on a turd. "Sweetheart? Can you and Peter make it inside? There's some friends of yours here." He listened a moment. His brow furrowed. "You signed the prenup, Charlotte," he said. "It's done. No. No you won't. I've got the keys."

He sat back down. He put a palm to his chin, cracked his neck in both directions, gave us an unfortunate smile. "She's snockered. Blotto when I got home from my evening run. I couldn't leave her home with Peter. They're out in the car." Henderson Gray was all lawyer now, a gamer, feeling in command as he sat back down and made stupid chitchat with Aretha about Houston for the minute and half it took for his wife to lurch into the Stockman with the little boy on her hip, wide-eyed and sucking a binky.

Gray said, "Sweetie? Over here."

His wife looked exhausted, tense, and none of this, as I should know, had been alleviated by all the alcohol that had scrambled her systems. Her eyes narrowed, tracked her grinning husband like a horse waiting for a chance to kick. As she came forth unsteadily, the child began to fuss and reach for his father. Charlotte Gray stopped at a distance, but the kid did a scary backbend in her arms to stay in view of Gray and resumed his crabbing from upside down.

"Do you remember, Honey, where I was a few days ago, around the time that Ringer girl died?"

That Ringer girl. Charlotte Gray flinched. She snuck a sullen look at me and pulled it back. Little Peter mewled behind the binky, pulled her off balance with another lunge toward Gray. "C'mere buddy," Gray said, and now he tried to take the child. Charlotte snarled and held on. There followed a truly awful moment where both parents pulled, little arms stretched, the binky fell to the floor, and the child began to screech, turning heads in the tavern. The struggle went on, Gray and his wife peeling one another's fingers, hissing low invective past the child's red ears, until at last Peter gripped his father's shirt with tiny fists. He kicked his mother in the chest, Gray lifted, and at last the transfer was made.

"Sweetheart," Gray repeated then, and he spoke slowly, "do you remember?"

But Charlotte Gray was frozen. She could only tremble, staring at the binky on the tavern floor as if she meant to pick it up but couldn't move.

Gray cradled his son inside a bony elbow. "Charlotte? It's important. These people suspect me of a terrible thing."

Still his wife wouldn't, couldn't, speak. Gray waited, shushing the boy. Aretha and I waited, passing grim glances. In this span of tavern time, as the Livingston night life resumed around us, little Peter reprised his habit of dissatisfaction. He wanted his binky back. He whimpered, squeezed his fists at the floor, began to squirm in his father's grip. "What is it, Tiger? Oh. That?" Gray bent. As he picked the binky up, Charlotte Gray spoke at last.

"That was on the floor," the woman mumbled. "That's dirty now."

Gray daubed the rubber nipple against his shirt sleeve. He returned the binky to his son's lips. "Everything's dirty, Sweetheart." He held his gaze on his wife until she looked up through her hair. She looked frightened now. "Everything," Gray said.

Now casual, supporting the happy boy in his arm, Gray erected a frame: "So from the morning of the twenty-first, through, say, evening of the following day? The twenty-second? Do you remember where I was? Charlotte? Darling? Or have you been snockered all week?"

Charlotte Gray had paled. She stared down where the binky had been on the floor. Then her head jerked up as Peter began to coo and giggle, wet sounds around a dirty pacifier. Her boy was grabbing at Gray's chin. As his father dodged and batted the tiny fists, the happy boy persisted. At last she said, "Sure. Yes. Of course you were at home, with us."

"Really? I'll have to trust you. Was that after I nearly caught that doe? And then I stepped in a hole and had to ice my ankle for a couple days?"

Before his wife could answer, Peter changed his mind and wanted back with his mother. He made gimme fists in the air, whimpered and squirmed. Henderson Gray held on, turned a sudden gummy grin on Aretha. "Kids. Aren't they great? It must have been terrible, being separated from your boy all those—"

"Yes," his wife blurted. Now she glared. All the slop had left her voice. "I told you I remember. You were home with us. The whole damn time."

Gray smiled benignly as he returned custody of Peter to his mother. Charlotte Gray clutched the child. She hung her head, began to shake, never looked up even when Sneed's mother took my arm and brushed past her. "Don't take that, sister," Aretha muttered as she swept me outside and into the night.

A Traffic Stop

At the Geyser Motel, I took one pillow and one bath towel and used the floor beneath the air conditioner. I had slept on harder surfaces, but never one grimier or more conducive to lurid dreams. About half the night I yearned for the Cruise Master and my path east, but in the long hours I began to crave the motel bed and Sneed's mother too, and so I rousted myself before dawn and fled into the nearest neighborhood, and there, thinking *look like a local*, I stole a truck.

At that relic Kwik Trip payphone, I found the sheriff's name in the book. The address was Big Timber and turned out to be a devolving ranchette a few hundred yards from Sweet Grass Creek.

I waited at a distance. By seven a.m., the sheriff had strapped on the O$_2$ cylinder and hobbled out to his cruiser, seeming to leave behind an argument with a younger-looking woman who lingered on the front porch, hands on hips, watching him go.

I followed Chubbuck back to Livingston on the interstate, then through town to his office. He did not leave the cruiser. Instead, he waited until Deputy Russell Crowe strolled from the station with a foam cup and a pastry. The sheriff accepted these items through his cruiser window and the two of them had a short meeting. Crowe took direction, apparently, and returned the empty cup inside.

Chubbuck headed out the way I hoped. He moseyed through the south end of town and along the 'Stone toward the park. It was too early for tourists. The highway was without issue except for a strew of fast food litter and beer cans just before Carter's Bridge. The sheriff slowed to inspect this mess while I eased around him into the awakening vault of the Paradise Valley.

The big river curved ahead through mountain shade cast upon the east flank of the valley, then swung west between fields of rolled hay, steaming in a new hot sun. I found a freshly graveled ranch road and turned around.

The sheriff crossed Carter's Bridge and just after Pine Creek headed up State 217 and from there into the Roam River valley. Not a mile in, at a turnout opposite the gated terminus of Tucker's twenty-five-mile fence, waited two black SUVs. I couldn't say if they were the same ones I had seen at the campground, but they were close.

Chubbuck stopped for a chat and I pulled up short beside the mailbox of a double-wide on the off-Tucker side, several hundred yards back. I dismounted, just for show, and as I circled the truck box I discovered I was bearing five bound stacks of today's *Bozeman Chronicle*.

What the hell—perfect. A flick of my pocket knife loosened one stack. I put a paper in the mailbox and drove on.

Now I played leapfrog with the sheriff as he maundered another three miles up the highway, driving as if he could not sustain pressure on his gas pedal. Somewhere just short of Tucker's gate, I stopped to deliver a newspaper to another across-the-road neighbor of the movie star. When I caught Chubbuck again, he had made a traffic stop.

The sheriff had the skinheads pulled over beside a spot where the Roam River snaked through bison-studded rangeland, reflecting the sky's pink-gray twizzle of sunlight and smoke. A portable dash light strobed in the window of Chubbuck's cruiser. The sheriff had found the energy to leave the vehicle. He wavered at the driver's window of the bleached-red Ford, hanging on to the side mirror as he appeared to chat with the boys inside.

I passed by with some idiotic face-blocking gesture, then glanced back to discover no interest in me whatsoever. I found a ranch road to ascend, turned my stolen truck around at enough altitude to see down as the chat went on. The two vehicles were dwarfed against the endless fence line and the entirety of Tucker's territory behind it. The Roam burrowed out of steppes and canyons to the south, and downstream it lazed open into the great grassy lap-folds of the Absaroka mountains. Dane Tucker's main gate was just south of the vehicles, and the movie star's ranch mansion was somewhere out of sight but directly east, ahead of me, where the miles-long driveway followed the river out of sight behind a hogback ridge.

Chubbuck's chat went on and on. At last the sheriff tottered away. He appeared to cast back a friendly wave to the skinheads before he toppled into his cruiser, turned it around, and headed back in the direction of Livingston and his buddies with the SUVs.

But the SUVs were gone now. Or not quite gone—but nearly so, jouncing fast across Tucker's land as if they had jumped the gate, which remained closed and locked behind them. Stunningly, they crashed across a shallow stretch of the Roam and rooted up the far bank, tires throwing sand. In a few seconds more, the vehicles were out of sight behind a ripple of land, no traces remaining but a gout of muddied water and a drifting cloud of dust.

Chubbuck never paused. He drove on. He drove all the way back into Livingston and then through town to a small private airstrip a few miles toward Bozeman. There he parked and seemed to rest for a bit before he climbed out, crossed the dirt runway, clawed his way into a battered single-engine Cessna, and promptly, expertly, put the damn thing into the sky.

I watched in wonder as the sheriff gained altitude and then banked the plane back the direction he had come from, over Tucker's land and the Roam River.

I left the truck there. I took a newspaper for my hike back to town.

An Avid Fly Fisherman

Sheriff's Illness Challenges Park County Law Enforcement

An anonymous source close to the Park County Sheriff's Department told the *Bozeman Chronicle* Thursday that several cases of lax procedure and unclear priorities could be linked to the illness of Sheriff Roy A. Chubbuck, 57, who was diagnosed with emphysema shortly after taking office six years ago. A former Park County deputy, Chubbuck became sheriff in a 2001 special election following a scandal and the subsequent suicide of his predecessor, Russell Crowe, Sr.

No clear policy guides the department in the case of a sheriff's incapacitation, said the source, who spoke on condition of anonymity. At the core of this difficulty, said the source, was the problem of determining at what point a sheriff might be unfit to serve. Chubbuck, a 25-year veteran who uses supplemental oxygen and is able to walk only short distances, acknowledged the severity of his illness in a telephone interview but

(continued)

denied that his leadership capacity was impaired or that his investigation into the recent murder of a Livingston woman had been compromised.

"Different people have different agendas," Chubbuck told the *Chronicle*. "It's easy to confuse disappointment over your agenda with incompetence or wrongdoing on the part of others."

The popular sheriff, who was recently re-elected to his third three-year term, said that the need for secrecy in ongoing investigations sometimes creates tension within a law enforcement unit as well as within the broader community. "Sometimes people just have to trust in the one they've elected and be patient," Chubbuck said. "If they don't like what's happening, there's always the next election."

But with the sheriff's health in rapid decline and the next election almost three years away, the time to position new leadership may be now, said the source, who pointed out that Chubbuck, an avid fly fisherman, had little time left to enjoy a long-anticipated retirement cut short by his disease. The source said, "Given his love of fishing, we all have tremendous sympathy for what the sheriff is going through. However, in the interest of justice and public safety in Park County . . ."

Trust Me

Deputy Russell Crowe's cruiser was parked at a jaunty angle in the Geyser Motel parking lot, engine running, A/C pumping, condensate dripping from the tailpipe. The deputy himself was nowhere in sight until Aretha Sneed's door flew open and she shoved him clear.

"Get out!"

"Ma'am, please listen."

"I know what you're going to do!"

"Ma'am, please—"

"Don't ma'am me. You're gonna kill my baby. Don't come in here talking all that liaison shit. And no, I never did think you were related to Russell Crowe the actor. What kind of fool would think that? Huh? You got the same damn name. All that makes you is an accident trying to jock somebody's style."

Sneed's mother was barefoot and her hair was unfixed. For a heart-leaping moment, I mistook the flatiron in her hand for the Smith and Wesson .38.

She wasn't done. "You think I must be related to some other famous Aretha? That make sense to you?"

Crowe raised his hands in defense. "I'm just here in my capacity as a representative of the department. I'm just conveying the news. The ambulance will be leaving the hospital shortly. I asked the sheriff if you could ride along. He said no."

Aretha glared at him, beginning to chew her un-glossed bottom lip. Crowe sensed me coming up behind him. He filled his chest with air, gave the space between me and him a little nudge with his Neanderthal jaw.

"Stand back, Mister Oglivie."

"What's up, Russell? Nice piece in the paper today."

"I haven't seen the paper."

"Sure," I said. "Okay, Russell."

"Stand back," he told me. "Ma'am, I am a trained law enforcement officer and I will be with your son the entire way. It will be just the nurse and me in the ambulance. I'll keep a good eye on him."

Sneed's mother dismissed him with a look of murderous disgust. To me she said, "They're gonna kill my baby!"

"We would never do that," Russell persisted. "We're doing everything possible to help him recover."

"They're gonna gas him," she told me.

"It's hyperbaric treatment," Russell tried to explain. "They're going to put him in a chamber—"

At that word, *chamber*, Sneed's strong and lovely mother wilted as if the whole of the Big Sky country had come down upon her. Her sharp shoulders gave up their edge, and her body seemed to sag into the mold of the middle age awaiting her. For a long moment, she seemed to drift through pain toward numbness. I touched her shoulder. "Aretha?" When her eyes found mine they were sunken and darkly circled, bruised by lack of sleep, perfect emblems of despair.

"They gonna put my baby in a gas chamber and kill him!"

Russell kept at it. "Not to worry," he said. "They're going to transport her son to Billings where they have a hyperbaric oxygen chamber. They force oxygen into the blood cells under high pressure. I guess it might reverse out some of the carbon monoxide damage. The doctor feels he's on the verge of making some improvements, so the sheriff feels it's worth a try—"

She lunged at the deputy. "Did you just say not to worry?"

Russell touched his gun belt, backed up. "You have to trust us. Trust the justice system."

"Black people know all about the justice system."

"I mean trust the doctors. The hospital."

"We know all about doctors, too. And hospitals. You ever heard of the Tuskegee Experiment? I know you didn't."

Russell took another step closer to his cruiser. "Well, hey," he jittered out, and incredibly, he smiled—at Aretha, at me, back at Aretha. "If anybody understands all that, it would be me." He panted a little, as if his brain were chasing his mouth. "So forget everything else, you guys, you know, and just trust me."

I stepped between to buffer. But Sneed's mother could not begin to process this. I watched her shut down rather than permit that nonsense inside.

"Oh . . . my . . . Lord."

She gripped herself in a hug and turned a circle—parking lot, heat-scorched range, distant Crazy Mountains—then tilted her head to the vast and empty smut-brown sky.

I walked Russell the rest of the way to his cruiser. I tucked the newspaper under my arm and put a hand on his shoulder.

"Nice piece. Seriously."

"I don't know what you're talking about."

"You got a day off coming up soon, Russell?"

He wouldn't look at me. His jaw was red. His voice was thin. "Sure. Tomorrow. Why?"

"You and me, we oughta go fishing."

Chicken Neck Down at the Bottom

"Hyperbaric oxygen is a real medical procedure," I told Aretha after she had thrown herself face down on the motel bed, after her lungs had stopped heaving. "I don't think it's even dangerous. And look at it this way. If he makes some improvement, maybe he'll tell us what happened."

"*Us?*" Her voice was a retch into the bedcovers. "He'll tell *them*, and they'll twist it into whatever *they* need."

"Don't they have what they need already?"

She was silent. Her neck and shoulders quaked. I ached to touch her again but didn't dare.

"If his case is as bad as you say, why bother with the procedure?"

"To kill him! Without a trial! Don't you see it?"

I passed a long moment that felt like floating in deep space. *What?* There was no air in this, no vision. *Could she truly mean those words?* Unknowns fell open between us, dark and cold, gulfs in experience and perception beyond my strength in knowing.

But I was who I was, and at last I had to speak: "No. I don't see it. I don't see it like that. Not at all."

Sneed's mother whipped around, knocked her hand bag over.

Her face was wet. With naked hope she croaked, "Really? Really, you think I'm wrong?"

"We didn't ask those boys enough questions," I told her as we drove that little Metro out along Tucker's fence once more, picking our spot to bait the skinheads.

"Maybe they can tell us if Sheriff Chubbuck has a deal with Tucker to fish the Roam. Maybe if we scare them enough they'll tell us why they threatened Jesse and your boy and burned his tent."

"Or maybe they won't fall for it again."

"Fair enough. Perhaps they learn."

"Though if you can't learn from Nazi Germany," she said, "then probably not."

She set back in to chewing hungrily. To allow her space, I had walked downtown from the motel, bought burgers and onion rings and Pepsi, walked back nursing a Swisher Sweet and studying the patterns of smoke across the sky. By the time I returned to the motel, Aretha had recovered, fixed her hair, refilled herself with a mother's rage and purpose. Now she drove with an onion ring in one hand and her pistol in the Louis Vuitton handbag, which rode like a third passenger between us. *Big Louis,* I decided to call the bag. I felt like smiling but held it back.

"I bet my fly rod those morons will fall for it again."

"But I don't want your fly rod."

"How would you know?"

"I don't care for fishing."

"What kind have you done?"

"My professor friend," she said, "likes to get out on this big reservoir outside Houston and sit there all day in a boat with a chicken neck on a hook down at the bottom while he quotes Farrakahn and cusses at some big old catfish he lost one day that never comes back." She took a bite of onion ring. "He calls that catfish Stravinsky."

"Hmm." Now I did smile. "Interesting."

"No, as a matter of fact it is not interesting. Not one bit."

"And that means fishing to you?"

She glanced at me, chewing. She didn't answer. Then, as her eyes moved back to the road, the onion ring flew from her hand and she shrieked.

A body, maimed and bloody, hung from Tucker's fence about fifty yards ahead. Aretha jerked the car over, then gassed it, then jerked it again toward the shoulder. "Oh, no. Oh, my Lord."

My pulse had jumped but I caught it. "It's okay. It's just a deer," I told her, fixing on the long brown torso that hung through the middle of the fence. I reached across, put the car in park to stabilize her.

"Nothing we can do. It's just a deer. It tried to clear the fence and got caught."

"Okay."

She gulped air. She put the car back in drive and we continued.

I told her, "Happens all the time, all these fences."

But the initial fear was still a coppery taste in my throat as I watched the carcass slide by. The animal had snagged on the top strand of the fence and become woven into barbed wire by its struggle. One haunch hung loose from the body, sliced almost clean. The tongue hung down. A crow hopped back from the eyeball, flew off ten feet and watched us pass.

"Just a pronghorn," I said, and watched Sneed's mother grip the wheel, murmur *pronghorn* and stiffen as she drove on, slow and silent, as if the car were made of lead.

At that awful pace we drove the entire twenty-five miles of Tucker's fence and then back again, pounding the intercom button both times without any sign of the skinheads and their pink truck. As the hours passed, the Roam River, where I could see it, became a beacon of shifting, heartbreaking beauty, the kind of water I fished in my mind.

"Odd," I said at last, when our final miles had failed to produce any trace of neo-Nazi fence minders.

"What isn't odd around here?"

"And this too," I said, as we backed up in tourist traffic on 89 in front of Sorgensen's Fly 'n' Float. "This surprises me."

Hilarious Sorgensen's rusty conversion van waited in the opposite lane for a chance to turn in. The big man was at the wheel, jabbering away, chucking peanuts in like punctuation marks. The odd thing, to me, was that his girl Lyndzee—represented by a plume of cigarette smoke and a tangle of too-bronze hair—rode in the passenger seat.

"Short trip to Memphis," I said. "Travel time, she couldn't have been there much more than twenty-four hours. Not much for a family visit."

"Hmm," Aretha said, seeming distracted. "Maybe they weren't home."

Then traffic loosened up and she said, "So that's not what you do? When you go fishing? You don't sit on a lake with a chicken neck down at the bottom?"

They Just Said

We picked up my fly rod at the Cruise Master, which was parked in Cord Cook's mother's driveway across from Sacagawea Park, Cook having agreed that my stuff could remain inside the vehicle until whenever.

Aretha and I spent a little time under a flood light on the grass. She wasn't bad for a true beginner. Most of such, in my experience, handle a fly rod like a hammer, with the water like a nail they just can't hit straight enough or hard enough. Sneed's mother—perhaps in her overload of worry and grief—had the advantage of paying no attention to my instructions. She rendered me lip service and went purely by feel, getting the line up okay and loading the rod a bit, and after a few minutes she was throwing a decent loop about twenty feet ahead.

"Not bad," I said.

"Except it's even more boring than the chicken neck."

"Well, it helps to have water."

"Where's your boat?"

"I stand in the water."

She let the loop drop. "You *what?*"

I reeled her up, walked her back over to the Cruise Master. Cord Cook came out, beer in hand, for minor pleasantries, mentioned second thoughts about our deal—did I know there was a pressure problem in the master cylinder?—and then the kid ambled back inside, left me hoping. I pulled my waders off the back of the galley bench and held them up. "I wear these and walk in the water."

Aretha shook her head. "Ain't nobody, nowhere, should wear a thing like that. Not even riding in a fire truck."

"Why not?"

"Don't even try to get me into a pair of those."

We spent a long moment trying to read each other through the dim light across a pair of patched-up, smelly waders. At last I said, "Okay. Well, not everybody has the guts to be that sexy," and she came back with, "Hoss?"

"Yeah?"

"You know something?"

"I probably don't."

"Well," she said, "sometimes you're kinda funny."

"You want to grab one too?" She paused at the motel door. "A shower?"

My heart giddied up. "Thanks. I'll dunk in the river."

"The river? Down where all those chicken necks are sitting?" She frowned at me. "Get in here," she said. "Take a shower. Let's order a pizza."

She went first. I yanked that swampy motel chair around, wedged it in between the air conditioner and the bed, where I could see the TV. From this position, I waited out one of the world's longest showers, a real marathon that seemed to reach deep into the local aquifer.

Or maybe I just hadn't been around a woman in a while. Maybe four years alone on the road, rinsing off in trout streams and encountering women mostly in the abstract, had shaved from memory some of the stickier pleasures of man-woman affiliation.

Always have a book to read, Dog. Maybe put a PhD in progress. Learn, and re-learn, to wait.

In any case, this is where we were—Aretha showering in triplicate, the Hoss-Dog ruminating, then giving in to a mildly incredulous scrutiny of the local ten o'clock news, on low sound—when Sneed appeared on the screen.

I jerked forward in the chair. The face was hardly recognizable—it was a booking shot, done with the poor kid all ashen and dopey in his hospital bed. I turned up the sound. From the talking bufflehead came real news: *". . . escaped from medical custody around eight o'clock this evening after receiving treatment in a Billings hospital, leaving an injured deputy and a frightened community in his wake . . ."*

I sprang up and pounded on the bathroom door.

"Do it outside!" Aretha hollered.

"He escaped! He's on Channel 2!"

"Dig a hole then!"

" . . . what doctors termed a successful treatment . . . armed and presumed dangerous . . ." intoned the bufflehead, his forehead gleaming, his smile turned upside-down, *" . . . do not confront . . . contact authorities immediately . . . and now, as Tracy Minor's going to tell us, that wasn't the only kind of breakaway in the news today, as high school football got underway this evening across the tri-county area . . ."*

The broadcast was over by the time Sneed's mother emerged fully dressed on a cloud bank of peach-scented steam, and she didn't believe me. I raced through the channels, trying to catch the story on another station, but it was all high school football, Dodge clearance, Subway low-carb sandwiches.

"How could that happen? Didn't they shackle him? Guard him? Are you sure?"

"I saw it." My pulse pounded, my brain scrambled. "They just said."

"He escaped from where?"

"They said the ambulance. After the treatment. Somewhere in Billings. They said he overpowered the deputy, who was injured."

"That . . . that . . . *him*?"

"Who else?"

"You're crazy. You must put crack in those cigars of yours."

"It was just on the news."

That stupid room, we were too close, yelling at each other from point blank like stiffs on a sitcom. Glistening drops flew from the nap of Aretha's hair and struck me as she shook her head. "I must be dreaming."

"Well, wake up. Half the people in this state are packing a gun. He's gonna get shot any minute now."

That stopped her. Now she believed me. I saw the buzz of panic rise inside her, widen her eyes and shorten her breath.

"Well . . . isn't that convenient . . . for them."

I stared at Sneed's mother. "Isn't it?" she demanded.

"I . . ."

"Shit." She circled the bed frantically. She came back. She reached into Big Louis. Out came that pistol. "We have to find him."

"Billings is an hour-and-a-half away. A hundred thousand people live there."

She was hopping into her sandals, aiming the gun around. "They said armed?"

"I guess he took Crowe's weapon."

"That's all the excuse they need. Hell, an actual gun in a black man's hand, they could send the military. Does he even know where he is?"

"How could he—" but tires squealed outside as I spoke "—he's never been to Billings, and his brain is—" *bang, bang, bang!* hammered a fist on the door.

A Roomful of Helpless Sumbitch Bear

"Baby!"

Aretha jumped at Sneed as he hesitated in the doorway. He flinched away and she stopped herself. "Baby, it's me. It's your mother."

"Come on, come on," panted Uncle Tick Judith, shoving Sneed in the back. "Get inside and close the sumbitch door."

I yanked Sneed by the arm, slammed the door behind Uncle Judith. "Is there a gun? Didn't they say he took a service revolver?"

Uncle Judith struggled to catch his breath. He was the Love Canal of snoose. A massive lip-bump had been buried and forgotten, sent a rich brown slime oozing unnoticed down his chin. "I threw that sumbitch down a sewer grate."

"You're bleeding. Oh, Baby, you're bleeding. Come here. Your mama's got first aid training."

Sneed shied away from his mother's attention. When she caught his arm, tried to find his injury, he struggled with what looked like real fear.

"Looked out the window," Uncle Judith went on, "saw that sumbitch wandering down the middle of Main Street with a gun in his hand."

"Main Street Billings?"

"The hell, Billings. Right here. Five minutes ago."

Sneed looked stronger. His color was better. The ashy-purplish skin of two days ago had made progress toward his normal rich brown. He looked somewhat agile despite the too-small slippers on his big feet. His arms and legs and butt stuck out powerfully from a pale green hospital robe as his mother, thwarted, raised her hands and backed away.

"You're hurt. Baby, who hurt you?"

"Said some lady drove him around then dropped him off." Uncle Judith shook his head at his own words. "Hell if I know."

The old bull rider gasped for air as he worked his brow with a bandana. Sneed's blood had streaked him everywhere.

"How hurt is he?"

"He ain't hurt at all." Instinct made Uncle Judith chuck a shirt cuff across his chin, approximately cleansing it without any sense of cause. "He's strong as hell." Immediately, the dribble of snoose returned. "I wrestled that sumbitch into the beer cooler for a minute so I could get the store closed up. He's bleeding from one or t'other of his hands but it don't seem to bother him much."

Aretha reached for Sneed's wrist. He put it behind him.

"Oh, Baby, please, it's me. It's your mama."

"He's not the same feller, though," Uncle Judith observed. "All that beer nearby and he didn't touch of a one of them."

"They'll come here." I said this to the group in general. "State Patrol, sheriff's deputies, whoever, they'll come right to this motel room and they'll be loaded for bear."

I made an anxious survey of the tiny space, thought the better of pinching back the curtain.

"And there's a roomful of bear right here."

"I ain't done nothing wrong," Uncle Judith said.

"You didn't turn him in."

Uncle Judith accidentally discovered his lump of Cope as he considered this. One could see both confusion and relief. His tongue sent word to his brain, upon receipt of which he spit neatly into his shirt pocket and tamped it flat. "Well you and she ain't done nothing wrong."

"Not yet. But we're not going to turn him in either."

"Damn straight we're not," Aretha confirmed. "That's right, Hoss."

Now everybody, even Sneed, looked at me like Hoss had a follow up, a plan, which Hoss did not.

"A roomful of helpless sumbitch bear," Uncle Judith summed up, wetting his pocket again.

Let's Just Go Find Out Why

Our silence lasted for an agonizing five minutes, until into that mute and anxious scramble penetrated the wail of a distant siren and Sneed offered, "Jesse dropped the boat."

"Where did Jesse drop the boat?"

"At the place."

"What place?"

"Over the line."

"Where is the line?"

"On the map."

"Where is the map?"

"In the locker."

"What locker?

"Jesse's."

Aretha jumped in, shook him by the shoulders: "Where is Jesse's locker? Come on, Baby. Tell us where it is."

Her words, her presence, her hands on him, the hardcore alertness, all of this seemed to tilt Sneed into mental freefall. His eyes glazed. "Oh, Baby," said his mother as a wet spot formed at the center of the robe and then the robe began to drip. The smell of urine on shag carpet rose strongly.

Then Uncle Judith broke in with, "Oh fer chrissake, I know where that sumbitch locker is at."

The headlights of Uncle Judith's pickup led us through the maze of a mini-storage facility on the far west end of town. Those same lights, if Uncle Judith stood aside just right, helped him key open the lock. They lit up an astonishing scene.

Someone had arranged the narrow interior of the storage locker like a living room that had been compacted. The headlights blazed upon a settee, paisley and frayed, that framed the rear of the space and was backed by a bookshelf with its trophies neatly arranged. Cramped at the sides of the locker were wing chairs, unmatched, that carried dirty lace doilies on their arms. All of it was powdered with dust and webbed by spiders.

"Holy hoosegow," Uncle Judith muttered. "I rented this to get Galen's stuff out of the house cuz I couldn't stand to look at it. Didn't tell nobody. I guess she found a key."

As I stepped inside the cramped and musty space, the taste of Jesse's grief rose in my throat. The girl had leaned framed photographs against the seats of the furniture, and in every one of those photographs, under my hand swipes, was a handsome bull rider in full regalia, or that same man and his little daughter, on horses, or in drift boats with fly rods, or at a soda counter, or on top of a massive hydroelectric dam. I wiped my hand on my pants. The dust would not come off.

"Ah, Jess," Uncle Judith moaned. He had opened a cedar chest. "You just couldn't get over it." He straightened painfully. "Shoulda burned it all, that's what. Shoulda tampered with the mail."

I moved deeper into the spray of the headlights. Crammed in the gap between the settee and a wing chair sat a poured-glass sideboard with liquor bottles glinting out through thick grime.

"Here come the sirens," Aretha said. "Once those boys get their noise on, they gotta do something. We have to get him out of here, hide him somewhere. Us too. Come on, Hoss. Quit gawking. And Baby, stop messing in there. Let's go."

I turned back to the foreground, where Sneed bent over a small heap of supplies, his hands moving aside dried food, water bottles, bedrolls. He searched slowly but certainly until he found what he was looking for: pants. *His* pants. He had only one hospital slipper by now, on his left foot, and this he kicked off into the dark outside the headlights. I knew a little about carbon monoxide poisoning from an industrial case in Brockton. In and out. On and off. Stable, then tippy. Or none of it, or all of it, prospects of a good recovery, or not, and not much—nothing, really, except the hyperbaric chamber—that anyone could do about it. I moved beside my buddy for support. First one hand gripped me, then the other, until he had the pants on. Then he went into the pile again and raised up with some small stretchy pink thing of Jesse's. With that in his hand, Sneed appeared to struggle with his thoughts for a long moment. Then he bent to the pile once more.

"I will be damned," Uncle Judith said, watching this, then toeing into the pile from the other side. "Looks like they were going on a trip. Errands, that girl said. She said she needed my truck for errands."

"Jesse dropped the boat," Sneed said, extending a map toward me.

I tipped it into the headlights. It was a section of a Forest Service topographic map, laminated, covering Tucker's property and the Roam River from its entire length, top to bottom. There was a black Sharpie circle far upstream on what looked like swamp-land, south inside Wyoming, near the boundary of Yellowstone Park. "What's this, Sneed?"

"The boat."

"Rubber one? Jesse borrowed it from Cord Cook?"

He blinked at me.

"Never mind." I pointed at a second black circle, thirty-some miles north from the first circle and a mile or two east of the Roam in the final downstream third of Tucker's property. "What was supposed to happen here?"

As Sneed frowned at the map, that glaze came over him. I cursed myself. *Pay attention, Dog. Learn. Learn fast.* Sneed had been somewhat tuned in—until I asked him to retrieve a past thought about a future event that would happen in a place he had never been. Now he trembled under the weight of his confusion.

"What is it, Baby?"

He turned his back, hung his head. The sirens had stopped. Moths ticked against Uncle Judy's headlights.

"Them sumbitches are at the motel," the old guy muttered. He was back into that cedar chest, working a huge cud of snoose and sifting what looked like letters.

I put a hand on my young buddy's shoulder. "Where were you going in the boat, Sneedy? Why?"

Tears had formed in his eyes when he looked up at me. "Dog?"

"Yup. It's me."

Sneed nodded. Then he raised open hands, dropped Jesse's pink thing, shook with the pain of forgetting everything else.

"Crazy," muttered Uncle Judith. He let the chest lid fall with a loud clap and a cloud of dust. He straightened up, all of us looking at him. Under this scrutiny, he became the Miss Manners of snoose. He turned demurely, spit in his hand, wiped it on his pants. "Them sumbitches think we're armed. They'll be shooting."

I looked at Sneed's mother. I saw the fire in her eyes, the spring in her posture. Her hand went into Big Louis. As a matter of fact she *was* armed, and there *would* be shooting, so there was only one thing left.

"Sneedy," I said, "never mind. Jesse dropped the boat. You and Jesse were going down the river."

I took his open hands in mine. I closed them.

"Let's just go find out why."

Looks Like We're On Our Way

We shoved off an hour before dawn from Sneed and Jesse's circle on the map, forty miles south on Forest Service land at the headwaters of the Roam River.

Tick Judith, having chosen to take his chances with the law rather than Dane Tucker and the river, cautiously toot-tooted good-bye and backed out the fire lane. Nervous brown jets squirted from his window. He was the Hansel and Gretel of snoose, leaving a trail as he disappeared into the woods—except on the Roam there would be no going backwards.

"Hoss?"

I couldn't see Aretha. For a long moment after the headlights were gone nothing remained but the hoots of swamp owls, the baying of a million billion frogs, and Sneed's heavy mouth-breathing.

"Yeah?"

"Can you swim, Hoss?"

"Yeah."

"Can you swim good?"

"Last time I checked."

The smells seeped back in—the piney muck, the coppery bog water—and as my eyes adjusted I saw that the first bluish threads of daylight had knit through a low fog to backlight the tamarack and red cedar as they rose jaggedly from acres of still black water.

"Well," Aretha said, "that makes one of us."

She resolved for me out of the darkness. She gripped her injured son by the tail of his new Jose Cuervo gimme shirt, outfitted by Uncle Judith from dregs behind the seat of his pickup. In her other hand, she gripped Big Louis. Her eyes gaped wide at the scene around us.

I shoved Cord Cook's yellow twelve-foot inflatable to the edge of the swampy black water. "Okay, let's go. See if you can get him in the boat."

"This ain't no boat, Hoss. This is some damn whoopee cushion."

"That's right," I said. "It will bounce off the rocks."

"Rocks?" Her voice echoed out of the swamp. "*Rocks?*"

I grabbed the last of Sneed and Jesse's gear: some plastic sacks from Food Country, stumpy little oars and an anchor, somehow no life jackets. Last in were a vest and a fly rod from the storage locker. Property of Galen Ringer, I was guessing. But if the Dog was going down, the Dog was going down fishing.

Aretha got Sneed on the boat bottom between the fore and aft rigid seats. She positioned herself in the casting chair, then leaned forward to straighten Sneed's shirt against the cool air. He twisted free, showed his back to her.

"Baby—what? It's your mama."

Sneed ignored this. He fingered Galen Ringer's fly rod as I laid it along the gunwale. "Dog?"

"Right here, buddy."

"We're going fishing?"

"You bet."

He smiled. I stowed gear around him. I felt Aretha's glare as I laid down the toy-like oars beneath their toy-like oarlocks.

"What are they hitting on, Dog?"

"They're swimming on their backs, Sneedy, slurping up grasshoppers."

This initiated a long pause. Then suddenly his eyes flooded, dropped tears, his expression abruptly desperate.

"Dog?"

"Yeah, buddy?"

He trembled. "What . . . what size . . . what size grasshopper?"

"They're on a feed, Sneedy. Any size you want."

"Okay." He seemed enormously relieved. Then his expression changed once more. "Shit, Dog." His face crumpled. He looked scared. "Listen to me. I'm . . . I'm like a . . . like a baby."

In ten more minutes I was ready. Sneed's mother still fixed me with what was most likely a jealous stare for keeping up a patter with her son while I slogged to the bow and yanked us off the boggy shore. The boat bottom dragged under Sneed's weight. I spun the stern toward me and shoved us out. Mud sucked at my boots. Swamp water climbed my legs as I broke off with Sneed and made an announcement: "We'll try to get across Tucker's property line in the next couple hours and then hide until dark. We'll float all night. By tomorrow morning we ought to be close to that spot on the map."

"You tell 'em, Pa." Aretha's tone was testy.

Now it's Pa? My retort: "Not my fault if he trusts me."

"And you've known him for all of what? All of three weeks?" She distributed her glare between the two of us. "I gave birth to this child. This child gave me a damn hemorrhoid longer than three weeks."

"Thanks for the information."

"You are just too damn welcome."

I looked at her. She straddled the seat, facing sideways so that she could be turned away from the two of us. I said, "Now here's some information for you."

"What?"

"Sit facing me in the middle of the seat with your feet spread apart."

"What for?"

"So you don't fall out."

"Okay," she said huskily, stomping her feet down in the center of the boat bottom. "Sure thing, Pa."

I shoved the boat ahead of me—*Really? Pa?*—four hundred pounds of payload under the strain of my back. As the sky grew lighter, the swamp around my hips grew deeper and colder. The bottom hardened. I shoved us through a vast reef of buckbean, and on the other side I sensed here and there the faintest push of water with someplace to go. Then, at once, the floor bottomed out and I dipped to my chin, my feet wheeling emptily in the flow of a river.

I kicked and clawed as the boat spun out of control and began to undulate on the wave forms of a heavy current. My head dunked once. My legs thrashed and scissored without effect upon the great gust of water. Then at last I found my wits, rested a moment, drifted, made a truce with my total lack of control— and then I heaved an arm over the gunwale and caught the webbing of my seat.

"Sonofabitch!"

I hauled my chest and then my belly over the pillowy stern. I threw a leg over. I toppled in, slopping cold water over Sneed and, as Aretha's shriek made clear, her too.

"Pretty smooth, Hoss."

"How about if you at least make up your mind?" I said back with gritted teeth. "Is it going to be Pa or Hoss?"

Her eyes were moving up and down the soaked shape of me. "Depends."

"On what?"

"On how I feel."

"Those are the choices?"

"So far."

I pawed the oars up from the boat bottom, fumbled them into the locks. I pried us around so I could see downstream. I was hacked off. "No Adam? No Little Joe? I can't be one of those guys?"

"Oh, no," she said. "Purnell Roberts? Michael Landon? Those boys were fly. I mean, for white boys."

Hell with that. Dog damn it. I cut the oars into rushing water. What I could make out ahead was that the river funneled toward a canyon, a strew of thinly submerged rocks in my path. I jabbed an oar too late. We bounced off a chalk-brown rock that skimmed the surface. I backpaddled the other oar to straighten the boat.

"And that defines the range, I take it, of your experience with white men."

"Except for cops," she said, "and jailers."

"Then I should consider myself lucky, really—" another bump and spin "— to have such a high-up station in your life."

Aretha regarded me with her head tipping one way, then the other. "Looks like we're on our way," was her comment.

"Yes, it does."

I fought the oars to keep us lined up for more dangerous water.

"And so what, if I may ask," she said, "is the range of your experience with black women?"

Redundant Security

An hour later at daybreak I was still mulling my answer as we portaged around a second, larger rapid. We led Sneed around first, sat him down on cool sand. Then we packed our gear around: three plastic sacks of beef jerky, Gatorade, bottled water, Snickers, packs of cigarettes, toilet paper, and a pair of fencing pliers—all the stuff left by Sneed and Jesse in her storage locker. Aretha carried her Smith and Wesson inside Big Louis, which also, she informed me, contained her "things." That was it.

Then we lifted the boat on our shoulders—one hundred-and-fifty pounds, but Aretha every bit the firewoman—and we hucked its awkward bulk over heavy cobble and masses of flotsam, thickets of nettle and huckleberry, all of it enough of a struggle in the end to make me consider floating the next big rapids, if they didn't come in darkness.

I was still considering various replies to Aretha's question as we set the boat on a skin of glass-clear water over multi-colored pebbles. The day was fresh and not yet scorching hot. It would have been a good time to fish, and the Roam looked receptive. I cracked a Gatorade, swigged, passed it to Sneed's mother.

"Well," I surrendered at last, "me and Pa and Hop-Sing once saw a colored woman get off the stage over in Nevada City."

"Mmm-hmm." She reached into Big Louis and surprised me with a lacy handkerchief. She wiped any trace of me off the rim of the Gatorade bottle. "That's about what I thought."

The float was peaceful then, for an hour or two, except for the *Fish, Dog, fish* chant that was mounting in my brain. The Roam slowly gathered itself in springs and rivulets through high-country meadows sparked with asters and thistles and joe-pye weed. Mayflies—they looked like pale morning duns—began to rise from the tails of long, clear pools, and a few small trout slapped after them. The big fish were staying down, it seemed, and Dog mind was busy seeking trout mind. Had there been a full-moon crayfish hatch? Were the big bellies full? I didn't think so. No—because for a long glide through riffle-run-riffle the whole river felt cocked, ready to go off. I knew the feeling. I needed to rig up, get ready. But I fought myself. For once this was truly *not* a fishing trip. Thinking of Sheriff Chubbuck, of what that man would do to fish this water, I kept my anxious mitts on the oars. Aretha trailed her fingers in the water, her eyes three-quarters closed. Poor Sneed slumbered hard in the boat bottom.

"So your professor friend, I take it, is a black man?"

"Mmm-hmm," she said. "Just ask him."

I oared close to a cut bank, looking for trout of heft. I thought I saw one dart beneath the boat.

"Would I need to ask him?"

"Just a glance in his direction is usually enough. He'll put all that in your face."

I set the oars, let us drift on gentle current between wide banks. Okay. I couldn't help myself. I was rigging the fly rod. I was just getting ready. That was all. That didn't mean I was going to fish.

"And your wife?" Aretha asked me. "She's a white woman?"

I glanced up. "More than you know."

"Oh, I know," Aretha said. "I do know."

She watched me fit the rod pieces and string the line and build a leader. "Pass me a chicken neck," I said when I was ready. She laughed. I saw her pretty teeth, saw the green flare in her eyes. "We do have beef jerky," she said. "How about that?"

"How about—" I snapped open one of Galen Ringer's old fly boxes, reached over Sneed "—one of these?"

"Wow," she said.

"Wow," I said too, startled by the tight, perfect rows of hand-tied flies. "This guy . . . wow." Then Aretha's pink-tipped finger was in there, probing through the tiny forest of hackles and wing posts and dubbings and tails—a hundred, maybe two hundred bristling Montana dry flies. "White folks sure can make things complicated," she murmured.

Now I laughed. "Your boy loves this stuff," I told her. "He just laps it up. Inside two weeks he knew which one of these to pick and how to put it on the water."

"He likes this? Really?"

"He loves it."

"So which one?"

"Any time now, I think we might see these." My finger entered the box beside hers. I tickled the tiny wingpost on one of Galen Ringer's trico mayflies, about a size 24, little more than black thread, a mote of white fluff from a duck's butt, and two long tail strands.

I nicked the fly out of the foam and balanced it on the tip of her finger.

"I see," Sneed's mother said. "So you all are trying to catch guppies."

I took the fly back. I tied it onto a 7x tippet with a clinch knot. Now I *was* going to fish. How could I not? "Okay," I said, "stay tuned for guppies."

We drifted down. I kept the rod ready. The Roam now flowed easily through a shallow canyon with spindly timber up the sides.

Larger trout had begun to dimple pocket water and spook from
the shallow tails of the biggest pools. "Any time now," I said, and
just then I saw the first cloud of insects, skimming and spiraling
over the next pool. I was right about tricos. A minute or two later,
I discerned noses of substance pushing through the glassy current.
"Here we go." I raised the rod and began to play line out in false
casts. I was picking out my guppy—about a sixteen-incher—when
through a gauzy twister of mating insects I spotted a tiny green
light on the trunk of a pine about fifty yards ahead.

And I confess at first I did nothing. Like the skinhead's tattoos,
I saw this unnatural thing, this anomaly, and I didn't see it. Then
I looked purposefully away. I muffed my first cast to the target
fish, landed the line downstream too far and dragged the fly like a
drunken water skier over the trout's lie. So that fish was down.

Now I had to look up for the next fish. There again, closer now,
was the green light. I should look at it, some part of me thought. *Dog,
that means something.* But between the light and the raft, a heavy cutthroat was porpoising through a current seam where spent insects
massed up. There was an easy mark. I had a chance for two, maybe
three quick drifts along the seam before we slid past into a tunnel
of pines. But again I botched the cast. An easy one. Yet somehow I
closed my back loop and my line jerked out short and tangled, a mess
on the water. So I looked hard, at last, at the light.

"Shit." I dropped the rod. I dug in with the oars. "We gotta
pull out."

Sneed jerked awake in the boat bottom.

"This is Tucker's property line. That green light, that's a camera mounted on a tree. It's got an infrared motion sensor—"

But now the easy current was defeating me, sucking me on a
risky tangent toward the camera's sight line. I had wasted time and
had no more to fuss with. I chocked the oars and rolled over the
gunwale, splashing down into thigh-high water, a human anchor.
I leaned against the current and let my feet drag bottom. Still the
water pushed me, but I had flattened the angle. We were going to
make it to shore without intersecting the beam.

"Laser." This was Sneed.

Aretha said, "Say what?"

"Laser," he repeated.

"Baby, how do you know that?" No reply. She appealed to me as I chugged through shallow water.

"Hunters use them to scout game—to get pictures of animals they want to shoot later. But this one is aimed across the river, to let Tucker know if anyone crosses onto his ranch. We're legal on the water. That's public. Montana law. But we can't let Tucker know we're here. We'll have to go around the camera."

I dragged up onto the last stretch of National Park land, ninety degrees out of the camera's line. Then I left Sneed and his mother and picked my way ashore, studied the camera from the back, across a four-wire fence hung with NO TRESPASSING signs and extending to a point of prohibitive steepness.

From my former life I knew a little about this technology too. It was very much like the high-tech junk I had once aimed down the hallways of a suburban Boston aerospace contractor: tamper proof box, laser trigger, digital memory card and playback screen. There were no wires on Tucker's camera, no instant relay, but a well-used narrow trail led down from high ground to the camera, so I was pretty sure our movie hero had a man ride out to look at the playback and radio in, or at least swap video cards and bring the used one home to download and view on a computer. By mid-day, I told Aretha, Tucker would have seen us coming.

"Good work, Hoss." She hesitated, looked away from me. "Or Pa," she said. "Or both. Whichever you like."

"Well, it's a big job, being all the white men in your life."

She returned her attention to me. "And for sure a thankless one, as well."

I shrugged. I looked where she had been looking. Her son was pissing in the river.

"Bladder control," I noted. "That's progress."

A hundred yards upslope from the Roam, we dropped our gear over the fence, eased the boat over barbed wire onto private land. Then we hiked further upslope into cool piney shade and eventually into rock rubble at the base of a bluff. Here, as I expected, Tucker's fence elided the steepness and picked up again on the mesa above. Maybe this was why Sneed and Jesse had packed the fencing pliers. I knelt with the intention of cutting the bottom two fence wires. But Sneed's hands intruded. He grabbed the pliers. Decisively, he cut the wires.

"There," he said, and we rolled under.

"Now we're illegal," I said.

"Good job, Baby," Sneed's mother said, trying to brush his back off as he walked away.

"Sneed," I said. He stopped. "Let your mother brush your back. She won't hurt you."

He waited. But she was pissed now. She marched right past him. "Who says I won't hurt nobody?" she called back as the steep slope grabbed her legs and made her skid, pitch her arms, and finally run.

When we were afloat again, legal, the sky was wide and blue above us, no traces of smoke in our view, and even though the trico hatch was over I felt like celebrating. I splashed water on my face. I filled my hat with the Roam and slopped it over my head. I cracked us a fresh Gatorade, this one pink, took a slug off the top, handed it to Sneed.

"Now pass it to your mama," I told him.

"Except his mama ain't thirsty."

"You'll get dehydrated."

"Hell I will."

"That'll make you cranky," I dared to say.

"I'll tell you what makes me cranky," she offered, but then she didn't disclose. Instead she let a mile of water pass, knifing her finger tips through the Roam, and finally she said, "So how come you're not home with your wife?"

"Because I'm on a fishing trip."

Sneed started a geeky laugh. "Four years long," he said, and I looked at him, gave him a shove with my foot. "Give me a warning, will you, when you're about to tune in?"

"I don't know, Dog. Sometimes I'm here and sometimes I'm not. But it's like there's a . . . like I'm a . . ." He looked crestfallen. "I don't know what it's like. I can't find the thought. And then I forget what I'm thinking about. I already have."

"Do you see where we are?"

He looked around, bewildered. "I've never been here?"

"That's right. We're on the Roam. Do you know why we're here?"

For a long moment he looked down at the boat bottom. "Dog," he said at last, "I'm really sorry. I . . . maybe . . . maybe I'll know when we get there."

"That'll be good enough, buddy. Don't worry. Okay?"

No answer. "Sneed?" He raised his head. I looked in his eyes. Gone. I had two shirts on. I laid one over his head to keep the sun off. We bounced and drifted and then the land flattened and the current backed up into a marshy lowland. I was allowing myself to think about casting beetles or crickets off the banks when Aretha spoke.

"You might have made a good father," she told me. She shaded her eyes and looked away into the marsh. I looked there too. Deep bog. My eyes stung.

"I thought I was."

"So what happened?"

"I wasn't good enough."

Aretha let out a long, low, and sympathetic sigh. "Whatever good enough is," she murmured. "Wherever the hell that place is. And can we get even close?"

"I wonder—"

But abruptly she raised a hand, made a downward motion to shush me and stop me from rowing. I followed her gaze. We had startled a bull moose grazing on arrowhead in a side channel. I stopped the boat and we watched him.

"I'll be damned," Aretha whispered. "Bullwinkle."

A breeze kicked up and the bull swung his head our way, his snout dangling a ream of arrowhead. His shoulder muscles twitched. His nostrils opened in a snort. Then he turned and sauntered away at a retreating angle, looking back as he reached solid ground. His legs just kept coming up and coming up out of the water—two full yards of legs—and when he had all that skinny bone beneath that massive body, those legs did nothing more than twitch—barely visible—and the bull leaped high over the trunk of a downed fir and vanished into boggy forest.

What I wondered was if I could ever go back, start over, make good enough. I had never even imagined it, truly, soberly, until now. But I kept quiet. I oared into the flow. I stared ahead at the point where the buckbean and the feathery swamp hemlocks gave way again to rangeland, current, dirt banks and sandbar willow.

Then, "Another one," Aretha said.

"Where?" I said, looking for moose.

"No," she said, pointing, and my heart sank. A second game camera. Redundant security. Serious stuff. And we were squarely in its sights.

You All Have a Nice Couple of Days

The camera was hard-cased, locked, impenetrable. So we were caught. As soon as someone from Tucker's place rode out to check the disk, we would face whatever defense the actor could bring to bear.

Grimly now, our whiff of amusement gone, we moved on to Plan B. We would keep advancing downstream. We would push hard, gambling on the next few hours as a window to get into what I figured was a steep canyon about ten miles ahead.

"What's that canyon going do except trap us?"

I was guessing wildly: "If we can get that far and escape actual contact with Tucker's people, the canyon should hide us until dark. Then a good night's float ought to bring us to this mark on the map."

I tucked the map back under me. I was sitting on it now. We could not lose it.

"And won't they just be waiting there?"

"Maybe." I stroked the oars hard. "If they know where we're going. But maybe not."

She scowled. "Then how long until we get out the other end, off the man's property?"

"Into the Yellowstone?"

"I guess."

"I don't know. It's about thirty miles. And there's a lot of kinks in this. Maybe two days."

She said nothing. She just looked at me like I had invented rivers and designed this one, drunk. Thinking maybe he knew, I said, "Sneed? Hey, buddy. Hey, Sneed."

He said nothing either. He didn't even move.

We rode a while in high tension. Maybe two miles into our race to the canyon, Aretha lost patience and stuck a toe into her son's side. She said, "Baby, that look on your face is getting old."

She toed him a little harder.

"I know I've changed, but can't you remember anything? Can't you remember Grandpappy's place, old sour apples Pappy smelled like his own poop and that dog used to lick your face? Can't you remember I used to sing you that chariot song? We had one good time. That was Pappy and Gramma Francine's place, after Atlanta when we went to Little Rock, remember? I am your *mother*, Baby." Another toe jab. "Tell us what we're doing out here." She shoved him, not quite roughly, with her whole foot. "You know me. Don't pretend. That's why you won't look at me."

Sneed twisted away from her.

"Dog?"

"Right here, buddy."

"Dog, where's Jesse?"

"Uhhhh!" exploded his mother. "Where is *who*?"

I shot Aretha a warning look to no effect. "Where's some trampy little white girl you knew for three weeks?" She had lunged forward, over him, tipping the boat. Her head worked side to side like a cobra's. "All blonde and smiley, skinny little ass like a weasel, little tiny voice like *I got jungle fever, can you help me?* Where is she? What are you talking about?"

Sneed hung his head. I could hear his breathing over the rush and slap of the water.

"Where is she? Child, let me tell you something: that bitch is *everywhere.*"

Sneed's mother slammed back against the boat's bulbous prow and burned holes in the back of her son's skull. "And your mother is right damn here." We floated along like that for a few hundred yards, cresting and dipping over a long run of submerged glacial boulders, some cream-colored, some black, some salt-and-pepper granite— and every damn one of them ready to rise up and kill us.

Then Sneed's mother said, "Well."

Her voice was tight with defiance.

"Well," she said again. "Everybody. Here it comes. I sure am sorry. But clearly you don't understand—"

Sneed's head snapped around to look at her squarely for the first time. I couldn't see what was in his eyes that stopped his mother, that held her emotions in limbo for a long moment until he turned away again.

"Oh, Baby . . ." Tears streaked her face. "I am sorry. For so many, many things. I am so sorry. I really am."

He let her touch his back.

"Oh my baby . . ."

I kept us floating, kept oaring that boat downriver, trying to realize our figment of safety in a canyon. I kept my eyes away from the two of them, tried to give what privacy was available between three people trapped inside twenty square feet of rubber and air, surrounded by pouring, pouring water. I became vigilant Hoss-Dog, keeping watch over everything: snags and rocks and shallows that would beach us; riders, gunmen on the river banks; signs of a lighting storm building in the smoke-clotted sky.

But nothing else came up through that long, tense morning—
nothing but scrappy yearling cutthroat trout gleaning the dregs of
the trico hatch, plus a few peckish rainbows jumping at phantoms,
and once—just achingly once—a monster German brown trout,
butter-flanked and kipe-jawed, that ascended to nip a frantic spider
from the scrambled currents of an eddy.

Nor were we spied on from above except by red-tailed hawks
in high thermals, and by occasional small clots of Tucker's hobby
bison sucking water at the bank. Once, where the river spread and
slowed, the spectacle of our passage spooked a mother pronghorn
off into a dry, vast grassland.

"Hey, Sneed!" I hollered, waking him, and I swiveled the boat
around, dragged the oars to slow us down, hoping he could watch as
the doe circled back, sniffing the wind, to recover her rattled fawn.

But he couldn't rouse himself in time, couldn't focus. When
he lay back down on the boat bottom, his mother said, "Has he
told you?"

"About what?"

"About pronghorns."

"He hasn't told me much of anything," I admitted.

"And what he did tell you, it was all my fault?"

"Pretty much."

"Well," she said, leveling her eyes on mine. "My mother's boyfriend raped me. So my motherhood just didn't get off to the best
kind of start."

"He did allude to that."

"Did he now? Well, that's something." She kept my eyes locked.
"Okay. Well, Hoss, there's been a lot of anger in my life, a lot of
things I shouldn't have reacted to in the ways I did. But I did what
I did and I'm sorry and I need to be forgiven."

I broke the grip of her eyes. I looked off where the mother
pronghorn had gone. She had sniffed out her fawn in the high
grass, was goading it away from us according to her own figments
of danger and safety.

"Well." I heaved a sigh that seemed to come from some tight, dark place at the root of me. "I guess we all need to be forgiven."

"Mm-hmm." Aretha's eyes had calmed a little. She looked at her son. "Him too. I know he's been suffering about what he did."

She waited for a reply from me, an acknowledgment. I oared on silently.

"But I guess he didn't tell you what this thing with the pronghorn is all about."

"Nope."

"Not a word?"

"Seemed like he would once. But I thought he was embarrassed, he didn't want Jesse to hear it."

I cringed as I said that. I figured Sneed's mother would bust up again, rake her anger once more over poor dead Jesse. But she checked it.

"Mm-hm. I can imagine that. If he cared for that girl, if he wanted her to like him, I can surely imagine that."

Sneed shifted, oblivious. He was mending, I hoped. All this sleep—or whatever it was—he was rebuilding brain cells, preparing for rebirth. That's what I hoped for, suddenly, wildly, at that moment. Hell, was that possible?

"So what is it?" I asked. "What is he sorry for?"

"He killed them."

"*What?*"

"He told you about his foster family? That funky old white man that raised deer? D'Ontay loved those animals. He took care of them. He would go absent from school and it was all like, where's this bad black boy, he must be out doing drugs, stealing stuff, committing all kind of crimes but no, that was me, that was his mother doing that shit. The school truant people would get their pants all up under their chins and every time, *every* time, they'd find out he just missed the bus on purpose and spent the day with those animals. I didn't know then but I guess they were pronghorn—little things, horns like a beetle, white on their chest and neck. They were like D'Ontay's friends, his family, until one day he killed them all."

I let the oars drop. My entire face must have shown my shock and confusion. "But he said . . ."

I couldn't finish. I didn't want to. This was all going to make some horrible kind of sense, but I didn't want to hear it. *They just stood there*, Sneed had told me, out of the blue, as we drove down from Great Falls one day and saw pronghorn on the range. *They just stared at me . . .*

Aretha said, "Well, Hoss, we were upstairs in the house fighting, me and that white family. See, I used to come once a week for a visit, one hour. I had a man friend would get me high and then drop me off, sit outside in the car and wait for me, maybe drive around a little, you know, sightsee how the white folks live. Then one time there's some burglaries in the neighborhood and guess who's busted for it? Because guess who tells the cops about this black man's been prowling the neighborhood? Mmm-hm. All righteous as hell, trying to take away my visitation cuz I'm in on the crime, you know? And maybe I was. I don't really remember. But that was this man Andre. He did me bad, that's for sure. I probably even knew he was casing places, driving around in there. But I just came storming into those white folks' house and I was gonna take my son. I'm screaming bloody murder. I don't care about the law. He's coming with me. Bitches. Raising my boy to be some tight-ass little snitch."

She caught her breath. With a wince, with a rueful shake of her head, she downshifted to her current self and spoke to the other one.

"Of course those people said no. Damn, 'Retha. They cared about him. At least more than you. But you—" she shook herself out of it "—but I said no, I'm taking him. I said they just wanted him for the comp money, the county foster allowance, and I starting screaming about he's mine, about how I'm gonna claim him on *my* welfare, I'm gonna take him away . . ."

She touched her son, then withdrew her hand. Sneed rolled groggily in the boat bottom, staring up into the sky.

"D'Ontay was downstairs, somewhere, hearing all this. And we were screaming back and forth about the law and about money, not paying attention to him. It wasn't even about him. And the cops were on their way. I was in trouble. I was going to be guilty of those burglaries too, going to jail again. I guess he figured all that, because that's just how I was."

The boat scraped a gravel shoal. I shoved, shoved, shoved us off, remembering how Sneed had told me: *I took care of them all that time. They were my friends, my family. But when I needed them, when I needed help, when I needed to know what do to, they just stood there. Doing nothing. Just fucking stupid animals, Dog. They just stared at me . . .*

"He sliced their throats."

Aretha's voice was hoarse suddenly, struggling to cut through grief.

"This poor boy did. I guess something snapped in him. He killed every one of them. He sliced their throats. Then he ran away while we were still fighting, and we never saw him again."

When I could manage, I took up the oars and tried to guide us. But there had been a shift, a slip. A half-mile of river had swept us along, but I hadn't noticed what dangers we had been lucky enough to avoid. In broad daylight, I suddenly felt blind, felt dread slide under and carry the boat.

The full scare caught up with us in just a few more minutes. We bumped along toward another rapids, heading for rocks that stood up like sentries in a maze of scrambled water. "Better hang on," I was telling Aretha, just as a boulder funneled the boat shoreward into shallow water and from behind the next rock flushed one of Tucker's skinheads.

"Grab them!" the fat radish bellowed, charging wild-eyed through waist-deep water to snatch our spinning prow. "Come on! Grab these motherfuckers!"

Out from the next boulder splashed the scrawny skin—Denny. The boat caught Denny square in the chest, plowed him under, but the impact slowed us enough for his partner to get one hand through the border-rope on the prow. I swung an oar but couldn't reach him.

"Got 'em! Mister Tucker! We got 'em!"

Aretha never hesitated. She twisted, made a fist, tried to hit his face but he went under. She pounded the fat skin's wet glove. He popped up, tried to punch Sneed's mother with his free hand, but Aretha was too quick. She grabbed that hand and bent it back while she hammered away at his grip. "Nigger bitch!" he tried, but that did not sit well. Aretha scissored her legs and lashed one foot across the gunwale, kicked the punk hard in the side of the head with a solid wet splat.

He shook himself like a mad dog. "Mister Tucker!" Now bleeding from the ear, the fat skin shot desperate looks toward the bank. As the boat slung out of his control, Comrade Denny popped up within my reach. His eyes went wide as my oar came down between his brows. He disappeared in swirl of pink water. Now it was just the fat kid, hanging on, swinging wildly and airing out his entire rancid storehouse of racist epithets as he tried to withstand Aretha and drag us ashore.

Aretha gave it back. "Peckerwood!" She pounded at his grip. "I'll break your damn arm, square-dancing motherfucker!"

A sharp whistle sliced the mash of churning water. A husky, broad-hatted rider crested the canyon rim on a sweating chestnut mare. Seeing us, he unsheathed a rifle and repeated the whistle as he goaded the horse onto a dicey switchback trail. Down they came, the rider yipping through his teeth. During this, perhaps inspired by it, the fat skinhead ducked behind Aretha and gained purchase on the river bottom. He beached us with one great heave, then backed away as if from a rattlesnake and rasped desperately at Aretha: "Coon!"

"Cave fungus!"

"Fuckin' porch monkey!"

"Saltine!"

"Hey!" shouted the rider. "Cut that out!"

When his horse reached river cobble, the rider dismounted and approached us, aiming that rifle at me, stopping just before his fancy boots got wet. Close up, there was no mistake: this was the cut-rate star himself, the B-movie hero, Dane Tucker. He had the skin tucks, the sun tan, the brand new hat, the big white teeth in a bullshit grin around a stagecraft lip of chaw—Dane Tucker.

"This nigger bitch—"

"Hey," Tucker repeated. There was acid in his voice. He grabbed the fat skinhead by his sopping shirtfront. "I said cut that out." He threw the kid away from us. "Go help out Denny. He's bleeding."

Tucker's rifle stayed on me, I noted, but his eyes went straight to Aretha. He drooled a short string of brown juice into the Roam. Guy needs a stunt man for the snoose, I was thinking. Not a star really, up close. More of a red dwarf.

"So golly," he lump-lipped, upending Sneed's mother as he yanked the boat another yard ashore. "I thought you all knew this is private land."

Aretha looked at me. "We're not on your land." I was out of breath, my voice tight. "We're on the water. The water's public. That's Montana law."

Tucker treated that bit of populism with a disgusted chuckle and then ignored me. "You," he said to Aretha, "have my deepest apologies. Please forgive these idiots. You are not deserving of such filthy language."

Her eyes blazed at him.

"You bet," he said. "You're a proud one. That's what I mean."

Aretha's right hand inched toward Big Louis where her Smith and Wesson was concealed.

"I detest that kind of language," Tucker said. "So unnecessary. So disrespectful."

I swung a leg over the gunwale, intending to shove us off. Tucker cocked the rifle, chased me back.

"That ancient tribal dignity," he purred at Aretha. "That's what you got."

He walked around the prow, appraising her from behind.

"And I'm guessing Watusi. Am I right? Mixed with some of that good West African Mandingo? Lovely stuff." Tucker grinned at her. "See, I don't get into this whole conflict. It's not necessary.

You people enslaved your own. That's where it started. We all need to let it go."

Having reached the other side of the boat, he used his boot to poke at Sneed, who slumped in a daze against the gunwale. "Who's this boy? He a retard?"

"Don't you touch him."

"Oh, we could wrestle, Sugar, you and me."

"Get away from him."

Tucker prodded Sneed with the rifle barrel. I felt the jolt of Aretha's tension down at my end of the boat. She had Big Louis's zipper halfway open.

"Back off," she warned him.

Tucker swung the rifle into her face. "Throw that bag on shore." He jerked his head toward the cobble behind him. "Go on."

I let a breath out as she tossed it. Tucker picked up Big Louis. He unzipped the bag the rest of the way and dumped out the pistol and all her things. Then he hurled Big Louis over my head into the Roam. It floated briefly, then filled and disappeared. Tucker kicked the Smith and Wesson up the red scree below the bluff. Then he zeroed back in on Aretha.

"So you got a name, Princess? Huh?"

The two wet skins crowded around.

"Come on. What is it? LaShaquille?" He savored it. "That'd be real pretty. Or how about Sha-Kobe? But I'm in the wrong time zone, huh? Let's see. Ebony? Diamond? Jazmin?"

"Maybe it's Whoopi." Denny liked this, slugged his buddy and snuffled amusement through his bloody nose.

"Shut up," Tucker told the pair. "Hang on to this marshmallow boat." He kept his gaze on Sneed's mother. "Hosanna? Tawanda?"

Sneed sat up suddenly, a massive scowl on his brow. "Aretha," his mother blurted as if to stop him from lurching into a bullet.

The skins fought snorts of delight. Tucker, too, seemed to be suppressing a jolt of amusement.

"Aretha." He played it around his mouth. "Yeah. Sure. Why not? Give it to me. R-E-S-P-E-C-T. You got it, baby."

Then abruptly he bent over the boat and plunged an arm between her legs. Aretha's thigh muscles jumped into sharp relief inside her pants. But she held back, watching Sneed closely as the film star came up with a sack of our supplies. Tucker hurled the sack ashore. As it tumbled, the bag spilled jerky and water bottles, plus a roll of toilet paper that bounced and unraveled among the rocks about twenty feet up.

"Now that up there, Princess Aretha," Tucker said, pointing to the bank where the supplies lay strewn, "is private property. *My* private property."

He leaned close. "You want permission to come aground, Sweetheart?"

"Fuck you."

Tucker drew back, sighed. "Stuck in the past," he sighed. "Oh well. So here's the deal. You so much as set one foot out of this river to wipe your pretty pink puss and I'm on you. You're a trespasser. You're mine."

Aretha kept her head down, her eyes now square on Tucker's chest.

"Captain Ahab or that retard touch my ground I'm just gonna shoot them dead and say they tried to rob my place."

Sneed began to take huge, hiccupping breaths. He began to mutter. But Aretha no longer looked his way. Her stillness was unsettling—*a lot of things I shouldn't have reacted to the in the ways I did*—and it bothered Tucker, too. He watched her carefully, inching back. "We're legal," I took the occasion to tell him. "We got on legally, upstream on Forest Service land, and we're legal all the way down to the Yellowstone."

Tucker's bronze cheeks puffed out. A droning in the sky made him look up—a small plane, high to the south. Then he lunged in, split Aretha's legs again and yanked up the other supply sacks and sent those to the same scattered fate among the rocks. He jumped back, this time the rifle on Sneed. He spoke to me.

"Okay, Captain. You're legal. But here's the deal. You're gonna get hungry, but you're not gonna eat. And you better not drink any

of this water because my bison shit all up it. Mistress Imani here
is going have to hang her pretty one off the boat. Wish I could be
there, but oh well. The next place you can legally touch dry ground
is twenty-seven miles down the river on the Yellowstone. And I *will*
have someone watching."

I glanced at the skinheads. They had their eyes on the airplane
as it banked over the western flank of the Absorakas. The chubby
skin said something into Tucker's ear.

"I don't care why they're here," Tucker responded. He snatched
up Galen Ringer's fly rod, snapped it on his knee, threw the pieces
ashore. I tucked the oars out of his reach—or at least he would have
to get his boots wet. He took another look down the rifle barrel at
Sneed and found Sneed staring back at him.

"What do you want?"

"Dane Tucker," said Sneed.

"I said what do you want?"

Sneed, as if in the middle of a conversation, as if in his perfectly
thoughtful and cogent self, as if he had struck a gold mine of brain
tissue, answered, "Fences keep your bison in. But they only survive
because you feed them in the winter. Those fences are bad for deer
and antelope. You don't feed them and they can't migrate. They're
going to starve."

We all stared at Sneed. Again he started the deep, hiccupping
breaths. Finally Tucker broke the silence. "I heard all that, but it
don't mean shit to me, Buckwheat. None of it. Never will."

Sneed's eyes blurred as his own air rose to choke him. The
movie star put a boot on the boat's prow. He took a last look at
Aretha. "Let it go, troupers," he told his skinheads, and he kicked
us out into the current.

"You all have a nice couple of days," Dane Tucker said.

A Million Pounds of Warer

"For the record," I began, after an hour of rage and rumina-
tion, after maybe three miles of wide and sluggish water, "I think
Aretha is a damn fine name."

"Well," she retorted, "I think that we're screwed."

"Oh, we were screwed a long time ago. Now we just know
how." I took an oar stroke. "You know what my real name is?
Ned. Can you believe that? Ned Oglivie. Now that is an example
of what a name should never be."

Aretha feigned interest, barely: "And that's why you're
Dog then?"

"Almost."

"What would you rather be?"

"I don't know. Ike. Elvis. Satchmo. Carlos."

Her eyes narrowed. "Go on. You think I haven't heard it all?"

"I mean it. Aretha. That is a kick-ass name."

"Next," she said, "you're gonna tell me how sexy it is."

"Well, I could." I performed an oar-shrug. "If it would
brighten your day."

She squashed that with an angry frown. "What would
brighten my day right now is some kind of damn plan."

I had been watching the sky.

"Okay," I said. "You want a plan? Here it is."

By means of stubby oar I maximized our speed through another five miles of river as meanwhile the temperature dropped twenty degrees under storm clouds and the Roam grew brawny and rough. Around us, the diorama had flipped by the quarter-mile: a searing jackpine scree became a shadow-cool matrix of angular volcanic stone, and that became a gusty plateau of brown bristlegrass, and now, as Aretha clawed at goosebumps on her arms, we plunged at a quickened pace toward a canyon where the river pitched and frothed beneath bulking thunderheads. "Here," I said just inside the mouth of the canyon, and I pulled us over where the river split around an island of rock rimmed with drifted wood and brushed with hawthorn and buffaloberry. Tucker's man, watching from horseback on the canyon rim, stopped with us.

Aretha did her part, collecting firewood while I hiked ahead along the treacherous riverbank to scout the X-factor of the canyon. It didn't look too bad, I decided. It looked dangerous but not impossible to navigate in the dark. Our plan was to light a fire and keep it burning a good hour or two into darkness, then build it up and leave it ablaze, holding our minder on the ridge while we slipped downriver, hopefully invisible, all the way to Sneed's mark on the map by dawn. With the heavy clouds—maybe even better with a storm—it was going to be *dark* dark at the bottom of the canyon. Our minder would never see us, never guess we'd gone.

I said when I returned, "You know what they say about the weather in Montana?"

"No, Hoss, I don't."

"You don't like it, just wait a few minutes."

Aretha dropped a heap of sun-bleached pine branches. "That's the same thing they say about the weather in Arkansas."

"Well, see, we're all one people."

"Mm-hmm." She moved off to collect more wood. "United by bullshit about the weather."

We raised the blaze to about six feet high sometime after midnight and then shoved off. Sneed lay as instructed in the bottom of the boat, half aware and three-quarters confused. Aretha twisted her arms through the side ropes and hung on. In this manner, graced by lucky bounces and timely spins, we endured a five-mile sequence of minor rapids and emerged an hour before a stormy daybreak into a long riffle, a smooth and speeding bullet train of water.

"We made it." Aretha yawned, shook the kinks out of her arms. "Good call, Hoss."

I didn't answer. I wasn't sure yet. The speed of the water was new, beyond my capacity to control the boat. I kept my eyes front. Overhead I felt the pressure of a storm about to break loose. I saw the next big rapids, felt its yank beneath me, just as thunder cracked and finally the rain came down.

"Hang on!" I shouted.

I back-oared, trying to slow us down and get a look ahead.

"Get him to hold something! Or sit on him, and you hold on! I think we can make this."

But in the downpour I could barely see beyond Aretha, and this new current felt like a knife blade under the boat that wanted to peel us up and flip us aside into the rocks.

I bent an oar. "Damn it!"

Aretha screamed as we hit a rock and spun one-eighty, giving her the view ahead as we sluiced into the rapid. She screamed again, sat down hard on her son and clutched the gunwale rope. I tucked the oars rather than lose them completely. This was a new game. This was pinball for our lives. "Two hands, everybody! Hang on!"

The boat bounced and spun. Lightning showed me sandstone

cliffs collapsed to a thirty-yard span, with Cruise Master-sized slabs of rock strewn in the river's path and drifted timber hung up like spikes and claws—then all was black and slashing rain.

There was no stopping, no control. We slung helplessly into the mess ahead.

Aretha's ragged voice reached me through the smashing water. "Hoss, what are you doing!"

"Nothing! I can't do anything!"

Not until we were upon it did I see the first big pine snag, wedged between behemoth stones in the center current, its dead limbs whipping and shaking in the water's frenzied onrush.

"Get down!" I roared at Aretha as we slid through a gap of air beneath the butt end of the snag.

A shattered branch-tip caught and snapped off in Aretha's hair—she shrieked and smothered Sneed—and an instant later the same branch, trimmed to a lethal thickness, tore my hat off but left my head where it was. *Lucky Dog.*

Then we were clear of that snag and spinning into the next danger. In the following instant there came a stomach-dropping lunge—a roller coaster plunge, as if the river were inhaling us—and then the boat slammed a rock broadside and careened into a new tangle of water and wood.

We did not luck through this one. We slammed in between branches and stuck fast, pinned by a million pounds of water. We were allowed one full breath of sickening stasis. Then the current simply pried the boat up into a vertical ass-stand and hung us there.

Aretha shrieked like a threatened cat. She and Sneed came slopping down through the mash of spray and water and vibrating rubber and landed hard upon me. Aretha grabbed me around the neck. "Baby! Where's my baby?" She wailed into my ear as the water levered us over into a full cartwheel. "Where is my baby?" she demanded.

But I felt the absence of Sneed as the boat flopped over us top-side-down and darkened everything.

Flotsam

I fought my head outside the boat. Lightning struck the cliff ahead and gave me a glimpse of Sneed clutching at a rock as he was swept past just yards ahead.

"Sneedy! Turn around! Grab the boat!"

But the Roam shoved us both along, converging, separating, converging one last time before suddenly the boat hung up once more in timber. "Sneed!" I yelled as he spun away into froth and slashing rain.

I ducked under the boat into Aretha's wail of terror. "He's okay," I lied. "He's fine. Let's get this thing flipped over. Hang on right here."

I left her at the flapping upstream edge of our predicament and hand-over-handed along the gunwale rope. The upside-down prow had jammed flush against a thick snag. Heavy current bowed my back around the snag, swept my legs beneath it. All around me the river raged and tore and sucked, and under this pressure the boat jittered madly. But all was in stasis, stuck in a balance of tremendous forces. I was flotsam now, a driftwood stick, or a shred of pondweed, Aretha and I both, and the boat, and we would stay right there, whipping and trailing in place until the river moved us along. We could be snagged there for hours, weeks, months. The levers of the river had locked. I had to unlock them.

"D'Ontay!"

"Stay there!"

"Where's my baby?"

"Hang on!"

I tried to bend my stomach muscles against the current. I couldn't. I tried to pull my legs through the rush of water to join the rest of my body on the upstream side of the log. I couldn't.

Flotsam, Dog. Flotsam.

I had to use my puniness. I had to leverage my frailty, not fight it. Hand over hand, letting my body trail limply, I worked my way back up to Aretha. There I spanned my arms to grab the rope on both gunwales and added my weight to hers to pull the flapping stern down against the current. "Go down to the other end and hold on," I rasped at Aretha. "No matter what. Hold on."

When she was in place, I worked one arm free of the gunwale rope. That side of the boat bounced up in the current, caught air and nearly tore out my still-bound arm before I caught the rope in my free fist and yanked the boat down flush.

Slowly, fearing a broken back or worse, I worked the other arm out of its engagement with the rope. Now I was in the same position as my original hang-up, but I was holding the upside-down boat against the water—my grip and nothing else.

So there we were. I held the mighty lever. I checked Aretha. She held on at the downstream end. "Son of a *bitch!*" I screamed, and I thrust my arms up and let the boat go.

The boat lifted away in a backbend over the snag with Aretha scooped up inside while my body, now in free float, swept out beneath the log. I raked through underwater branches and popped up on the other side just as the boat sailed over me and splatted face-up, Aretha jumbled inside, on a short patch of fast, smooth water. In an instant, streaked by a sideways crackle of lightning, Aretha and the boat were gone, safely or not, downstream.

"Son of a *bitch!*" I screamed again, kicking with numb legs toward an eddy on the east canyon wall where Sneed floated face down.

This is the End of Us

So how come you're not home with your wife?

A good, hard question. But just try me. The Dog doesn't say much about the past. The Dog lives not to think about it, endeavors to fish hard, to drink hard, and to sleep like ancient mud. There exists, out there, an endlessly open tap of trout water, a cool and intoxicating wilderness of clear waters along blue highways. And when all this ceases to soothe me, there is always the Big Two-Hearted. But now and then memory does lay siege. And then God help me. I would, I could, do anything to fight back, to conquer the past. I would die. Of course I would. I would offer up myself.

"Can't you hear me? Ned? Can't you just respond?"

My sweet bride Mary Jane calls me from too far away in the house, a practice I abhor. Injured somehow, she has gone away to clatter in the kitchen and now she tests me, wanting me to follow, seeing if I won't. I post a numb and angry won't, vigorously thumbing a seam on the couch cushion and feeling trapped. What haven't I done? What haven't I provided? What demon has gotten in past my guard? What the hell is her problem?

The upstairs water has stopped some time ago. The pipes are silent in the wall behind me. I haven't noticed.

It is April. Our fight is about her mother, and about my father, and about six red tulips. These are the coordinates.

Crime is up in Boston. My business is good. We have just upgraded to a three-story, turreted, nineteenth-century textile merchant's mansion in West Newton. Her mother is sick with what turns out to be uterine cysts, painful but benign. My father, on the other hand, has been sick all his life in certain ways that a scrupulously fault-free girl like Mary Jane cannot reference.

"Ned, can't you just respond to me? I'm asking you where is Eamon?"

Of course, I don't like the tone. I post a silence, and one small, internal breakdown in diction: bitch.

Irate, slamming things, my wife repeats, "Ned, I'm asking you: where is Eamon?"

I wonder suddenly: when have the pipes stopped hissing and hammering in the wall? I have no idea. "He went up to take a bath."

"By himself?"

"Yes."

"And you think that's a good idea?"

"Obviously, I do."

"I can't hear you. What did you say?"

I am too tired for this. "Come in here and talk to me. I don't have to follow you around." *And here is the twist, the tangle that costs us. She arrives angrily. Returning to our original topic, I say,* "I did what I thought was a good idea. Dad was happy with it, and your mother doesn't really mind, she just talks, so what is the problem?"

Things mix up, but I don't budge. What is the problem? If the water is off, then Eamon hasn't overflowed the tub. What else is there to worry about? Tulips? Shall we worry about the six red tulips? Eamon is a smart kid. He's a Manta Ray at swim lessons.

Now my wife steps in front of me, crosses her arms. Interrogation. "He wanted to take a bath himself. He said he knew how."

"And you think that's a good idea?"

I say again, "Obviously I do."

"He is four."

"Yes he is."

"Jesus, Ned."

Mary Jane is just exactly the woman you would expect out of the Dog in those days. A tall blonde, angular and fragile beneath a big bust, the daily authoress of an edgy, clingy, classical beauty that can disappear in a flash. And I am just the man to match. I am a quivering side of corporate beef. I wear expensive suits. I work out and then afterwards I eat and drink too much. I just barely keep my pants on around the hotties on my office staff—all of them young women I've hired because I own the company, all of them young women who look like my wife before she became a mother. I am, as we sometimes say, a piece of work.

At home, ever wary, I have learned to read Mary Jane's quicksilver moods like a seaman reads a barometer. I fix on the text of her face. I check it every minute, trying to spot harbingers of the change that could come any moment. Her brow and lips and skin tone, how much freedom her hair dares to assume—any of these can shift suddenly and spook me, summoning guilt and reparations on my part. A year or so later in my life, hearing of this kabuki-like arrangement, a shrink will paint a picture of yours truly in the image of a pet dog—and hence I name myself—a slave to the external, a creature eternally unsure from one moment to the next whether he is good or bad. Only later will I understand. Only later—too much later—will the Dog go bad, gloriously bad, snap the chain, and run.

But poor Mary Jane. Really. And poor me, too.

This isn't what we need.

And lately I have had enough of her, enough of myself, and enough of us. I have begun to snarl. I can't believe how stupid we are. I tell her, "I never meant to offend anybody—"

"Well, congratulations, Neddy. That's quite an aspiration."

"I don't know where you get this shit."

"I married it."

"Jesus, Mary Jane. Settle down."

"*Those were my red tulips,*" *she storms.* "*I planted them in front of my house. I watered them. They complemented the color of the house. I did not want to cut them. It was a sacrifice.*"

"*But I heard you say about a hundred times, 'Mother would so love these red tulips.' Then my dad called. He didn't know your mother was sick. I told him. He said, 'Neddy, I'll take her some flowers. What kind of flowers does she like?' I remembered the red tulips, and that you said your mother would love them. Something clicks. I tell Dad, 'Go to the florist and get some red tulips. M.J.'s mother loves red tulips.' I thought it was a good idea.*"

Mary Jane squeezes her narrow fists and interrupts me with a growling sound. Her hair has come undone and her hyper-sensitive skin has exploded in a rash below the jaw.

"*Ned,*" *she said,* "*Ned, that is not a thought. That is, like, half a thought.*"

"*Why is it such a big deal?*"

"*Ned. Ned, don't you see the sacrifice I've made here? For nothing? Thanks to you? Don't you see that I cut my red tulips? The ones that I planted. That I watered. That I would have liked to keep in front of my house, where I planted them. That I cut anyway, to give to my mother, who is sick?*" *My wife stops herself. For an unconscious moment she is a human female gyroscope, centering her anxiety. Then she shrieks toward the ceiling,* "*Eamon! What are you doing? Are you okay? Eamon? Eamon, answer me!*"

"*I told you, he's taking a bath.*"

"*I don't hear anything.*"

"*He's okay.*"

"*You know that?*"

"*I'll check in a minute.*"

She scowls at me.

"*Finish your sad story,*" *I say.*

"*I cut them. My red tulips, Ned. I didn't want to, but I believed that Mother would be pleased, so I cut them and I took them to the hospital in a vase. I gave them to my mother. And she says, 'Oh, red tulips. More red tulips. It must be red tulip day. Neddy's father dropped off*

some red tulips just like that. Now I've got more red tulips than I know
what to do with.' Jesus, Ned. Thanks a lot."

I stand up.

I can be enormously more sensitive than my wife will ever bother
to know. It is me now—not my wife in her tulip rage—who senses that
things have taken a fatal turn.

"Mary Jane," I say, "I'm sorry. I'm really, really sorry."

Halfway up the stairs that afternoon in April I stop, overwhelmed
by a dread all out of proportion to a fight over tulips. No one in our
family is more sensitive than little Eamon. That boy's skin can change
five shades in a minute. That boy will crawl into my lap, feeling my
sadness before I do. He just knows. And how long have Mary Jane and
I been fighting? How many hours, months, years?

I bellow from the steps, "Eamon, answer your mother!"

From the entire upstairs comes a vaulted silence, drifting down on
the iron smell of Boston bathwater. Then a single blink of sound—one
drip from that old faucet onto a skin of perfect stillness.

"Eamon!" I roar.

I take the last flight of steps in threes. That sweet little boy has left
the door wide open, the way he does when he poops, because he isn't
ready for privacy yet, not even when—

"Oh, God! Eamon!"

"Ned," Mary Jane calls from downstairs, "what is it?"

I skid on his discarded t-shirt. The hand I fling for balance rakes
toothbrushes and deodorants and cosmetics from the vanity. Our
crap flies everywhere. A pink plastic razor hits the water and breaks
the perfect seal beneath which lies our boy in a white-skinned embry-
onic curl.

"Ned? What's wrong?"

"Oh, God. Mary Jane—"

"There'd better not be a mess all over."

I tear our boy from tepid water. His skin is cold. His green eyes
fix randomly on the direction from which his mother will arrive. His
little body fits in the sink. The inside of his mouth is warm. I shove
my own desperate breath in there. Snotty warmish water spews from

his nose. I stick a finger between his little ribs and feel no movement. I have no idea what I'm doing. I haven't rehearsed this. Nothing like this can ever happen.

No!

I whip around and slam the bathroom door. I lock it. This is the end of us. The end of me. This is the end.

"Eamon," I whisper, "please . . ."

Again and Again and Again

Dawn, bottled up by the storm, now tore through a cataclysm between cliff and sky. Sneed spun slowly in the eye of a foam-flecked eddy against a shallow rung of sun-red rock. Then he rolled himself over, spouted faintly, and sank beneath the swirl of his Jose Cuervo shirt.

I fought to the outer seam of the eddy, but the current pulled me past him. I stopped my thrashing and dove.

Underwater, my eyes stung and blurred, but there was light and I saw the shape of him—curled and sinking into the bottom of a hole where a pod of big trout finned aside in silhouette as he settled gently down. I burrowed hard into the swirling water, but Sneed's limp arm slipped through my grasp and the river pulled me downstream.

I got air and whipped my head around. This picture is fixed forever: The rain had lifted. The air was cold. A spotlight sunrise beamed beneath the bulbous, skidding clouds to illuminate Sneed's mother and the boat as they drifted through a long, smooth bend and out of sight.

And meanwhile the relentless current spun me, shoved me into chest-deep water where the bottom cobble was slick as bowling balls. I kicked at those stones, backpedaling. I saw Sneed come up again—slow and still, passive as death—but as his face cycled through the world of air, he spouted again and sucked air feebly before he went back down to join the fish.

There had to be a way. I smashed ashore. Downstream of the eddy, the cliff had crumbled and laddered into a skree that I could I climb. Breathless, I squished across a treacherous shelf of rock and came even with Sneed, then upstream of him, trying to read the current, trying to time it and lead myself—*Go, Dog, go!*—he wouldn't last another minute.

I gathered a fifty-pound flake of sandstone in my arms, raised it overhead against the twirling, green-and-silver sky. Then I tipped into an awkward plunging dive that keeled my legs over and buckled my spine and slammed me straight down to murky mid-depth in the eddy. Everything slowed down. The water chilled. I seesawed to the river bottom.

Big trout bumped me as they glided aside. I let go of the rock and snatched Sneed by the back of his pants. I kicked up and clamped an arm across his chest, which now heaved and hiccupped with startling strength. We went under again. For a long moment I had no traction, no direction. Then I kicked for the fast lane at the margin of the eddy and let the thrusting water have its way, tumbling us into the bowling-ball zone where I got my feet down and steered with desperate tiptoes.

Down the Roam we bounced and twisted, downstream, downstream, Sneed puking water across the side of my head and gripping my neck so strongly that when we finally struck shallow water I took two zigzag staggers toward shore, tore his hands off, and dropped him

I pounced on him then. I jammed my fingers through his teeth and saw the blood as he bit me. I cracked his mouth like a nut and rammed my lips inside and pinched his nose. I had forced myself to study CPR after Eamon's death. I pounded breath against Sneed's throat. Water—cold and acidic—pushed back and I spilled him over, yanked him on his belly, drained his lungs into the cobble.

Then I fought his clenching jaws again. I blew air in, fast and hard. I pulled back, rolled him again, just in time as he puked bile and Gatorade and river water across my arm. Again I forced my air, again and again and again, until at last I felt his chest push back and I raised up, my brain black and tangled, to spit and take my own deep breath.

The sky boomed. A cold gust. Now it hailed. A stinging sheet of white advanced across the river as I watched over Sneed. He was taking air—and then, as hail lashed his face, he hiccupped violently and stopped. I blocked the onslaught with my body and burrowed back through his defenses. Hailstones stung my back, bounced madly about our faces as I stayed in for ten breaths, then fifty, then a hundred. Then at last, pressed together, we calmed. A rhythm came. The nipping, clattering hail settled around us like a blanket, a screen that closed out all else, and Sneed focused, worked with me. He pulled in my air, timed it, relaxed the clenching of his chest. I stayed . . . stayed . . . then eased away and sat back.

Sneed pulled air in . . . out . . . in . . . out. His eyes opened. At first, and for many minutes, he looked at nothing. Gradually the storm lidded past, opening a scrubbed blue sky over rapidly warming air. Sneed looked around. He hiccupped twice, then seemed to find the off switch. He found rocks with his hands and pushed himself up. He looked at me in puzzlement. I thought it was the old shakes again, the ones I couldn't control.

"Where is she?" he asked.

Pretty Good Short Term

I pulled Sneed under a narrow ceiling of overhanging rock. Cliff swallows swerved and chittered around us, defending their holes. Once more, in a final spasm, hail pulsed across the scene in front of us, pocking the river, rattling and bouncing off the rocks, then letting up for good, making way for a brilliant stroke of sunlight that glittered every surface in the canyon.

I stayed hard on Sneed for an hour or more, monitoring. I knew nothing about his type of brain damage, only that many things were possible, few of them good. I feared that any moment a circuit would shut down and those bright eyes—weren't they brighter now?—would melt away like the hailstones in the river rocks around us.

I prodded him. I shook him. I talked to him. I avoided an answer to *where is she*, knowing that one *she* was dead and fearing for the other. I talked about—what else?—fishing. "You know after a storm like this, Sneedy, the water level rises. And I don't know why for sure, but trout feed good in rising water. My guess is they are masters of anticipation."

He repeated me: "Masters of anticipation."

"Right. I mean, how else would a trout know that a hatch is about to happen?"

"About to happen."

"Yeah. Not happening. *About* to happen. They sense it. They take their stations. Then it happens. I've seen it a thousand times. They don't eat my damn fly—"

"Damn fly."

"—earlier in the day, because they anticipate something better later."

"Later."

"Yeah. Later. What are you, some kind of parrot?" I gave him a nudge on the shoulder. He gave me one back. I said, "Eventually, rising water washes food into the river. Worms. Spiders caught napping in the rocks. Ants and beetles on streamside grass that is suddenly pulled under. See?"

Yearling trout slapped the fast edge of the mirrored pool before us, where a seam of earth-stained foam steadily bulked itself one bit of fluff at a time. "They better watch out," I said. "Big old Uncle Brown Trout's gonna come up and eat them."

Sneed waited about thirty seconds. "They better watch out," he said then, seeming to listen to himself. "That's pretty good short term, huh Dog?"

"Yes, it—"

But he broke into violent hiccups. He choked. He slammed his fist against his sternum. When finally he caught his breath Sneed slumped against me, slid down until his head was on my lap. "God damn it," he sobbed, and threw an arm over his face.

I felt his lungs expand and contract against my legs. After a few minutes, I tried a joke.

"So this big brown trout we all talk about, what's his first name?" I jostled him. "Huh, Sneedy? What about James Brown?"

He tried a slow breath that worked okay. He tried to laugh.

"What about Cleveland Brown?"

"Foxy Brown," Sneed managed.

"Girl fish. Sure. But how about Charlie? Charlie Brown. I think I caught that guy a few times."

This time Sneed managed a faint but legitimate laugh.

"And John Brown," I said. "Know who he was?"

"Huh-uh."

"Abolitionist."

"Huh-uh. But what about Encyclopedia Brown. Can't catch that guy, Dog. No how. Too smart for you."

Now I laughed. I added, "Hubie Brown. Larry Brown. Gilbert Brown. Paul Brown. Jim Brown. Dee Brown."

"Huh?"

"Sports."

"I don't do sports, Dog. I . . . I think I paint bridges."

"And sometimes water towers."

"Yeah." His chest heaved up and down. "Yeah. Water towers. Hey, what about Bobby Brown?"

"Don't know him."

"Singer. R&B. I like that. And Foxy Brown."

"You said Foxy Brown."

Sneed posted a long silence before he said, "I know. Just checking your short term, Dog."

"You like Foxy Brown?"

"Like to catch her one time," Sneed said. "That's all."

"Yeah? What fly? Wooly bugger? Humpy? Bead head scud?"

Sneed pulled that arm off his eyes, looked at me. He grinned. "Damn, Dog. You're a sick old man."

"And you, my friend, might be a good bit better."

The possibility of this seemed to dawn slowly on Sneed as well. He sat up, leaned his back against the warming rock, tipped his face into the sun. "But all the time I feel like puking," he told me. "Or you ever been real carsick, Dog? *Real* carsick? Like you don't care, you ready to jump out the window at sixty miles per hour? That's what it's like." He gulped. "Don't give me a gun, man. I don't know what I'd do."

I stared at him, thinking of the dead pronghorns, thinking of Jesse on the ground. Sneed blinked back. "What?" he said.

I let my breath out. "Nothing. But your thinking's coming back a little, Sneedy. I can tell. Your memory."

"Well—"

His confidence seemed to waffle. At least that's what I guessed. Maybe the fatigue, the nausea, those waves he talked about had washed out brain function. I watched him carefully. He stared past me toward the river. Should I tell him about Jesse? Ask him about Jesse? Now? But something was moving inside him. He winced. He squinted. He twitched. Then he said, "Well . . . my memory . . . maybe so. Cuz I know that's my mama."

It was. She was. Up that sparkling canyon battled Aretha Sneed, negotiating a rocky downstream bend with Cord Cook's tattered boat half on her back, half snagging behind.

"Hey!" I hollered. I waved an arm. "Aretha! Over here!"

She looked our way and stopped. She let down the boat and I saw her shoulders droop. Then she sat down hard in the rocks. I stood. Sneed struggled to his knees beside me. "Hey!" Aretha had just dropped her face into her hands when the first shot rang down from the canyon rim.

Atta Boy, Hoss

Rock dust jetted up behind her. The second shot hit a chamber of the boat, fizzled it down to a limp yellow sack.

"No!" I screamed as by instinct Aretha crawled under the remainder of the boat. A third shot pierced the thick rubber bottom. "Get out and run!"

I caught Sneed from the back, hooked his armpits, dragged him back to the canyon wall.

"Stay."

"Dog—"

"Damn it, Sneed. You're not that better. Listen to me. Don't move until I come back."

I charged out across an ankle-twisting chaos of wet rocks. Aretha hadn't reappeared from beneath the boat. A fourth shot hit the bulbous prow, popped it like a balloon. I glanced over my shoulder, saw the pink pickup on the rim, two gunmen standing up on the hood. The fifth shot—as I flung the boat off Aretha—hit me and I went down.

I lay face to panting face with Sneed's mother in the rocks. "I got him," I gasped. "I got your boy. He's okay. He's over there, warming up in the sun."

Her eyes went wild.

"He's out of sight," I said. "They're above him."

I rolled over. We were in the wide open, no cover nearby, but the hood of the pickup was free of gunmen. I tried to figure where I was hit, but the whole left side of my torso was buzzing into numbness. "You okay? They didn't hit you?"

Aretha nodded. "You?"

"Not sure."

She felt along my left side, found pain and blood around my shoulder.

"You're hit."

"Not much."

She made a face at me—incredulous, mocking, hopeful.

"Really," I said. "Flesh wound."

She peeled back my torn sleeve, winced on my behalf. I took the wet red shred from her fingers and ripped it free. "Turn around," I said. "I have an idea how we're going to get out of this."

Aretha sat still as I dabbed and smeared my blood across her back and neck. As she lay face down in the rocks, her voice was fierce and grim.

"Atta boy, Hoss."

Playing dead is an easy thing to talk about, but a harder thing to do. Aretha and I stayed face down in those rocks watching the last of the hailstones melt for what seemed like hours before the skinheads made it down to the river bottom.

We could hear them. They came bitching all the way—the gist being that they were supposed to pop the boat and not hit us, this derived from verbal vomit in the configuration that Denny, goddamnit, should have held his fire because he couldn't hit a nigger in a barbeque shack—or alternately, that Gunter—and here the fat radish received a proper *nom de Nazi*—should have quit bugging Denny while Denny was trying to shoot because Denny could hit that big fucking boat already—who couldn't?—except that some mudpuppy like Gunter was assing up inside Denny's ear like some kind of Jewboy fag.

I heard a rock click between Aretha's clenched teeth, suppressing a snarl. Not a bad idea, I thought.

"Well now they're fucking dead, you asshole, and we're in trouble."

"They were gonna drown anyway."

"Exactly, you moron." Gunter was spitting mad. "That's why we don't need to shoot them. What did this bitch call you? A cave fungus? Jesus Christ, Denny. You don't make much of a case for white power."

"Well   they're dead, ain't they?"

"You see this one?" Gunter toed me. "This one here, this is what we call a *white man*, right here." Gunter gave me stiff, steel-toed shot to the ribs. "He may be a nigger lover, Denny, but we still *do not shoot white people*. Got it?"

Denny dodged lateral. "I'm gonna finish off this boat now," he announced, and this drove Gunter wild. "Do we *need* to shoot the boat now? Huh? If they're dead? Think about it, Denny, do we—"

We had a signal, Aretha and I. My thumb was an inch from her face, and when I twitched that thumb, we jumped.

She took Denny's legs out, me Gunter's, and the two skins slapped face against rock and had rifles in their necks before either one could blame the other.

"Well . . . that . . . was easy."

I caught my breath. I carefully fit the snout of Gunter's rifle over the bump of Gunter's seventh vertebra. Aretha did pretty much the same with Denny. But she also worked her foot up under Denny's crotch, found a testicle and made ready to pop it like a grape.

I said, "You fellas think this would be a good time to have another chat?"

We All Drowned in the Canyon

I didn't know where Aretha got her next idea—it had to be *Bonanza*, didn't it?—but she found each boy his own forty-pound river rock to hold with two hands or else we would head on back to crushed testicles, bullets to the spine, all that. This kept the children busy.

"That rock is ancient sea bed," I told them. "About forty million years old. Isn't that fascinating?"

Then, after collecting Sneed, we marched them, holding their bits of ancient sea bed, up a narrow trail to the faded-red Ford pickup on the canyon rim. Up there, all that rain and hail had accomplished little. It had balled up dust around a mini moonscape of raindrop craters, no more.

"No, you cannot put your rock down."

Aretha snapped this in response to Gunter's fat boy whining. Without discussion, she had assumed the position of supervisor in all matters pertaining to confinement and coercion.

"No, you cannot sit down. Oh, you're tired?" She got in Gunter's face. "Well, how about if you stand there about another two hundred years, so you can get some idea how tired the rest feel about you all?"

She gave me a nod. "Go ahead, Hoss. Ask away. But talk slowly."
Denny groaned.

"And use a lot of words," Aretha added.

The sentiment was right, but I tried to make it quick, efficient. I
was not done bleeding, and there was more to Tucker's game, surely,
than Denny and Gunter. So my first question constellated the film
star, his affairs on the ranch, the fanatic denial of trespassers, and this
fence that seemed to come up over and again in various contexts.

"We don't know nothing about a fence," Gunter averred
eagerly, ignoring the other dimensions of my inquiry and thus giving me focus.

"Really?"

"What fence?"

"Does Tucker have a deal to let the sheriff on his land? For
fishing?"

"The sheriff? Fishing? Hell no."

"So who else is in here, besides Tucker and you boys?"

He didn't want to say. Not at all. Neither of them. But
Aretha solved that by stacking on additional samples of
Ordovician sea floor.

"Bunch of whatyacallums—natives," Denny offered in a
whimper over his rocks.

"Natives?"

Gunter grunted a correction: "Nativ*ists*."

"Which are?"

Rushing at it now, getting it over with. Nativists represented
the real Americans, Gunter huffed out. The original white people
who built the country. "They come together with Mister Tucker
to fight off the Aztlan conspiracy." He flicked a dark glance at me,
managed a simper of disgust at my confusion. "And the North
American Union. All that shit that's coming over the border."

Aretha and I traded looks. "I guess we haven't been visiting the
right websites," I told Gunter. "You want to fill that in a little?"

"No."

I shrugged. Aretha collected additional sea floor. "We'll wait."

"Mexicans!" Denny blurted. He hiked one knee up under his rocks, struggling desperately against Aretha's reminder of a rifle at his chest. "Illegal immigration! It's a plan to take over everything from Colorado to Texas and give it back to Mexico—"

Gunter sneered. "That or make the U.S., Mexico, and Canada all one country." He hunkered defiantly under his own rock pile. "Change the dollar to the 'Amero.' Bullshit like that. Mister Tucker's against it—"

"He might be governor of Arizona—"

"He's got a ranch in Arizona but all these fucking wetbacks, they, they—"

"He clears all this shit up once and for all, Mister Tucker's gonna run for president," Gunter concluded. "We'll be Secret Service." Sweat ran down his fat cheeks and tattooed temples. He hitched up his rocks and spat defiantly. "Folks like you probably ought to learn to suck dick before then, that'd be my advice."

I took another look at Aretha. "I'm having a hard time believing people like this exist."

"Yeah?" Her return glance cut me no slack. "Well it's about time you got over it."

Gunter enjoyed that. He spat again. I gun-nuzzled a pudgy spot just above his rocks. "So there's nativists in here? At Tucker's place? Why?"

"Training camp," he grunted.

"Para-military," Denny squeaked. "They go down in units and do cockroach control on the border. Cuz the government—" he nearly dropped his load, looked up in pleading at Aretha, which was a mistake that brought another rock "—the government won't do the job. Won't protect us. So Mister Tucker . . . Mister Tucker . . ."

I waved him off. Next topic. "Who's in the airplane?"

"Mexican spies."

"Who sent you to burn my buddy's tent and leave him that note?"

"The—"

"Shut up, Denny. We ain't been paid yet."

"The lawyer," Denny gasped. "That guy that used to work for Mister Tucker but got fired for building the fence. Gray Henderson."

"Henderson Gray." I glanced at Aretha. She wasn't buying it either. "Why?"

"Because he promised to pay us."

"Why did he promise to pay you?"

"I don't know."

"We don't know."

"But we didn't do it right away. We were busy working for Mister Tucker. Then when we did it, the lawyer said it was too late, they were dead already, and he jewed us."

I nodded for Aretha to cover both specimens. I walked over to the pickup. "You following any of this, Sneedy?"

He nodded. "Uh-huh. My mama's going to kill some crackers."

"I hope not." I found what I wanted in the truck box—a greasy rope about thirty feet long—and in the cab—a two-way radio.

I dropped the rope at Gunter's feet. I opened a channel on the radio and put it to the side of his head. "Call in. Tell whoever that it looks like we all drowned in the canyon, and you're out here just making sure. You'll be back in a couple of hours."

Nearly broken, Gunter did as instructed. Then I had those boys move back to back. I tied them tightly that way, like two bits of fishing line, one thin, one fat, cinched up in a giant nail knot. Aretha permitted me to take her rifle and stow it, unloaded, in the truck box. She permitted the boys, at that point, to drop their rocks.

"Watch your toes."

"Ouch! Fuck!"

"You're free to go," I told them. They fell in a squabbling heap that was quickly enveloped in dust as Sneed and his mother and I drove off downstream in the pickup.

Maybe I Am

I had to work from memory. We were along the lower third of the Roam River now, and my sense was that the black circle on Sneed and Jesse's map was maybe another ten or so miles north as the crow flies and then a mile, at least, east of the river. Maybe. I could only drive and hope. I held on to the thrashing wheel as the truck hammered over raw rangeland in a way that spoke well for the Fords of yesteryear. Meanwhile Sneed and Aretha, squeezed together on the bench seat beside me, engaged in a prickly kind of rapprochement.

"I'm not going to bite you." Aretha glowered at her son from frighteningly close range. "I'm your own mother, for God's sake."

Sneed maintained a forward gaze on a stiff neck planted between pinched-in shoulders. "There's no money in me now," he said.

"Funny how out of everything, you remember that. But since you do remember that, let me tell you about—"

"Dog!" Sneed blurted, appealing for help.

"Hang in there, Sneedy. Just listen."

"—while I—"

"Tell me all about yourself." Sneed piped this hotly and then covered his ears.

Aretha drew her head back and narrowed her eyes. She moved her head side to side, that cobra again, looking to strike.

"Well," she said. "Well, well, well. Listen to you."

He lowered his hands. "Why *don't* you listen to me?"

"You sound like an angry little child."

Now Sneed made fists in his lap. "Maybe I am."

The truck pounded onward another hundred yards, lurching over prairie dog holes and mowing down sage brush, me looking for a place to cross the river.

"Maybe I am," Sneed blurted again. "And maybe you are too."

His mother gathered those words into a long and stony silence. Meanwhile I found some long-gone rancher's poured-gravel ford across the Roam River. I ripped through about a foot of water to the eastern bank, an eroded dirt scarp that the truck angled up with a great amount of revving, spinning, and clanking along the undercarriage.

"Glad it's not my truck," I put in, hoping to lighten the mood.

We had to be getting somewhere close—but close to what? Sneed was insensate with stress right then. I let him be. I glanced at Aretha, thinking I would need her shortly. She was biting her lower lip, digging absently with her painted thumbnail at some hardened piece of ranch muck glued to the wing window in front of her. Stalemate. Dog running solo.

"Well," Sneed's mother said again after another half mile, and she blasted us with a sigh. "Well, well, well."

"Well what?" her son said.

"Well, maybe I am what you said. Maybe you're right. Maybe both of us just had the world cave in on us at about the same time."

She bit her lip again, hard, and let it go.

"I'm okay now." This sounded like a claim, tenuous, but submitted for Sneed to believe. "I built my health back up. I have a job that's hard but I got another woman in the fire station with me and so don't mind it too much. I make decent money. I'm taking classes at a college. I'm meeting lots of smart people—" she glanced at me "—who say I might make law school."

I just smiled at her. Why not? She released another, lighter sigh while I steered up a stump-littered hogback ridge.

"But I think I should start by talking about you, D'Ontay, and how what you did, no matter how much pain it caused you or how bad you feel about it, talking about how what you did saved me. I mean, child, you don't realize that you saved my—"

"There they are!" shouted Sneed, cutting off his mother and nearly jumping off his seat. "Dog! There they are! It's not too late!" He thrashed side to side as if looking for something. Then he struck a fist down on the dashboard.

"Damn it! We lost the fence cutters!"

That Bastard . . . That Cheater

From the crest of that hogback ridge I witnessed a sight that I will credit to the grit and compassion and guilt of my young buddy D'Ontario Sneed for the rest of my life.

From the narrow piece of flat land below the ridge, along a fence line to the north for nearly a quarter mile, stretched a milling mass of pronghorn antelope—hundreds in all, so crowded and so close below that we could smell them, could hear their grunts and whistles and scrapings along the barrier of the fence.

"Dog, I knew it," Sneed was blurting into my ear. "They're not herding animals. That's one way they avoid disease and starvation. They travel in small family groups. This is not a herd. They're just piled up here. They're stuck. They can't move."

"Travel where?" his mother wanted to know.

"They're migrating . . . trying to migrate . . . to the Red Desert in Wyoming."

He was breathing too hard. I saw the hiccups strike him, then the dizziness. His eyes glazed and for a moment, I thought Sneed would pass out. "Shit," he muttered. "Oh, shit. Why?"

I opened the door, pulled him out across the bench seat, made him lie down in the thin hot shade of the truck box. I could read the demand in Aretha's eyes. *What the hell is going on?*

"They're stuck at Tucker's fence," I told her. "It went up last year on Henderson Gray's orders. Tucker got in trouble with activists and Gray lost his job over it. Then Tucker got stubborn and wouldn't take it down. Gray and Sneedy—"

I gazed down at the milling pronghorn. Their distress was palpable. The air buzzed with animal energy.

"When Jesse introduced those two, Gray and your son, D'Ontay must have heard about the fence. Gray said they clashed. This is why. D'Ontay didn't like it."

"But it's just a little fence."

"Mama, pronghorn can't jump," mumbled Sneed, trying to sit up. "That fence . . . it blocks the corridor. They can't . . . they have to . . ."

I raised up to study the landscape. Where the pronghorn wanted to cross was a dry wash that led up into the lap of the Abrosakas, the rugged, snow-capped range they would have to cross to reach their lowland winter grounds in Wyoming. Not that a human eye could tell, but up there somewhere had to be the easiest route through this part of the mountains, a route discovered and made into memory by a million years of tightly threaded pronghorn steps.

"They hit this fence and have to backtrack?"

I was asking Sneed. He nodded.

"But they don't want to backtrack," I said. I could feel this now. It was so simple, really. It was like salmon with a dam in their way, contemplating the unknown of a fish ladder. "They stall and stress," I explained to Aretha. "They waste time and energy. They don't want to take a different route that's not as good. They're conflicted."

"Yes." Sneed was staying with me through a mighty mental effort. "They can't stay here. Wolves will get them. They can't run . . . in so much . . . snow."

Aretha had figured it out—not just the animal behavior, but now, fully, our mission down the river, the injured soul of her son.

She knelt beside and cradled his head. "Oh, Baby." She blew a horsefly off his face. "I see, Baby," she murmured. "I know."

I called back from the cab, "No problem with the cutters, Sneedy. There's a pair right here in the glove box."

Sneed limped between his mother and me like an injured athlete to the fence. The pronghorn shied and scattered, leaving behind the half dozen or so that had tried to crawl under, had gotten snagged, and were dead or dying.

"That bastard," Sneed muttered. "That cheater. He runs them up against here."

He did not observe the symmetry or the ceremony of the moment as he labored with his weak grip to cut through the six strands of overzealous barbed-wire. But I felt it. I know Aretha felt it. Her tears fell silently as she helped him, peeling away each wire strand on her side, tugging it back twenty feet to the next steel post, where it could be crudely wrapped and kept out of the way.

I did the same on my side. We did not speak.

Then Aretha went to her son. She sat beside him in the dirt. She enveloped him in her arms. I stepped away, giving space, heading for the truck. I planned to wait for the creatures to settle and sniff and process what had happened. I hoped it would not take too long and that we would see them move. We could linger for an hour, I figured, but not much more before we would have to clear off Tucker's land.

But the eager pronghorn surprised me. They didn't wait. Not even one minute. A bold pair skittered through, yards from human mother and son, and then turned, nostrils flaring, flanks twitching. Then through that proven breach sprinted a juvenile buck, kicking dust on Sneed as he passed, and off into a joyful, grass-munching zig-zag went this little family group on their long trek to the winter grounds.

It was beautiful. Another family followed, then another, and another, until a stream of hooves and flanks and horns flowed

around Sneed and his mother, on and on, the animals both nervous and bold, picking their way precisely around the two strange
creatures entwined and weeping in the dust.

On and on this went—and on, it seemed, for an eternal
moment that stretches now across my entire memory, my entire
imagination, and infuses every scrap of my time, past and present,
with a new type of end-all river, with loveliness and hope and above
all, for me, with the miracle of sadness.

I could cut loose and cry at this. I could. I could just fucking weep.

And I would have—except just then across the rangeland
appeared the twisted sprinting shape of Henderson Gray.

World-Record Brook Trout

Gray at first was a speck, an odd neon bug crawling across the vast landscape with his scooting, arm-flapping, ultra-marathoner's gait. But in truth he came on with desperate speed over the hogback ridge, down the near side, and into the wild dispersion of pronghorn.

Once immersed among the animals, he zipped open his fanny pack and withdrew a camera. He photographed, even seemed to take video. Having captured their images in his camera, Gray charged at various juveniles—and once at a gimpy older buck—trying to split them out. But each of these animals simply squirted away in the direction of the general migration. Each of these animals pogo-hopped for a hundred yards or so, then turned to inspect Gray with placid ungulate curiosity.

Gray persisted. Time and again amidst the moving mass he singled out an animal, photographed it, stashed the camera in his fanny pack and lit out after the antelope. But time and again that pronghorn sprang away easily in the direction of the herd, leading Gray to abandon a chase that should have gone on—if I understood deer-running correctly—for several miles until the animal collapsed and surrendered to the Blackfoot brave or the Tarahumaran warrior.

Not without the fence, though. Not for Henderson Gray. Not without the confusion and stress of animals forced to go against their prehistoric grain.

Gray threw his red harrier's beanie to the ground and stamped toward me, shouting something long before I could hear him, shouting it again and again until he kinked right up into my face. "What the hell?" he squawked. I gripped one scrawny, freckled arm and slammed him against the skinheads' pickup.

"You tell me."

"Who the hell cut this fence?"

"We did. Who the hell put it up? That's the question. And why?"

"You're trespassing," Gray sputtered at me.

"So are you. Tucker fired you a year ago."

He tried to wrestle free, but I had him. He gave up pulling and tried to shove me off my feet. But I could hold my ground in some of the biggest rivers in America. Core strength, I believe they call it these days. I didn't budge. Not for that jerking weasel. Not a bit.

"Now I see it," I told him.

"See what?" he panted.

"You had your thing with Jesse. She wouldn't let you go. She wanted you to do something for her father. She stalked you, bothered you, whatever. Poor guy. You can have that. Jesse was like that. It's all true."

Gray stopped wriggling. He tried to reassemble the game face of a big-time lawyer. "This is aggravated assault," he tried out for size. "This is an unprovoked attack."

"I saw the same TV show," I told him.

"You'll be sued to the bone in civil court."

"You're looking at the bone, pal. This is it."

We stayed nose to nose. Meanwhile I began to hear a faint low thumping, like the drumming of a prairie chicken.

I nodded toward Sneed and his mother. "Down there too. Bone. We got nothing to lose. So let's talk about something else."

Aretha noticed us. She stood up, grabbed her son beneath the armpits and hauled him up too. As they began to make their way in our direction, Gray thrashed hard, made me catch him up by his chicken neck.

"Here's how I see it. Correct me if I'm wrong. Jesse thought maybe she could use Sneed to make you jealous. Then you'd come back to her, at least as far as helping her appeal her father's sentence. But that didn't work out. Instead what happened is that you told Sneed about your deer running. Probably Jesse told you about his interest in pronghorn. You sensed his interest, and so you told him about this fence. He didn't like it."

"I . . . I . . ."

I eased up on Gray's throat. He spat. "I didn't know about the whole migration thing. Until he told me."

"Like hell you didn't. You knew they would pool up here and get weak. Then all you had to do was pick one out and chase it back in the direction it didn't want to go. That would make it easy."

His temper flared at that. "Easy? It's not easy. It's never been done, never been proven to have been done. Only stories. That's how easy it is."

"So you'd be famous. You'd be a real hero."

"I already am. In some circles."

The thump-thumping grew louder. It came from the sky in the direction of Livingston. I glanced back. There was nothing in the air.

"Really? You're famous? For what, for *almost* running down a pronghorn? Like I'm famous for *almost* catching a world-record brook trout?"

He glared. No effect on the Dog.

"My guess is that you're more famous for being a fool and a liar, for hacking off a bunch of scientists who want you to prove your stupid idea, and to get that monkey off your back, you decided to cheat."

Down the ridge, Aretha was now wrestling with Sneed. "No, Baby. Just take it easy. Dog is going to handle it. Baby, take it easy."

"It's not cheating," Gray claimed, keeping an eye on mother and son.

"No? And I guess it wouldn't be cheating if I trapped that world-record brook trout behind a dam, let it starve a couple weeks, then tossed in a nightcrawler? How would that look? Because that's what people are going to know about you when we get out of here."

"Let me go," he seethed, and I saw no reason not to. But I stayed in front of him while he shook out his legs and began to jog minutely in place. The thump-thumping grew louder in the sky.

"You didn't anticipate that Sneed would react to your fence the way he did. Then you figured out he was either going to expose you, or he was going to stop you by cutting the fence and letting the pronghorn out. First Jesse was a problem, now Sneed too. You paid those skinheads to scare them off, but it didn't work. So you found a way to get rid of them both."

By now, Sneed and his mother had reached the truck. She had him contained, she thought. "You wait in there." With an application of her firewoman's brawn, she stuffed him in.

Then we all looked up. The thumping was helicopters, two of them, government maybe, skimming fast up the Roam River from the Paradise Valley. As they hammered toward us, the pronghorn bolted en masse to the south. On came the copters until the down-draft from the rotors enveloped us in a stinging, blinding dust storm—and inside of this storm, Henderson Gray broke past me and darted off across the scrubby rangeland.

And there would be no catching him—not now, I thought—until Sneed started the pickup.

And Then What?

"Sneed!"

"Baby, no!"

But he jacked the gear shift into drive and spun the tires, slung the box around so hard that his mother and I had to bail or be crushed. He squared the truck in Gray's direction and floored it. "Jump in the back!" I hollered at Aretha, and we just made it.

"Baby!" She pounded on the cab window, clawed at it. But it was an old truck. Nothing moved, nothing opened. A jolting swerve threw her down beside me. "What do we do, Hoss?"

"I guess we hang on."

The next several minutes were wild enough that no real thoughts entered my head except this one: Gray could outrun the truck over rough terrain, like a pronghorn could easily outpace a human, but for short distances only, and the truck had as much endurance as it had fuel—and the gasoline gauge, visible over Sneed's shoulder, said plenty. Sneed would catch him. And then what?

Aretha and I hung on to the box sides and dodged the various sliding pieces of skinhead junk—some iron fence posts, a bale of wire, a few dozen empty beer cans, and the two empty rifles. A toppled oil drum sloshed and slammed side to side each time Sneed slung around a rock pile or pounded through a gully in pursuit of Henderson Gray.

Twice Sneed had the grill six feet from Gray's bony ass, was about to bury him under the truck until Gray zagged like antelope and escaped.

"He'll cross the river," I predicted, and soon after, Gray did just that, slogging in, then falling in, then wallowing with a spastic overhead crawl to the far bank.

Sneed did not hesitate. He gunned down a long sand spit until he found a marginally shallow spot, where he plunged the truck into the Roam and fishtailed across. Emerging at the far bank, he buried the truck's grill in a dirt hump and had to reverse. I jumped out, tried to rip his door open. But Sneed saw me coming, cranked the window up, hammered down the button lock. He rooted the truck free with a to-and-fro motion that spat dirt and rocks back into the river. Just in time, Aretha caught my arm and hauled me back in.

"I told him his girlfriend was dead," she shouted half in wonderment at one point. She watched Gray stumble up a rise through sage brush. "So he killed her? And hurt my baby?"

"Looks like they both know it," I shouted back, "don't they?"

I yanked her aside as Sneed bucked up the rise and the oil drum skidded down from the tailgate. *What the hell, Dog?* I kicked the tailgate open, jerked the barrel around, and on the next uphill the damn thing spun out and bounced free, spewing loops of oil down a dusty draw.

"He's going to get away," Aretha hollered.

"That'd be good," I hollered back. "We wouldn't get our necks broken and he'd be caught soon enough." At that I pounded on the cab roof and pleaded for the tenth time, "Sneed! It's okay! Let him go!"

But the chase went on. There was little time to wonder how Sneed stayed focused for so long, but he did. He and Gray played

out their crazy crisscross over the entire western floodplain of the
Roam until at last Tucker's roadside fence rose on the horizon, with
Gray having opened a good half-mile lead.

"This will do it," I told Aretha, and for an entire ten seconds
I was sure of Gray's escape. But the ground leveled out and Sneed
gained velocity. He was only a few hundred yards behind when
Gray decided to take the fence. The deer runner cut right, tried to
hurdle the four-strand barbed wire. He snagged his back foot and
fell hard. Gray recovered, hobbled away—and not a half-minute
later Sneed blew right through the fence and summarily closed the
distance to a few frightening yards.

Gray had made a terrible error, obviously. Now the chase was
down the highway, down a corridor of heavy fencing that Gray
was too exhausted and too injured to hurdle a second time. Still
he labored along the shoulder on the right side, his runner's gait a
broken, desperate catastrophe. "Just pull alongside him, Sneed!" I
reached around the cab and hammered on the window. "Just stop
the truck and I'll grab him!"

Sneed slowed and looked at me once—that was it. He was
flooded with adrenaline, looked fully alive. Then he turned back
to Gray, regained his losses, and swerved the truck onto the narrow, sloping gravel shoulder and nipped at Gray's heels. Gray's head
hung, flapped to the right, and his gaze remained locked on the
road three feet ahead even when a sedan and then a panel van
flashed by in the opposite lane.

Now I knew this would end in blood. A third vehicle, a school
bus, lumbered around a curve toward us. I prayed without hope
that Gray would look up, would wave, appeal for help, for mercy.
I pleaded into the barren wretchedness of that doomed moment
that Sneed would be contained, would lose focus or pass out, that
order would be restored, and justice would come through for us.
But instead Sneed seemed to be calculating, timing something,
maybe waiting for a flat stretch of shoulder, or one so steep that it
would force Gray back onto the pavement. "Gray! Sneed! Damn
it, stop!"

Aretha pounded the cab roof. "Baby, stop!"

She had just turned back to me, aggrieved and desperate, when I slammed an iron fence post through the cab's back window. Glass popped, hailed against Sneed's head and onto the dashboard. I shoved my legs through, wrenched the rest of me after.

"Sneed, you don't need to do this!"

I fought him for the wheel. The swerving truck lost ground— ten yards, twenty yards, then a cushion of forty that might have given Gray a few moments to collect his wits, dodge back the other way, stop some traffic and get help.

But Henderson Gray plowed on, his head dangling down as if on a broken neck, even as a fourth chance, a black SUV, sped toward him.

Sneed caught me good on the bridge of the nose, knocked me back. He flattened the gas pedal. That old pink Ford roared up to speed, dragging a hundred feet of fence and poles. Gray's new lead disappeared in seconds and the roadway narrowed into a chute of rock. His problem was insurmountable now—until he solved it, neatly and with horrible suddenness, by darting into the grill of the oncoming SUV.

A Pair of Café Americanos

Tom Gorman was the name of the hulking, phlegmatic U.S. Border Patrol agent who fetched us at the Geyser Motel the next morning in a Park County Meals-on-Wheels van because his federal-issue SUV had been totaled.

"I've hit deer before," he announced to Aretha and me as we sat touch-close, still traumatized, in his back seat. "But never a deer runner."

Aretha took my hand for the hundredth time, squeezed it and held on. The van smelled like lasagna.

"Gosh," Tom Gorman said. "What was that guy thinking?"

I was still seeing the loose sack of skin that was Gray's body as he sprawled in the center of the road. Sneed had slammed the brakes and spun the truck. With that iron fencepost in hand, he had vaulted from the skinheads' truck. But his legs had crumpled beneath him the moment his feet touched the pavement. He lay on his back, gasping at the sky.

Now he was back in custody, in the hospital, and neither his mother nor I had slept. After a lengthy period of questioning by law enforcement agencies from the FBI all the way down to a frazzled and fumbling Russell Crowe, we had sat up side by side on

Aretha's motel bed, staring at the television and sometimes talk-ing. Around dawn, I managed to tell her, finally, what it was she needed to know about me and my family, and Aretha thanked me for filling her in, told me how sorry she was and how things didn't feel quite so terribly awful for her after hearing it. Her son was alive and would get off without any too-serious charges, she decided, whereas my son, well . . . you know . . . and it was shortly after that wordless moment, as the sun came up on the Crazy Mountains, that this touchy-feely hand-squeezing thing got started. And damn did I like it. I really did.

Tom Gorman rumbled on. "Went up the mountainside this morning to give my condolences to the widow. Hell's bells, that's an awful thing to have to do, you know?"

He looked at me in his mirror. He had taken a pretty good shot from the airbag and wore a faint racoon mask of bruises around his eyes. But I gathered that a man of his phenomenal obtuseness had taken worse hits from the various doors in his life.

"It's not like, hey, sorry, I ran over your dog, you know? But then again, dogs don't murder people . . . so hey, what are you gonna do?"

He gave us a second to post the silence that a man like him took for agreement.

"I told the woman her husband didn't suffer. I figured that would help."

He pulled the van into the Livingston hospital parking lot. "Helluva thing though, all this from top to bottom. Your Sheriff Chubbuck's going to be a hero around here, if he makes it. Hell, even it he doesn't make it. Posthumously, right?"

Aretha let go of my hand was we climbed from the van. She whispered in my ear, "Hoss, can you translate?"

Sheriff Roy Chubbuck had collapsed in his driveway the morn-ing before. Now he wanted to talk to us. It was slow going. There were no tubes in his nose, just one large one, withdrawn from his windpipe so he could talk. His wife, in a chair beside the bed, fed him ice shavings to lubricate his voice. As the sheriff wheezed and whispered from his hospital bed, the various events that had made my last seven days a baffling mosaic began to come into focus, and Chubbuck resolved before my eyes as a man of startling vision and courage.

Toxicology tests on Sneed had taken time, he told us, and despite the public rush to judgment, despite his public statements to the contrary, he had never closed out the option that someone other than Sneed had killed Jesse. Nor had he let on that he was still considering other suspects. Including me. Only when I wouldn't leave Livingston did he check me off as someone who was simply going to be in his way.

We had to wait while a nurse came in to take Chubbuck's pulse and blood pressure. He would need the breathing tube in a few minutes, she said.

When the result came back that Sneed had traces of animal tranquilizer in his system, Chubbuck said he had suspected Henderson Gray, whose efforts to run down a pronghorn had disturbed the sheriff for some years.

"Asinine," Chubbuck wheezed, and he used precious breath to add: "How was he going to prove it? I asked him once. He was going to have to photograph the animal before, then somehow show himself side by side with that same animal, clearly alive, in a different place, later. And those little buggers all look alike don't they? How was he gonna prove anything?"

He went on, exhausting himself on speculation. I told him about the doubtful scientist and the ear tag, and how Gray would have to show the placement of that in corroborating video before, during, and after the deer was up and moving again. But no pronghorn, the sheriff figured, no matter how tired, was going to sit still as long as it would take Gray to set up a camera shot and tag its ear. So a syringe of the same tranquilizer found yesterday in Gray's fanny pack spoke plainly for Sneed's innocence. When Gray's wife had retracted her support for his alibi, the deal was done.

He asked for my hand and gripped it. I think it was a hand-shake. "Those skinhead punks were never suspects," Chubbuck whispered, "because we were watching them. We knew where they were when Jesse Ringer was killed. I didn't want you to get mixed up in it and spook the operation on Tucker's ranch. I worked on that too long."

He rested a while. His wife left the room for more ice shavings. Chubbuck made a painful sound to clear his throat. "And I got it. The Roam River is ours again. Dane Tucker's land . . ." was on its way into a public trust, he managed to explain over the next precious half hour. Fishermen would be able to access public water, the way it was intended. Montana boys and girls could grow up fishing the Roam again—"fishing the best river God ever made," the sheriff said, "like I did."

I said with my eyes to Aretha: *No, this isn't clear to me either.* Across the room, Tom Gorman fiddled with the pump on a blood pressure cuff until a new nurse arrived and took it away from him.

"Grief—" The sheriff startled us with a loud rasp. He tried to lift his head from the pillow. His buzzard eye was fixed on Aretha. "Grief . . . is like . . ."

He couldn't finish the statement. But he couldn't let it go. He fought it for a long and pathetic moment until his wife put an ice chip to his lips.

"I'm gonna miss the land," he whispered.

He closed his eyes as they teared up. He swallowed with difficulty.

"So much. Damn it all. That's my grief. This land. This water. The fish. The birds. The goddamn wind. I'm going to miss all of it so much."

The nurse tried to re-insert his respirator tube, but Sheriff Chubbuck batted it away. She turned up the drip into his left arm. He worked his feeble hands and squeezed his red-rimmed eyes.

"Go fishing for me," were his last words before the faintest smile shaped his dry lips and he faded into morphine dreams.

"Well, yeah," Tom Gorman said with a shrug in the hallway.

"We're keeping this out of the media for now. But probably the gal from Alabama can explain it best."

Agent Gorman dropped us at Chad's on Main Street, rumbled off toward God knows what destination in that Meals-on-Wheels van.

The gal from Alabama was Melissa Pines, a hefty young woman of apparently mixed race who sat down with us on one of Chad's funky sofas.

"Sheriff Chubbuck brought us all together this last year and a half," she said. "He got a tip that Dane Tucker was using his land for paramilitary training. Vigilante border patrol, actually. It's all the rage lately. The sheriff might have gone in on weapons charges, but that would have done nothing vis-à-vis the land. He wanted the land."

She smiled. Her hair was reddish and kinky. Her skin was caramel. She wore jeans and a flawlessly ironed men's shirt. There was pretty handmade jewelry on her hands, wrists, and ears. She backed up to clarify for us.

"I'm an attorney with something called the Southern Poverty Law Center. I don't know if you've heard of us?"

We hadn't.

"Our civil lawsuits have bankrupted more than ten major hate groups. We kick ass and take assets." She smiled at Aretha. "When Sheriff Chubbuck learned that Dane Tucker was running a 'border patrol' training camp on his ranch, he got in touch with U.S. Customs and Border Protection and the Arizona State Police. They didn't know about this particular group. But they started watching for them."

Melissa Pines sipped her latte, leaving a faint stripe of steamed milk on her lip.

"It's the latest thing these days, nativism and vigilante border patrol. There are probably ten or twenty groups like Tucker's roaming the Mexican border right now, going after anything with brown skin. They tend to shoot first and ask questions later. It's just plain murder, mostly. Hate crime. But these guys are legends in their own minds."

Another sip. Another smile for Aretha. "So that big guy, Tom Gorman? He was assigned to track Tucker's group. Meanwhile Sheriff Chubbuck got in touch with us too, and we worked in an advisory capacity as to how this could all go down."

In the interest of form, Aretha and I also had ordered our own special coffees. Clueless, we had copied each other, going for a pair of Café Americanos. Now neither of us was really sure what to do with what we had. We watched each other, waiting for the first move.

"As they always do," Melissa Pines said, "one of the units trained on Tucker's ranch eventually committed a crime, along with a serious civil rights violation. They attacked a man named Jose Rafael Ramirez, a U.S. citizen who ran a farm machinery repair business and was driving from Douglas to Nogales—this is in Arizona, along the border—to fix an irrigation pump. His truck broke down and he tried to hitchhike back to Douglas. He was shot once, stabbed twice, and beaten. Mister Ramirez died of his injuries last week."

She glanced at her watch. She scooted up to the edge of the dingy corduroy sofa.

"So it goes like this. In civil rights and hate crimes law, the actions of that unit go back to Dane Tucker. He's accountable. The raid by the feds yesterday put that beyond any question. Since Mister Tucker's property was essentially used in the commission of this crime, our lawsuit on behalf of Mister Ramirez's family will ask for Mister Tucker's ranch property, all of it, to be confiscated in the judgment, and the family has agreed to sell that land to the state of Montana, who has agreed to buy it and put it into a trust that stipulates public access."

I picked up my cup. So did Aretha. I sniffed. She did too.

"The vision behind all of this is Sheriff Chubbuck's," Melissa Pines said. "And all of this is specified in our lawsuit." Her cup was empty. "*My* lawsuit," she clarified. "Which I will win."

She looked at us in puzzlement. "Is your coffee not good?"

Dropping Like Flies

Change at the Park County Sheriff's Department was in the news the next day. I grabbed a *Bozeman Chronicle* at the motel office and brought it back.

The county board of supervisors, including Rita Crowe, had put Sheriff Roy Chubbuck on indefinite medical leave and initiated an investigation of departmental priorities and procedures. Clearly nothing of Chubbuck's play for Tucker's land had been disclosed to county office holders.

The paper said the new Acting Interim Sheriff, Deputy Russell Crowe, was recovering well from minor injuries sustained in the recent escape of detainee D'Ontario Sneed, formerly a suspect in the murder of Jesse Ringer. Charges against Sneed had been reduced by the Park County DA from first-degree murder to resisting an officer, and Sneed would be released on signature pending investigation into a further charge of reckless vehicular endangerment. Acting Interim Sheriff Crowe, the paper said, had been the shcriff's loyal right-hand man and was the presumed front-runner in a special election for sheriff to be held in the coming months.

"Maybe that coffee-drinking chica can sue this bunch of goofballs too," Aretha suggested.

"Do you really think—" there was something bothering me "—that D'Ontay could have overpowered Russell Crowe? A trained and armed sheriff's deputy? And wasn't there also a nurse in that ambulance, an orderly, anyone? And how did he end up in Livingston so fast? On Main Street? Right where Tick Judith would find him?"

"At this point, do I really care?" Aretha asked. "That's the better question."

We were private enough—at a picnic table in Sacagawea Park, practicing knots—that when my mind wouldn't settle she grabbed my hand and squeezed it. Damn. I liked that.

"Come on, Hoss. It's over."

She had the clinch knot down. It was easy. Gray just wasn't a fisherman. We were moving on to the surgeon's knot. But I couldn't let it rest.

"Do you remember Hilarious Sorgensen saying D'Ontay and Jesse stole a fly rod? And that's why he fired them? Why would they do that?"

Aretha rolled her eyes. "That girl did drugs, Hoss. Where I'm from, that explains about ninety percent of all bad shit that happens. Money for drugs. The other ten percent is just for fun."

I was thinking of Cord Cook being minus a boat, looking across the park at my Cruise Master gathering dust in the kid's driveway, when Aretha gave me a stiff but playful shove.

"What's the point in being a trout bum," she wondered, "if you're going to carry the world around on your shoulders? Come on. It's over. Let's get busy here. I want to get the hang of this fly fishing game before D'Ontay gets out of the hospital. He thinks he's something. I am going to blow that child away."

We stood at the bank of the Yellowstone. "See, grass in the park just sits there, but water moves. It never stops. No time outs. That's the challenge."

"You're saying I'm not ready for it?"

"You're not ready for it."

"So get me ready." She waded barefoot in ankle-deep water, her jeans rolled up, hot sun striking white shirt against brown skin, sweat on her forehead and a smile for me.

"I . . . this is awkward . . . do you mind?"

"Should I mind?"

I moved stiffly behind her and matched my arms to her arms, fit my hands over hers, and we began to cast and strip, cast and strip, until we found a rhythm together.

"You got it?"

"Hmmm," she said. "Not quite yet."

When I left Aretha at the Geyser in the late afternoon she was threatening to freshen up for supper. It seemed okay now to drive her rental car out to Sorgensen's Fly 'n' Float to catch the arrival of the guides and their clients.

There were no fisticuffs today. Instead there was the general giddiness of a good day on the river. When the fish were on, there was water for everyone. I picked Cord Cook out of a small crowd around a tailgate and a beer cooler.

"Hey," he said, raising his can as I approached. "How you doing?"

"Hey," slurred one of his new clients, raising his can as well, "how you doing? I do everything Cord does, see? Guy's a helluva guide. Do what Cord does, that's the ticket. Jesusmaryandjoseph did we stick the fish today. Cord was right on 'em. How you doing guy? You catch any?"

"My veterinarians," Cook said.

"Veterinary surgeons," the second guy corrected, and guffawed. "Brad Verona and Brad Hawn. Great guys. From Minneapolis."

"Saint Paul," the second guy corrected, and guffawed louder.

"Still haven't driven that vehicle of yours." Cook seemed apologetic.

"That's all right. Can I talk to you just a minute?"

"Don't give away our secret spots!" one of them bellowed at our backs as we moved away toward the dumpsters beside Sorgensen's shop.

"Don't know if that was a fair deal," Cook continued. "Especially seeing as I can reprint that photo. Hell, I can put it on the internet. Russell Crowe is mine for life. Plus I'm not even using the vehicle."

"You're a good guy, Cord. Sorry about your boat. Does that even things up?"

"I don't know. What's that vehicle worth?"

I shrugged. "Scrap."

He laughed. "I hated that boat. It rode too low. The oars sucked."

"I noticed that."

"Season's over for me anyway. School starts next week. Next summer I'm probably going to intern at a place in Denver." He reached into his pocket. He tossed me the keys to the Cruise Master. "Here. Gas just went up to three-fifty a gallon. She's all yours."

We were quiet a moment, watching Cook's veterinary surgeons root in a cooler for more beer. It was a sweet evening, cool enough that the forest fire smoke had a pleasant campfire essence, slightly crisp. The sun had plunged behind the Gallatins and we were in shadow beneath a pink-ribbed sky. For a change, the tall spruce windbreak out-fragranced Sorgensen's dumpsters.

"I guess things worked out okay for your friend," Cook said. "The black dude."

"If he gets his health back."

"I mean. Yeah. And it doesn't surprise me about that lawyer. Jesse had a way of snagging guys like that. She didn't mean to, she just . . ."

"Is Gray the one she dumped you for?"

Cook toed the gravel. "Yeah." He looked off toward the 'Stone. "Well. He was one of them. You never really knew with Jesse. But oh well. So what do we need to talk about?"

I told him I had come to follow up on Sorgensen's story about Sneed and Jesse stealing a fly rod. Had he heard about that?

"Oh, sure," Cook said. "Sorgensen announced it to the whole world. He made sure every guide in the business heard they were stealing from our vehicles. That's a huge deal with us, you know, because we trust the shuttle drivers with our keys. Shit, half the time it's the car key, the house key, everything, we hand it over to them on the faith they're going to do nothing else but drive the vehicle, park it, and hide the keys where we ask them to."

He finished his beer and tossed the can into the dumpster. He nodded toward his veterinary surgeons. The Brads were raising toasts to their fishing success.

"Hell, Dog, half these knuckleheads bring along their own keys too, their wallets, their credit cards, their hotel pass cards, the five-thousand-dollar bamboo rod that they just want to show off, it's all sitting there available to the shuttle driver. If something gets stolen, we all know who did it."

I thought about it. "So it's a serious trust thing, like bonded workers, only—"

Cook laughed. "They're mostly just college kids or drunks or both. But, knock-on-wood, it tends to work out."

"So Sneed and Jesse ruined their reputations?"

"More like Sorgensen did."

"Doesn't it hurt his too?"

"Somewhat, I guess. Funny thing was, none of us had a rod stolen that we knew of. None of the clients either. And I mean, because it was Jesse—"

His eyes followed the St. Paul Brads. They were bumping chests. "Well, she was in enough trouble, so I asked around. I was going to blame the black dude and stick up for Jesse. That's what everybody thought anyway. But it turned out that nobody had lost anything. Not that I could find out."

"So why . . .?"

Cord Cook shrugged. "Maybe he made it up," he said, looking over as the door to Sorgensen's Fly 'n' Float banged open and out flung Sorgensen's girl Lyndzee with her battered suitcases. "Like one time this Blackfoot driver Ronny Beaver got accused of siphoning gas. Sorgensen just didn't want him around."

Cook and I were out of sight and yet close enough to hear Lyndzee grumbling as she hauled the suitcases across the porch, where she ripped off old baggage tags and tossed them in the dumpster. Her voice sounded like a rake on gravel.

"Who the hell has that much family?"

"*What?*" challenged Hilarious Sorgensen as he swayed onto the porch with his peanuts and his van keys.

I could see up through the slats of the deck rail—more than I wanted to. This girl Lyndzee had pale, bruisy legs and not a stitch of underpants. This close, she vibrated with what looked like rage or fear—or maybe it was a just a screaming amphetamine high.

"I said who the hell has that much family?"

"You do," the big man replied, rattling his peanut jar. "You got family all over. They're dropping like flies."

"I swear, Larry. I'm not going."

Sorgensen shrugged, tossed peanuts into his mouth. He side-saddled down the porch steps. He opened the rear doors of his van and waited. Lyndzee stood her ground on the deck for a full five seconds. Then she lifted her suitcases, tossed back her frazzled mess of coppery hair, and marched to the van.

"God damn," Cook muttered beside me, "am I glad to be out of that."

His eyes followed Lyndzee into the van. He shook his head.

"That buzz. You get to be a slave to it, you know?"

Acting Interim Sheriff Russell Crowe

Ninety percent is money for drugs. The rest is just for fun.

I had no grounds to debate Aretha's premise. I just didn't want to believe it. It didn't seem right. I had a sense of drug crimes as being obvious, impulsive, brutal, and stupid—not like the subtle set-up of Jesse's death—and I had a fatigue for the whole drug excuse as well. The world had become a television show, I was thinking, and everything was about drugs, even falsely stolen fly rods.

Hilarious Sorgensen held his cell phone to his ear, shifted painfully foot to foot beside his van for a full five minutes while inside Lyndzee reamed through radio stations before latching onto Fleetwood Mac's "Rhiannon."

Finally Sorgensen snapped his phone shut. He nearly flattened his shocks getting into the van. As he was turning around, Acting Interim Sheriff Russell Crowe pulled in off the highway. He circled Aretha's jade-green Metro before parking in front of it, blocking my way out.

Sorgensen matched him window to window. They chatted for a half-minute before Sorgensen squirted gravel behind him and headed for the Bozeman airport with "Rhiannon" sailing out the window.

Cook was watching as I reached down into Sorgensen's dumpster. Down among the beer cans and yellowjackets, I picked out the discarded baggage tags: *Toledo*. Not Memphis. *Toledo.*

"Isn't Toledo where your dentists the other day were from?" I asked Cook. "White Fang and Top Gum?"

"Yup."

"But wasn't Sorgensen talking about Memphis?"

"Dunno. Don't listen to the man."

Acting Interim Sheriff Russell Crowe strolled up. He had a minor black eye and a bandage on his forehead. Fingers on his left hand were splinted and wrapped. "Evening, boys. How'd you do on the river today, Cord Cook?"

"Not bad. Even the veterinarians caught fish."

"I never asked you, Russell," I said. "Do you fish?"

The acting interim sheriff frowned, swung the jaw bone my way. "Yes, you did ask me. And yes, I do fish."

"Really?" Cook was surprised. "I never heard that before, Russell."

Russell levered open a smile. "Well, boys, you're hearing it here. Grew up fishing the Missouri River."

Again Cook was startled. "Really? What section?"

"Pretty much all of it."

Cook nodded. His cool grey eyes—the ones that must have attracted Jesse—stayed on Crowe's face. "I'll bet your favorite stretch is west of Holter Dam toward Wolf Creek."

"Absolutely," Crowe said. "Beautiful water. Caught an eight-pound brown in there." He turned to me. "Now, Mister Oglivie, I am sorry but this is your fourth offense driving without a license. That's automatic jail time without bail."

He tossed his shock of black hair, still smiling. He touched the side of his black eye and winced.

"Just to show you what a good guy I am, though, I'm gonna let you drive away. But lax enforcement is not going to fly anymore with the county board. They've had enough. I see you behind the wheel in Park County again, I'm afraid I'll have to—"

Cord Cook stopped him. "This isn't necessary, Russell."

Acting Interim Sheriff Crowe switched jaw angles. "Huh?"

"There is no stretch of the Missouri River west of Holter Dam toward Wolf Creek," Cook said. "The river runs north-south through there, and it's sheer rock up to Flesher Pass." Cook paused. "You always tried too hard to be a man, Russell. But just to show you what a nice guy I am, I won't tell anyone how full of shit you still are."

Crowe put his splinted hand to his belt, fixed his eyes on the mid-distant Yellowstone River, striking a pose that attempted an Andy Griffith-style affectionate weariness with the shenanigans of his people. But it played as a smirk—and I slapped it off him with a stiff clap to the shoulder.

"*Now* I remember what it was I never asked you," I said. "Guy like you, Russell, I'll bet you had a go or two at Jesse, huh? Am I right? And she dumped you?"

Crowe's eyes closed to slits. His chin moved side to side on the twin booms of his fabulous jaw bone. We waited. He offered no answer, so Cord Cook told me, "Actually, I heard his mother said he couldn't get anywhere near to Jesse. So I wonder how that party picture would sit with her."

Now Cook clapped the acting interim sheriff on his other shoulder.

"But anyway, Russell, what vehicle?"

"Uh—" Russell stuck his chin at the little green Metro.

"Oh, that's me," Cook said. "I drove that one. And whatever else after this point you think my friend Dog here might be driving."

Sudden Inexplicable Death

"I've got money. Why don't we all go out for a good old ranch-style supper?"

This was Aretha's suggestion after Cord Cook delivered the Cruise Master to the Geyser Motel and took off on a jog toward home.

"I mean steak . . . and what? Beans? And whiskey? And hmm, what else to they have on *Bonanza*?"

I didn't answer that right away, could not read the sincerity of her tone in my current mood, so I just stepped in and hauled my buddy Sneed off the bed and hugged him long and hard.

"Be careful!" Aretha scolded me as she separated us. "Headache, dizziness, confusion, convulsions, kidney failure, respiratory arrest, memory loss, dementia, irritability—" she recovered the doctor's handout from a spanking new hand bag, Big Louis II, and shoved me further away from Sneed "—blindness, gait and balance problems, speech disturbance, loss of higher intellectual function, heart arrhythmia—"

She stopped short. She gripped me rather desperately by both arms, hustled me into the bathroom and closed the door so Sneed couldn't hear. Her hazel eyes popped with color. She shook me.

"*Sudden inexplicable death!*" she whispered.

Peering through dim light at my menu in the swanky Livingston
Bar and Grill, I decided to say, "Well, isn't it true about *Bonanza*
that Hop Sing could make damn near anything?"

Aretha looked at me over her menu. I said, "Don't I remember
lobster bisque and Yorkshire pudding?"

"Were you in juvie too or what?"

"Why do you ask?"

"All that time for television."

I shrugged. "For white boys, the equivalent is college." I tapped
my menu. "That's what I'm having. Lobster bisque and Yorkshire
pudding."

Sneed started banging his silverware together like a three-year-
old, as if the sound was new. Aretha took the fork and knife away
and gave him a piece of sourdough bread—and a kiss on the temple. She looked well satisfied as she returned her attention to me.

"Did I ever tell you that my mother is now in Seattle? No?
Why do I mention it? Because that's where lobsters come from.
Not Montana. You eat a lobster here, Hoss, that thing's got fre-
quent flier miles."

"Well, actually lobsters come from Maine," I said. "But your
point is well taken."

She sighted me in with a scowl. "My mother eats lobster
in Seattle."

"Crab?"

"She says lobster."

"Then maybe you ought to go straighten her out."

Aretha raised the menu in front of her face. "What do you
know, you old coffee boiler."

"I know that only a greenhorn shave tail mixes up the coasts."

From behind the menu: "Aw, hobble your lip, you durn flan-
nel mouth."

"Curly wolf."

"Four flusher."

"Mudsill."

"Odd stick."

Sneed let out a snort of sourdough crumbs. Me too. "*Odd stick?*" I pulled her menu down. "All right," I demanded, "out with it."

And so Aretha finally told me the *Bonanza* story over her Thai charred-beef salad, my grilled Montana squab, Sneed's burger and fries, and the bottle of 1996 Domaine du Caillou Reserve Chateauneuf-du-Pape that our waiter somehow finessed onto the tab.

She was fifteen when she got pregnant. Aretha began here while we waited for our food. It was unclear if Sneed—in-and-out at her side—was listening, but she seemed to hope so this time as she detailed in plain, calm language an act of midnight violence in her bedroom that was every bit as gruesome and barbaric as something from the true wild West.

She touched her son's arm. "So you see, at first, I didn't want you. I was scared, I was angry, and I was ashamed. There was no person inside me then, just a problem that I didn't know how to solve. Can you understand that, Baby?"

Sneed nodded. But then his nodding didn't stop.

Aretha sighed. She stopped him gently. Here was the wine. "What makes you think I'm not paying for it?" she asked the waiter when he offered me the cork. "Because I am."

She went on through the terrible first months of her secret until the moment when a school friend came to her in tears and blurted out, "Retha, help me, I'm pregnant!"

"So we ended up together in this home for bad girls that weren't allowed to embarrass everybody by staying in school. That home was supposed to be a school itself, but we girls, all we did was eat and talk and watch TV and feel our babies growing."

Our food came. For a while, the taste of it made us monosyllabic, like cave people, gulping it down on five-dollar swallows of wine. Aretha was afraid that Sneed would choke, so she carefully cut his burger into bits, then his fries, until Sneed raised doubt about his "loss of higher intellectual function" by blurting out, "Nobody here has a job, right?"

He looked at his mother. "Right? Did you ask for a leave?"

"No, Baby. I just left."

"And Dog, you . . ." He frowned. As if he had forgotten how to describe it, how to describe *me* in relation to employment, he just raised his hands and started to laugh. He laughed right through his next question: "So what are we going to do?"

Aretha and I traded looks. Do? We? There wasn't any answer. There wasn't even any question. All that *do* and *we* stuff was worlds apart and miles ahead, in a realm his mother and I could not access.

"Well, what do you think, Baby?"

"I think we should stay here," Sneed pronounced. "I like this place."

He looked from me to his mother, then suddenly he was crestfallen. "I had a plan," he said, "for staying here, but I can't remember it."

Lost in private thoughts, we ate quietly until were full as ticks and poking around the last precious remnants of our meals. Privately, knowing Aretha wasn't interested, I was still working over possibilities involving Russell Crowe, and Crowe's mother, and Jesse. So—what had happened? Had Sneed punched Crowe in the eye, smashed the service pistol out of his *left* hand—the one that was splinted now? And then Sneed—a black man, in hospital dress?—had gotten picked up hitchhiking? And dropped off on Main Street in Livingston?

At last I shook it all away and said, "So that's where you got into *Bonanza*? At the bad girls' home?"

Aretha chewed slowly and then smiled, warming from the memory.

"Those girls," she said, "were wonderful. They were my first real friends, and my last ones for a long, long time. I am *still* looking for friends like that." She sighed and pushed away her plate. "You want the rest?"

"Oh, God. I'm stuffed. But I've been eyeing that this whole time."

"Go ahead."

I took a forkful of Thai beef. "Much obliged."

"I remember it was winter and that was the one time it did snow in Arkansas. But that big old house was warm, and full of girls and their babies, and we were eating and laughing and watching old re-runs on TV and then what happened with us black girls, see, is we started goofing a little. You know, the truth is there are a few good-looking white men out there. We black girls are just not supposed to think so. But there were no black men on TV anyway, and we were naughty girls already, and that house was like some cruise ship at sea. We were alone, nobody watching us, no idea where we really were or where we were going. So we started hunting around the TV for cute white men we could play a crush on. It took some damn work, I'll tell you. They had to be on a series, because we had to see them enough to really check them out, so we're looking at Hogan and Gilligan and Maxwell Smart and this was just *not* working out."

She poured the last of the Chateauneuf-du-Pape into my glass and waved the bottle in the air like you might a beer glass in a saloon.

"Are you sure—"

"Yes, I'm sure." She looked at me square, didn't seem one bit drunk. "It's just sinking in to me, right now. *Sudden inexplicable death.* It could just as well be me." She smiled somewhat sadly as she encouraged me to finish the wine. "Or you. Or any of us. Really, couldn't it?"

I wasn't so sure about *inexplicable*, in my case, but I nodded. There was my boy Eamon, after all—how would I ever manage to explain, to my own satisfaction, *that*?

"Oh, yeah." She was moving again. "And we tried out Hawkeye and Trapper and Radar. He got a few nibbles—Radar did. But we weren't looking for teddy bears, you know. We were looking for some *ummph*."

She confirmed that we were having another bottle, giving the waiter's look right back at him.

"He's decided my check is going to bounce," she told me. "But anyway, then, *then*, we find *Bonanza*. We find Adam, that's Purnell Roberts, and we find Little Joe, that's Michael Landon, and those boys are fly. They got those silky cowboy clothes, nice and tight in the back, with their shirts open. They got curly hair and nice smiles. Pretty soon that is *all we watch*, girls screaming when their boys come on, crying when they get hurt, fighting with each other when Adam and Little Joe get into it on the TV. It was a scene, oh my."

Her eyes glittered from the memory. "I'll let my assistant do it this time," she told the waiter, vis-à-vis the cork.

"We had the Adam camp and we had the Little Joe camp," she said.

"And you?"

"And I," she said, "had a secret."

Let's Not Go Backwards

A secret, mind you, that she withheld for the purpose of toying with the Hoss-Dog—but withheld also, I could tell, because she was stuck on something else, something serious inside her.

She looked a little troubled as she paid out five crisp fifties onto the bill tray, failing to take full and proper appreciation of the effect this had on our waiter.

I asked her outside, "Not to be nosy. But where did you get the cash?"

"Russell Crowe," she answered. Her pace quickened and she spurted ahead.

"Aretha, what the hell? Russell Crowe personally?" I caught up, grabbed her arm. "Or Russell Crowe sheriff?"

"He said he was still my liaison." She was stiff to my touch. "He said it was money to help us get back home."

I stopped her. "Aretha, listen. Did anyone see him give you the money? Were you with anyone? Do you know if it's his money or the county's?"

"He didn't say."

"Were you alone with him?"

"I was at the motel. About an hour before you got there. He

knocked on the door. D'Ontay was asleep. He said he paid off the motel bill and then he gave me the cash."

"How much?"

She walked ahead without an answer.

"Aretha, this may not be over."

"It's over for me."

"Aretha, how much?"

"You are an odd stick. *Sudden inexplicable death*, Hoss. Don't you get it? Money is money. Let's not go backwards."

"Aretha—"

She faced me. "I have come a long way," she said, trying to control a tremulous voice. "A *long* way. And I am very, very close to a place I never thought I would be."

Then she wheeled and walked away, all the way up to the corner of Main and Park, and turned right toward the Geyser.

Sneed trailed behind. I grabbed him, shook him a little. "Sneedy, are you with me?"

"What's up, Dog?"

"I need you to tell me about your ride back to Livingston, after the ambulance. Do you remember? You think so? My guess is Deputy Crowe suddenly pushed you outside, is that right? Can you remember?"

He shook his head. "I was in an ambulance?"

"Yes. Then you were outside. Then a lady picked you up and drove you here."

He thought a moment. Then he nodded. "Yeah. Okay."

"I need you to think about that ride with the lady. Anything you can remember. Anything at all. Sights, smells, something you heard. Just relax and try to be in there again."

He closed his eyes. He was trying. He backed up against the Livingston Bar and Grill, slid down the bricks until he sat on the sidewalk.

I turned a circle, attempting to calm myself.

"Sure," Sneed said behind me.

"What is it, Sneedy?"

"Dog, I think . . . pine cones?"

I Am Telling You I Am Innocent

Backward I went then, at full tilt. I walked Sneed home to the Geyser and returned downtown by Cruise Master, parked in an alley and came up behind Uncle Tick Judith locking up the liquor store. "Hey." He was the greater Montana sage grouse of snoose— startled, ballistic, spit flying into the window.

"Sumbitch . . . you. . . thought you'd left town."

"I'm still here."

Inside, he thumped a fifth of Smirnoff's vodka onto the counter.

"Bet you need a . . . big old sumbitch . . . jug for the road."

"I need some basic facts," I said. "Some history."

In ten minutes we were back at Jesse's mini-storage, lit by Uncle Judith's headlights. "Just about every letter she ever got from some point, whether it be from her dad or a boyfriend, seems it's gonna be in here." Uncle Judith rapped his knuckles on the top of the cedar chest. He coughed in a sad attempt to laugh. "Guess she's had that key a while. So much for my supervision."

I opened it: Jesse had tossed letters and other keepsakes in randomly, it seemed, until her memories were at least a foot thick and jumbled.

"Probably cuz I snooped a little, opened things."

Uncle Judith went in deeper. He stopped in front of the little glass-faced china cabinet, back left, and said, "Move your shadow, will ya?" From the cabinet he brought forth a statuesque bottle of Galliano and flopped down on the settee. He put his boots up on an ottoman. Now I saw that he had carried forth an old Colt pistol from his truck. He laid the pistol on the settee beside him. Then he wiped dust off that fancy high-top bottle, took a pull. "You always was a fancy pants," he muttered, as if someone sat beside him. He held the Galliano out for me.

"You're gonna find this out anyway," he said on a gust of what sounded like regret. "You'll know from reading all them letters. The way he denies it every chance he gets."

I declined the bottle. Uncle Judith took another gulp of yellow liqueur. He was the David Copperfield of snoose. Where had that brown gob gone to? How could he drink with it in there? And what was it that I would know?

"Read them letters I'm guessing what you'll find out is that Bozeman guide down at Otter Creek didn't read Galen exactly right and called him a faggot. And Galen will swear to his girl that being no such thing as a faggot, he had no cause to kill the man. Therefore he is innocent."

He took another swash.

"And that is one part true. Galen Ringer sure as hell is no faggot." He snuck a timid glance at me. "This sumbitch world has always been confused between a homosexual and a faggot. No man likes to be called a faggot. Sure as hell not Galen. And not yours truly one bit neither."

"Wait a minute," I said. "What?"

Now Uncle Judith straightened up, eyed me as if I'd offended him. My gaze skipped to the Colt. He said, "A faggot's another thing. I know plenty of faggots that go with women. It ain't about that. Me and Galen is real men."

Then abruptly he tipped his hat down over his face and said from behind it, "Now I done said it. I guess I surprised ya."

"Well . . . I never gave it much . . . yeah, you did."

"We raised that girl, me and Galen. Her rightful mother wanted nothing to do with it. Galen went with that woman before . . . you know, before he . . . well, see, I . . ."

His chest began to shake. From under his hat he said, "Now I lost them both. I lost my entire family." He sputtered. "I been carrying this pistol around these last couple days everywhere I go. It just seems to end up in my hand."

I waited. But that was it. He seemed to be done talking. I offered a conflicted and stillborn "I'm sorry" toward the snuffling behind the hat.

"Uncle Judith, who did kill that guide at Otter Creek? Do you know?"

"Galen did. For chrissake, who the hell else?"

Now the hat trembled. His gnarled hands gripped the knees of his jeans. I could reach the Colt, and I did so, unopposed. I unloaded it.

"I do thank you for that," Uncle Judith managed.

He was silent for so long then that I tried to refocus: what mattered here, why I came, was to see where Acting Interim Sheriff Russell Crowe fit into the Jesse picture. I began to sort the letters and memorabilia: father in one stack, boyfriends in the other. I looked for Crowe among the notes and scraps and movie stubs and sometimes red-hot missives of love or hate or restraining orders from boyfriends. Nothing came up right away. This was going to take a while. I had decided this just as there came a great gasp and Uncle Judith's hat fell off, landed on the neck of the Galliano bottle.

"Well that's that," he concluded, wiping a sleeve across his nose. "All the rage these days, of course, sumbitch movies and all."

He looked every place but into my eyes. I needed to say something: "You wanna help me read these?"

"I do not read," he pronounced. He recovered his hat. He

sniffed the Galliano, put the cap on. "Galen read a magazine now and then. Myself, I recognize, but I do not read."

That clarified, he turned sideways on the settee. His compact body fit just right with his boots up and crossed on the far arm.

"Turn those headlights off, willya? There's a flashlight in the cubby."

Then he was the sandman of snoose. He raised up to access the can in his back pocket. He packed in a goodnight pinch the size of a minor cow flop. In ten seconds he was snoring.

After two hours I had found no trace of Russell Crowe among Jesse's mementos. Many of these keepsakes, I thought, came to seem like evidence, like testimony as to how much Jesse Ringer mattered to a wide assortment of men and boys. Henderson Gray was one among several to say that he loved her. But her letters from Gray delineated a steady retraction of that love, terminating in a blunt demand that Jesse back off and leave him alone.

Gray hadn't lied about the relationship—not to me, anyway. Clearly, Jesse mistook him as someone who could lawyer up on the state and free her father. Clearly, she felt Gray had promised to do so. But he wrote at one point, "Fucking is not a promise. Fucking is fucking." I dropped the letter and turned away, too sad for Jesse to continue.

Anyway, Crowe was not in the Jesse Ringer boys club. Could I let it go then?

I tried.

I told myself that all the games Crowe and his mother had played around the margins of the Sneed-Jesse tragedy were moves in an opportunistic scheme to embarrass and discredit Chubbuck and return the mantle of Park County Sheriff to the Crowe family—for whatever reasons they had. And the scheme had worked, more or less. But so what? Was this my concern? Russell and Rita Crowe did not cause the tragedy. I was certain. They simply, clumsily, successfully exploited it.

As Uncle Judith snored into the early morning hours, I moved on to the father-daughter correspondence—or at least Galen Ringer's half of it, stamped by the Deer Lodge prison. What startled me right away was the shallowness of Ringer's tone, the paucity of specifics in the claims he made to his daughter. He was innocent. This was the central declaration in each and every letter. *I am telling you I am innocent.* This was the phrase he repeated. And: *why would I care what anyone called me if it wasn't true?* Jesse had to believe him. She was his daughter. This was the logic. Apparently she begged him for proof, facts, names, people who could help her, but Galen Ringer always replied *Faith is stronger than facts Jesse you know that and your my daughter you just have to trust me.*

God help me if this did not go on and on—months, years— the poor girl graduating from high school, planning to go to college but backing out for lack of funds, getting hired as a bartender, a smokejumper, a camp counselor, a mini-stop cashier, a bartender again, getting engaged, once, twice, and at each of these junctures her father echoing her accomplishments back at her, setting them up in scoffing capital letters, replying, *PROMOTION TO NIGHT MANAGER. Well thats fine and good about your big success but here I am an innocent man in prison so what is happening with my defense?*

Why Don't We Fish the Roam?

Okay, Dog. Your wheels are spinning. It's sad. It's over. Let it go.

I slumped at my galley table in the Geyser Motel parking lot. I parted my grimy curtain to watch the sun come up through a stand of yellowing cottonwoods over the top of Aretha's room.

Time for vitamins, Dog, and rest.

I fixed a whopper v-and-T.

Time to go, Dog, go.

I took my socks off. The cup was empty.

She woke me around noon, banging on the door and then coming right in. I sat up to Aretha tugging on my foot and telling me, "This place needs room service, Hoss."

She looked good. She smelled good. I sat up in my bunk, hit my head like I hadn't slept there more than two thousand nights.

"He remembered," she told me gaily.

Confusion. "Remembered what?" I had to piss like a Russian racehorse. My mind scrambled for options. Cottonwoods, I thought. Or the room. "Where is he?"

"Watching Oprah."

I was urgent. "Can we talk in there?"

"What's going on?" she demanded, looking under the bunk and into the cab. "Hoss, you got a lady in here?"

The box of Sneed's personal property, recovered from Jesse's car and dropped off by Aretha's liaison, Acting Interim Sheriff Russell Crowe, had produced a paid receipt for a Livingston business called Printing for Less.

I could think now, my bladder empty. But I could not connect. Printing what for less?

She had taken Sneed there, his mother said, and they had picked up a finished order of fliers advertising a new guide shuttle service, Sneed's Car Ferry, and giving Jesse's cell phone number as the contact.

"That's my plan," Sneed told me, his eyes bright, "for how I'm gonna live here."

"Obviously we're going to help him," Aretha informed me.

That *we* hung there. She sent up another one.

"And also," she said, "we're going on a fishing trip. I am going to show off my skills."

I turned the flier over. Orange paper, blank on the back. The front said *Cheap Rates! Reliable Drivers! Satisfaction Guaranteed!*

"Don't look so troubled, Hoss. D'Ontay explained it to me. The service is essential. There's no skills or overhead. You just drive the vehicles wherever the fishing guides want, park and leave the keys, drive back and do it again until you're done. They call D'Ontay, they don't have to go through the outfitter, so it's cheaper. It's a simple business."

"What about Sorgensen?"

"Nobody likes him," Sneed said.

"I don't mean that. What about his business?"

"It's a free country," Aretha said.

"Inside a small town," I said back.

Her head went side to side, like she was about to go cobra on me. But then she nodded.

"Then let's talk to him." She snapped off the TV. "Life is ninety percent money. Let's just cut him a deal."

Sorgensen was amped up and jolly. It was mid-day. All his guides were out. All his shuttles had run. There was rain on the way, and you could not drive along any road outside of town, could not take all that bug meat on glass, and miss the fact that the grasshoppers were in. Therefore the guides now worked hopper-droppers and everyone caught fish. Life could not be a whole lot better in the outfitting business.

We found Sorgensen grease-smeared and heaving for breath beside the propped-up hood of his van, but not even engine trouble could darken the revival of some particularly antic smile from the rodeo days.

"Good to see you folks again." Sneed took a slap on the shoulder. "How you doing, kid? You look like new."

Sneed had the orange flier in his hand. But he was carsick and seemed to struggle to recall the purpose of our visit.

"Say, one of you mind reaching in the engine here and grabbing that wrench? Dropped that little shit and couldn't get to it."

He gusted a peanuty laugh. I easily recovered the wrench from a crevice behind the oil cap. All it took was a regular physique.

"Ah, you're a lifesaver. You folks looking to fish today?"

Aretha said, "Actually—"

"All my guides are out by now, but what say I call this retired fella I know and you folks do a little thing like Emigrant to Grey Owl?"

Aretha said again, "Actually—"

"You want I call this retired fella? Why don't you come into the shop? Let's get you what you need."

"We don't want to fish. We want to talk."

Aretha might have been a bull. Sorgensen's mouth began to run in crazy zig-zags.

"Hell, I was supposed to be someplace an hour ago but my car-buretor has some dang thing flopping open too wide and flooding the engine—You folks ought to fish today. They're on—Or maybe it ain't the carburetor, heck I ain't a mechanic—One of you got the time?— You think they'd make a watch band for larger people? Heck no—Noon?—Goddurnit, I'm way late. I gotta go. You're looking good, kid. You folks weren't interested in fishing?"

I just stood back, watched the speed work and the peanuts fly. Eventually Aretha got Sneed's flier into Sorgensen's hands and the idea into his head: he had competition on the shuttle end of his business. That was the off switch.

"Hell I do."

He nearly handed the flier back. Then he seemed to actually read it, his lips moving, his pupils no bigger than pencil tips, slid-ing back and forth. It took a while.

"Hell now. Ain't that a thing. Well."

Managing the flier in a slit between fingers, he rattled a hand-ful of peanuts, mashed them, gobbed them down and went for more. He mumbled as he chewed. About a thousand calories later he handed the flier back with his odd and unexpected response. "Blessings upon you then." A magnanimous clownly bow, utterly difficult to look at. "It ain't actually a business so much as a pain in my ass. You can have the durn thing."

"We'll give you a cut," Sneed piped up, tuning in too late and drawing a sharp elbow from his mother. Her scowl said *keep your loss of higher intellectual function to yourself.*

"A cut? Will you now?" Sorgensen said, ruffling a greasy, pea-nuty hand up through his beard.

I didn't listen, but after thirty minutes Aretha had somehow wrestled Sorgensen down from his ridiculous opening position at half of all profits to ten percent for the first season, five for the sec-ond, and none after that. Then a Bozeman taxi pulled into the lot. A cigarette end-over-ended out the window. Lyndzee skittered out in a denim mini skirt and clip-clop heels that were dicey on gravel.

I was there when the trunk popped. I lifted out her suitcases, getting a look at the baggage tags. "How was Saint Paul?"

She looked grimly surprised. "Heavenly."

"Hilarious had engine trouble."

"Fucker's got more trouble than that," she rasped, and wobbled off between the suitcases.

I followed her back to the scene of negotiations and found that Aretha and Sorgensen had settled and were now on amicable terms, discussing our prospects for a fishing trip in the Cruise Master.

Lyndzee's voice dragged out. "Hello, I'm back."

"How were things in Denver, Zee-Zee Doll?"

"Mile high."

"And Uncle Irvin?"

She turned, started toward the house. "Uncle Who?" she said, sounding like the gravel had risen from her feet to her throat.

Sorgensen laughed. "She's got so much goldurned family."

More peanuts ensued, flying into that great shaggy head. He tried to pass the jar around. I said, "Why don't we fish the Roam?"

Sorgensen looked doubtful. Aretha too. Even Sneed.

"We know a spot where the fence is down," I said. "And the ground is flat and hard a good mile back in there." I was talking to Aretha, really, wanting to persuade her. "Then there's a rancher's road that's better than a lot of places my vehicle's been. We can fish our way down and then park by the river, sleep to the sound of it."

I read her mind. "I don't think Tucker's going to bother us. He wouldn't dare now."

Sorgensen intervened: "You set up properly to camp, the three of you?"

"We're good," I told him, though the truth was we would need to take Aretha's credit card to Pamida and pick up a few things.

"Got heat?" Sorgensen persisted. "The weather's turning. It's gonna get down to forty tonight and then rain later tomorrow. Probably knock these fires back finally."

Aretha had her eyes wide, her mouth open. "Forty? Forty degrees? Hoss, we better have heat in that thing."

Body heat ran through my mind. But I checked the thought and unhooked my eyes from Aretha. Sorgensen took it upon himself to inject his huge body through the side door of the Cruise Master, apparently to check the status of my long-dormant gas heater.

"Well, it's all there, so you're good to go, heat wise." He left the Cruise Master rocking on its sloppy shocks as he side-stepped down.

I relented. "I'll take a tank of LP."

Sorgensen heaved off to provide. "On me," he puffed when he had the tank secured on its bracket. "You folks are good people," he said, "and I wish you the best."

Obvious to a Woman

Acting Interim Sheriff Russell Crowe pulled the Cruise Master over at one half mile after Carter's Bridge and executed such a perfect chin-first saunter up to my window that I decided he had forgotten about my immunity in his deal with Cord Cook.

But instead his voice had an ornery pipsqueak edge to it: "You all didn't say goodbye!"

"We're not leaving."

"Oh," he said. "Not yet. Right."

"Maybe not ever," Aretha said.

"Oh."

"My baby likes it here. We're going into that guide shuttling business."

"But—"

"We talked to Sorgensen. He said take it."

Crowe had sunglasses on. The clue was in the chin. It zoomed out another quarter inch, like something from a 3-D movie screen.

"So where you all headed now?"

The Roam was the stuff of any fly fishermen's dreams: sinuous and slick, reflecting the gorgeous pinks and purples of a smoke-addled sunset sky, trout rising everywhere. I struck out in a performance mode, cocky for Aretha, dropping long and lovely show casts into feeding lanes, launching drifts to break a hard man's heart.

Nothing. Not a bump.

I changed flies. I went to a thinner tippet.

No.

Dog damn it.

I shortened up. I trailed a nymph.

Nyet.

"What's the matter, Hoss?"

"Hang on just a minute. I think it's an emerger. I'll figure it out."

But I continued emptily upstream, unable to reproduce even inklings of the hook-ups I had imagined. Now I was just trying to find anything that worked—parachutes, comparaduns, floating nymphs, midge clusters—trying to pry the lid off the cookie jar before I turned Sneed and his mother loose.

Nothing.

The trout kept rising. They rose everywhere, and then they rose in everywhere's face, pummeling the surface. It didn't help me to hear Aretha yelling, "There's one, Hoss! Get it!" every time a nose came up. And there was the distraction of Sneed, veering and stumbling along the bank badly enough to make me think he would break either the fly rod I loaned him or his ankle, and quite possibly both.

Dog damn it. Bear down.

I lit a Swisher and dropped the mental flaps. I went back to basics, back to first intentions, made good offers. I shot cast after loving cast across that perfect, pink-on-pewter water, insinuating a pale evening dun into the feeding lanes of large, rising trout— every one of which nosed fussily around my offerings as if it were an old spinster rejecting bummed fruit at the supermarket.

I bit through my Swisher and then Aretha gave up on me. "I'm going to fish right here!" she called, wading into a run I had fished about forty yards ago.

Grunt.

"I'm going to use this fuzzy-butt pink thingy!"

Snort.

"Tie a clinch knot, right?"

Whatever.

I did not even turn around to watch it happen. I didn't need to, because it happened so vividly, so perfectly, in my mind. I just stood there crotch-deep, scowling upriver, sucking on my broken Swisher and cussing through the countdown. And sure enough, it was not quite three minutes before Aretha began to yell— "Hoss! Hoss, I got one!"—whereupon I unsnapped my net and waded back to corral her trout and tweezer the bead head Pink Squirrel from its big kipe jaw.

"That's a rainbow?"

"That's a rainbow."

"Oh . . . my . . . Lord. It is so pretty!"

I slipped a hand beneath the trout's belly and swept the net out. Sneed came clomping to us with two good ankles but, as predicted, a broken rod.

"He's a nice one."

"Your mama caught him, Sneedy."

"Damn right." Aretha wanted high fives. "Hoo!"

I held his tail, moved the trout forward and back to send water through his tired gills.

"It's a boy?"

"It's a boy."

"Oh . . . my . . . Lord," Aretha said again, but this time she had straightened her back and widened her vision to take in the scene. This time she was seeing it—seeing the whole fish in the earth and sky and water. She was seeing the landscape that bled silver and pink and blue into her fish, that built those great straps of live muscle. She was gazing in awe at the snowcapped mountains that bred speed and instinct and brilliance into her fish as it faced upstream, upstream, like the twitching tail of a dream.

"Oh . . . my . . . Lord. Baby . . . look!"

"What, Mama? Where?"

"Everywhere, Baby!"

"Now watch this," I said, and I let the trout go.

"What did you do!" Aretha shrieked. She slugged me flat in the chest. "What in the hell did you just do?"

She was still fuming when I handed her a partitioned aluminum mess kit plate with a sausage, some macaroni and cheese, and baby carrots. A significant vodka-Tang could not assuage her.

"Some pig died for this," she ranted with the sausage on the end of her fork. "Some innocent animal got trucked around the country, got its throat cut, got itself ground up and mixed with its own damn feet and ears, got wrapped in Styrofoam and cellophane—but you won't kill a fish right out of pure clean water? Lord help me. White people sure are crazy."

I sat on a flat, sun-warmed river rock. Actually, she had me laughing. I wanted her to go on and on, chopping me up like another doomed pig, but that lovely jilted fisherwoman just tensed there in my lawn chair, in firelight, and wanted push-back, wanted to fight, so I said, "You are about ninety-nine per-cent right," and sure enough, Aretha Sneed wanted to excavate the other one percent, using very sharp tools.

My reply: "I just can't kill them."

"Why not?"

"I just can't."

"I see. You need somebody that looks like me to do your killing for you, that's what you need."

"I *can* kill," I claimed. "I just don't."

She waved the sausage in my face. "Dead," she said. "Correct? And I'm not political, but let's take Vietnam, Iraq, any of that, and you're saying you are off the hook because you, you personally, don't kill? And you can sleep on that?"

"Well, I do drink a lot."

Now she was laughing—but just a little. "This stuff is actually not so bad," she admitted, raising her tin cup for another sploosh of vodka-Tang.

"You make false analogies," I told her. Silently, I called myself a fool for prolonging this. But my self surprised me, came back with *It's okay, Dog, trust her . . .*

"People aren't commodities. There's no market for them." Her eyes flashed hot. "Anymore," I tacked on. "Not as food anyway." And more: "Those hogs are raised to die."

Jesus, Dog. Are you drunk?

Yes, I am.

Then shut up.

No, it's okay, really. Trust her.

"I . . . okay, listen, please . . . there are explanations . . . biological . . . you know, resource issues . . . conservation, fish don't feel pain, studies, all that . . . but at a time like that . . . at a time like that one we just had, that beautiful rainbow in my hands, remember it?"

"Mm," she said.

"At a time like that, I cannot take life. I can only share it. I can touch it, feel it. I can come *so close* to something that is just *so much* like this thing inside me . . . are you listening?"

"Mm."

"I don't know, a wild trout is this perfect live *thing* that is . . . it's like the spirit of something inside me . . . but inside me that spirit is trapped . . . it can't speak . . . it can't live enough, can't get enough to eat, can't jump like it should . . . but the trout does, the trout lives all that . . . and I . . . I have enough trouble, Aretha, really . . . and I just can't kill . . . can't kill *that*."

I looked at her. "Can I?"

She was completely still and silent. Sneed's eyes were wide upon me from across the fire, sausage grease reflecting from his lips.

Oh, shit. Dog damn it. Drunken bum speaks gibberish, appeals for meaning from listener.

It's okay. Trust her.

No, it's not okay. Why don't we just all go to a bar and yell at faces?

Because it's different out here. Things change. They open up.

Sure they do. I think I'll just drink a bunch more and hibernate until it's over.

You don't need to. It's fine.

Who the hell are you, anyway? Where did you come from all of a sudden?

I thrashed myself free. "Never mind," I blurted into the glowing, honey-brown side of Aretha's head. "You're completely right," I told her. "One hundred percent."

She turned. She smiled.

"You know what, Hoss? So are you."

She rose a bit unsteadily from the lawn chair and sat down beside me on my warm, flat rock. She took my hand but didn't squeeze this time. This was a different touch. My mouth went dry.

She said, "And now I think you deserve to know a secret."

This intruding inner voice persisted: *In. Out. In. Out. Breathe, Dog. Do it now.*

"Yeah?" It was barely a squeak, all I could do. "So what's your secret?"

"The first part is who it's a secret from." She held on to my hand as she drew her knees up and knocked gently against my shoulder.

"A secret from me?"

"Absolutely. But not originally."

Wait. Breathe. That's all you have to do.

"The original secret was a big one. I mean, I could *not* let it out. Those girls at the bad girl home, they would have teased me to death. But we watched about a hundred episodes of *Bonanza*, and after all that, in my mind, and my heart, if I was to give myself to any one of those boys . . ."

Wait. Breathe. Count. Whatever.

Aretha sighed, shook her head. Firelight gleamed in her eyes. "Oh, my girlfriends would have laughed. And I was so embarrassed, calling myself crazy, and believing I was crazy right up to a pretty short time ago. But . . . you know?"

"No," I managed in a whisper. "I don't know."

"Yes, you do."

"I don't."

"You've seen the show."

"I have."

"Adam was gay. Good Lord, anybody could see that. He was going to sneak out on a girl and you-know-what. And Little Joe was spoiled. Little Joe wasn't ever gonna grow up. Some poor woman was gonna have to powder his precious ass her whole damn life. So really, a person watches enough *Bonanza*, men-wise, it becomes obvious."

She put her head to my shoulder.

"I mean, obvious to a *woman*."

She let out a breath she might have been holding twenty years. I held mine tight.

"My secret choice," she whispered to my neck, "was Hoss."

Immersed, Together, Breathing

Imagine Sneed then. That poor kid was tickled and disgusted and confused and excited—and all of this taking place inside a brain full of sink holes and dead ends and infused with a high degree of loopiness.

"Argawagawbbk!" he said, coming at us with apparently violent intent—though if he was violently angry or violently happy was hard to tell.

But then, mid-assault, balance and gait problems paid Sneed a visit. He listed to his downriver side and walked into my lawn chair. Unable to change course, he trampled it flat, dragged it around his ankle beyond the circle of firelight. Over there, in the darkness by the Cruise Master, he started to laugh, and then, free of the chair, he wrenched open the Cruise Master door and stumbled inside.

"There are so many barriers in life," Aretha mused, keeping her head against my shoulder. I put my arm around her, felt warm muscle, hard rib, and the inward squeeze of her elbow. "And most of those barriers we can't even see."

I agreed with that. "And sometimes the things that we see aren't actually barriers."

"Yeah. I guess so." She traced the bones on the back of my hand. "I'm sad, Dog. I'm sad that certain things have happened to me. I'm sad that I got into drugs and that I screwed up as a mother. I'm sad that D'Ontay suffered and that he's like this now. It's gonna be hard. Real hard. I'm gonna have to give up a lot to take care of him. None of this needy radical professor bullshit twisting my mind around, I'll tell you that. I'm sad about that too, though. I'm sad about my time, my options tightening up. I'm sad about all the experiences, all the memories lost to D'Ontay that he may never share with me . . ."

"That kid jumped off a bridge. I don't think I ever told you that."

"*What?*"

"I mean for fun. As the perfect way of quitting his job. I couldn't say no when he asked to go fishing with me. My guess is he'll still have that spirit, no matter what."

"And maybe die any moment," Aretha said. "That scares me so much. Oh my Lord, Dog, that scares me. But couldn't we all die at any moment? Really? Isn't that exactly the way life really is?"

"Especially when you wade big rivers."

She sighed. "Dog, this is all big rivers. Layers of big rivers, going every which way. Some day one is gonna get you. But you know what?"

She was looking at me, so close. I squeezed her. "Fortunately, I'm never quite sure what I know, with you. So tell me."

"Inside all this trouble I feel happy. And the reason is that for the first time in my life, I feel like I see."

She was so close. I turned and we were eye to eye, one hand span apart. She reached and brushed something from my cheek.

"You know?" she said. "I mean, I see somebody, and I under-stand something."

Of course we were caught kissing when Sneed lurched back out of the Cruise Master with the ratty pup tent and the spare sleeping bag I kept under the galley bench.

"Don't mind me," he said, kiting off into the darkness with a false agility that raised his mother out of my arms.

We caught up with him pitching the tent on a scrubby rise from which the road was visible but the Cruise Master was not. Out there toward Livingston, a few stray cars moved through the darkness, past the gash in Tucker's fence, and onward in their private directions.

"You're a good kid," his mother told my buddy Sneed. "You always were."

He pounded stakes with a rock. The ground was dry and hard. A stake bent. Sneed dropped everything. He looked up. "You like Dog?" he asked his mother.

She nodded. "Isn't that funny? It turns out that I do."

Sneed picked up the bent stake, sharp at the point. He picked up the heavy rock he used as a hammer. He placed the rock in front of him, focused the center of the stake's concave surface over the opposite arc of the rock, and he bent the stake straight.

He told his mother, "I didn't think so about you, not really, not at first. But you have a lot of potential."

Then he turned away and resumed his efforts with the tent.

"It's going to be cold, Baby."

"I'm fine."

"You didn't eat much, either."

"I'm fine."

I moved and stood beside her, gathered her shoulders in my arm. "Baby, don't you want help putting up that tent?"

"Mother," he said sharply, "I'm *fine*."

"Is it going to be cold in here too?"

I lifted Aretha's shirt away from her waist, touched her beneath. "I never use the heat in here. And I especially don't think we'll need it tonight."

She pecked me on the forehead, raised her arms overhead. "Go on," she said. "See what I got on."

It was a brassiere in green-brown camouflage, and I, of course, was speechless.

"I bought it to piss off the professor," she said.

"Oh."

"Does it work for you too?"

"So much," I said, "that I'm going to have to remove it right away."

In my bunk, after a long time just nuzzling, kissing, taking our time because it felt like we had known each other for years, we finally went just so far as to move me to my knees between her, my hands and her hands tangling up as we put pieces together, and then something—a barrier? a non-barrier?—something stopped us, and in rushed the sound of the Roam.

In that silence, the first true silence of our time together, the river roared in our ears. But it roared with a delicate complexity, a denseness and a cool warmth, truly not one sound but a weave of sounds, as if there were a thousand rivers out there, a million rivers out there, and we were in them, immersed, together, breathing.

"Do you hear that?" I whispered.

"I can't hear anything else."

Her hands moved again, found me pulsing.

She said, "I don't ever want to hear anything else."

Then she found center. I moaned.

"Except that," she said. "Come on, Dog. Let me hear some more of that."

Knocked Around in the
Clown Barrel Too Much

We dozed a bit, and I dreamed that the river was a highway. Aretha
and I needed roadside help. We were trying to have a picnic but
we had no peanut butter. Cars whipped past us until finally one
stopped. In my dream I spent the longest time trying to stand up,
see who it was, but I could not find my balance and Aretha kept
pulling me down, pulling me down, trying to make love right then
and there.

"Why don't we do it in the road?"

"Not on the highway."

"Huh? What?"

She was sitting up, for real, over me.

"Nothing. Stupid dream."

We did make love then, for real, a second time, but it was
strangely unlike our first. Something felt off-center in our bodies.
Somehow the flesh felt distant, like we were touching each other
with protective mittens across a glass divider. Aretha tried to take
me from the top. I do remember that. I remember the seasick feeling. I remember Aretha's strokes felt erratic and faintly painful.
And I remember a weird numbness in my mouth when she came

down to kiss me, murmuring, "Dog? Sweetie? You okay? Tell me what you like."

I remember that I felt panicky. I couldn't feel much. I didn't know what I liked. I could not form words. I don't remember what Aretha did about it, but I know that at some point she soon became a blank, a dumb weight that smacked down on top of me—but that is all I can pull back from those early, telltale moments. I still shake and sweat when I try.

When it happened, it happened fast. It happened inside me on the level of instinct, with the kind of headlong adrenaline magic that sends a trout up a waterfall.

Something woke me. It may have been Aretha gagging against my chest. Or it may have been the jolt to the Cruise Master when Hilarious Sorgensen jammed a two-by-four under the outside door latch and began to kick the other end down into the hard dirt.

But I turned Aretha off me and sat up in a head-spinning lunge. The heater gas was on but the pilot wasn't lit. That was the insight of instinct. I never meant to use the heater. I never touched it. Therefore the pilot valve had been opened already, sometime before, and the valve on the outside tank was open now. That one small string of logic appeared from nowhere into my hampered brain and sent me naked over the edge of the bunk.

My legs collapsed beneath me. I tore skin from my back against the corner of the galley table. I got onto hands and knees and spent a weird ten seconds looking for my instant Folgers— somehow I thought making coffee would solve the problem— and then for an even more bizarre stretch of time, having found my jar of Folgers, I crawled around the floor looking for matches. It was the most frightening kind of accident that I did not find them. It was blind luck that I spiraled back to an earlier thought: the heater gas was open and the pilot wasn't lit.

I hurt Aretha, the way I yanked her off the bunk and to the floor. She cried and mumbled and looped a fist at me. Then she threw up between my hands and knees and I crawled right through it. But the Cruise Master's side door wouldn't open. Something blocked it.

I crawled back through the galley and into the cab. Sorgensen blurred through moonlight past the windshield and put his weight against the passenger door as I tried to push it open. I was weak, impaired. The monster checked me easily. Then, desperate, my mind skipped rails. I thought Sorgensen was helping me—the good man—but the job was just too tough for the two of us.

I think it was the appearance of little Lyndzee—running into my vision, screaming at Sorgensen, hitting him, kicking his legs and knocking him down—that tipped me off to the true nature of our situation.

I bulled the door open and staggered out. Real air was a shock, like cold water, and now Lyndzee was screaming at me, shoving me along the outside of the Cruise Master while she tried to keep Sorgensen on the ground with a flurry of sharp-booted kicks. He caught her leg finally, pulled her down with him in the dust.

"Forget me!" Lyndzee screamed. "Get her out!"

I kicked out the two-by-four. My side door swung open. I wasn't smart enough to move aside and so took a massive hit of propane that dropped me to my knees. But I saw Aretha's hand reach out. I grabbed it. I pulled, and it seemed that she came to me like a heavy, lovely, played-out fish. Still alive.

Stupid me: I took the time to kiss her.

And now Hilarious Sorgensen had broken some piece of Lyndzee, made her shriek in pain, and the sloppy fat man had wallowed upright. Where his shotgun came into the picture, I have no idea. It must have been there, on the dirt between us, knocked loose by Lyndzee and for me to pick up while I was kissing Aretha.

Sorgensen aimed it at me. He could barely breathe. "Both . . . of you . . . stand . . . together."

I had no idea I was naked. I kneed up shakily, stood in front of Aretha, understanding, somehow, that *she* was.

"Give me that," I said, and I wobbled straight into the shotgun barrel, solid proof that natural gas causes brain damage.

Sorgensen's beard ruffled with each word. "I'll . . . give you . . . this."

Anyone's guess where my next words came from: "You musta got knocked around in the clown barrel too much."

"Git back and . . . go stand next to her."

I was pure blind synapses, fish up a waterfall: "I guess you only got one shell in there, huh? That's why you need us together?" Maybe Sorgensen hadn't understood his own logic. Now he saw it. Uncertainty made those buried pig eyes begin to reach and dart. "There's three of us here," I threw out. "Four if you count my buddy. Look."

Sneed had awakened and come to the rim of the rise above us. He was a dark shape. "Go back to the tent," I hollered at him. "Get your . . . weapon."

Of course Sneed was confused, frightened—what weapon?—at a loss for what to do next. So was Sorgensen.

"Lyndzee!" he bellowed, not daring to turn and look for her. "Go to the van!"

She was moving, crawling. But I said, "She can't help you."

Aretha began to vomit behind me. Sneed had taken my order and gone back toward the tent. I took a nude step toward Sorgensen, freezing him. Meanwhile, Lyndzee had lifted herself from the dirt. Hopping like an injured bird, she had made it to Sorgensen's van.

I took another step, staying on the fat man's mind.

"Better shoot me soon. Sneed'll be back any second. And you know his brain is damaged. His boundaries are down."

"Lyndzee, damnit woman, get my sidearm!" Sorgensen began to tremble with the ferocity of panic and rage. One more step closer for me. "*Now!*"

But Lyndzee had the sidearm already, was hopping out with a heavy pistol, aimed square on Sorgensen's back. I worried about angles. Behind me Aretha had risen to her knees, bleeding freely from one arm, and she began to rant about fire safety in a tone that was both loopy and vicious, as though she were on a public service visit to the Ku Klux Kindergarten. "Look," I said to Sorgensen. Across rangeland from the highway bounced headlights, coming fast.

"Just lay it down," I said. "Spare us. Lyndzee's about to blow a hole in all that."

Sorgensen jerked around to look at her. She was only ten feet behind him. I had the reptile sense to dive beneath the Cruise Master and pull Aretha with me. Hilarious Sorgensen began, "You stupid, crazy little—" and she pulled the trigger.

Wham! The sound nearly cracked my head open. Lyndzee flew back one way and Sorgensen blew apart in the other direction and it was over.

Acting Interim Sheriff Russell Crowe filled the next few dreamlike moments by slamming out of his cruiser with pistol drawn, barking commands that nobody followed except for Sneed, who dropped the stick he had carried over the ridge.

Then in gasping bursts Lyndzee said to all of us, "Just because I'm a drug addict doesn't make me a bad person. Nobody can make me a bad person. Nobody can do that. I decided that. It won't happen."

None of us objected. But she repeated her resolution three times before she limped up and shot Sorgensen again.

No Harm Done?

Sheriff Roy Chubbuck, vanquisher of Dane Tucker and liberator of the Roam River, and Hilarious Sorgensen, behemoth, beast, outfitter, ex-clown, and dealer of substances A-Z, died on the same day and with approximately opposite degrees of grief and fanfare.

Sheriff Chubbuck died predictably and quietly with his wife and grown-up daughters at his side, causing murmurs of sorrow and relief to ripple through Park County and beyond.

What a story, people said. Their Sheriff was a good, quiet, hardworking man who with his last stores of energy had managed a successful counterattack against several kinds of evil and pulled it off. Over the next few days, the national media would discover the Dane Tucker bust and come in sniffing and prodding, pontificating from Livingston street corners into their wind-baffled microphones. Folks just walked on by.

The sheriff's funeral at St. Mary's Catholic Church in Livingston drew six hundred people, including a shell-shocked yours truly, plus a shell-shocked Aretha and Sneed, as among those who could not fit into the church and so participated from outside, listening through the windows and soaking in the first day of a slow, blessed, three-day rain that drowned out the forest fires for good.

Sorgensen died alone under a surgeon's racing fingers in a scarcely human puddle of blood and guts and fat, disappointing no one but a small cadre of local death penalty advocates who were regrouping after the loss of Sneed as their poster boy. I saw in the newspaper that Sorgensen's funeral was in Big Timber. I cannot tell you who was there.

And poor Lyndzee Peterson, only twenty-seven after all, had crossed her Rubicon, drug-wise, all over state and local newspapers and television with her "story"—her confessions of crime and addiction and her promise to herself and to God and to her family (Clyde Park, Ringling, and Belgrade) to clean up her life. For good this time.

In the details, the drug story was a new one entirely, interesting for everyone involved.

Lyndzee came clean on her part. She was the one who stole drugs for Sorgensen. Not the *only* one, she was quick to point out, because she and Hilarious had only been together two years, and there were plenty of other girls before her who took those quick-hitting trips around the country to raid the clinics and pharmacies and pet hospitals of Sorgensen's fly fishing clients.

As for the rest, Acting Interim Sheriff Russell Crowe invited me and Sneed and Aretha to visit him in Chubbuck's office, whereupon he revealed a multi-layered agenda that began with an over-reaching description of combat wounds to his head (bruised eye socket) and left arm (not a break, fortunately, but painful, and in the sling for a couple weeks).

"But you folks are okay, I hope, no harm done?"

"You mean no harm done by you?"

Russell gave a little shrug and tried to charm us with a smile. "You know what I mean. Things have worked out okay, right? Why shouldn't we just leave things as they are?"

A long, long silence. I could sense Aretha's blood heating up. I gazed around the office at Chubbuck's artifacts from a lifetime of enmeshment with the land. Then, "Russell," I said, "just how are things, exactly?"

He sat back in the sheriff's chair. He put his hands—both—behind his head and his boots on the desk corner. Then he quickly dismantled all that, realigned his sling, and leaned over the desk to press the intercom button. "Ms. Park-Ford?"

"What."

"Could we get a round of sodas in here?"

There was no answer, just a click of static. Moments later Chubbuck's fireplug receptionist bustled in and out, leaving four wet Sprites on the desk exactly in front of Russell. "No thanks," all three of us said to his offer.

He cracked his can, refreshed himself with a sip.

"We've been onto Sorgensen for a long time."

Aretha and I traded glances at the "we." Crowe caught it, read it, forged on with the sale.

"Of course we knew he was dealing. He was dealing as far back as twenty years ago on the rodeo circuit. But something about his set up at the Fly 'n' Float seemed different to us. And so we—"

"Russell," I interrupted, "you made those injuries to yourself, right? After you let Sneed out of that transport ambulance?"

He tried to off me with a silly-Dog smile. His Sprite can clanked against his teeth.

"And speaking of we, your mother picked Sneed up in Billings, drove him around until you were ready, then set him down in Livingston. Chubbuck was going to look incompetent. You were going to catch Sneed on Main Street and look like a wounded hero. And you just missed him, right? Tick Judith snapped him up before you saw where he went."

"That's over," Crowe said.

"Do you plan to run for real sheriff, Russell?"

"What do you mean?"

"Because if you do, and we hear about it, it is most definitely *not* over." I traded looks with Aretha. "I think we'll see to that."

Nothing from Russell. He looked down at the Sprite rings on Chubbuck's desk.

"What happened with your father, Russell?"

We waited. Russell said to the desk: "He built Ma a nice place in the Paradise Valley, next door to Michael Keaton. The county board accused him of embezzlement."

"Of course he was innocent."

A long pause, now fingerpainting with the water on the desk: "So I hear."

"He was set up, I'll bet. By his enemies. Is that also what you hear? And that therefore all this is okay?"

Russell didn't answer. Finally he pushed the intercom again. "Ms. Park-Ford?"

"I'm here. I'm here every day all day long."

"Great. And how about Investigator Collins? Is he still here?"

Silence again on the other end—and our end too until this Collins came in. He was a handsome young black man, wearing an expensive suit and looking as if he had been pulled away from something more important. He was FBI from Denver, Crowe informed us. "Because, you know, this is interstate. Probably Investigator Collins is the best person to answer your questions. I mean, instead of you making a lot of assumptions."

I smiled inside. We had him. Russell Crowe was ours. Sneed was out of legal trouble. Meanwhile Collins looked around in dismay as if to say *answer whose questions why?* But Russell offered him a Sprite, and Collins, ever-so-slightly gracious, proceeded wholesale to get the Sorgensen story over with.

What was different with Sorgensen, he said, was the drugs. The variety, he said. I saw him glance at Aretha. She nodded.

Collins said, "Most guys deal coke, or weed, or meth—you know, they specialize, they have basically a vertical network. You bust someone at the right place on the totem pole, you can bring the whole thing down."

He checked on Aretha: still nodding.

"But Sorgensen was like a black market pharmacy. He could

sell you morphine, oxy-contin, amphetamines, animal tranquilizers, growth hormones, Prozac, Viagra, I forget the name of some crap they inject bulls with, you name it. And he seemed to have no chain, no one above or below him. Local law enforcement would bust a user, like . . ."

"Like Jesse," Aretha helped out.

Collins seemed unclear who that was. The dead girl, Aretha told him. He smiled.

"Yes. Like Jesse. Local would bust a user and get nothing, no story, no ups. None of his users knew a thing except to see this Sorgensen about taking a float down the river. He would say his guides were all out and did you want him to go inside and call this retired guy he knew. Your Sheriff Chubbuck, smart man that he was—" and here the acting interim cleared his throat, found a tissue, began to wipe Sprite circles off Chubbuck's desk—"was determined to bring the whole thing down, so rather than scare Sorgensen into inactivity, he backed off."

Collins looked at Aretha and provided a footnote: "We weren't in this yet. It was a local matter."

"I see."

"We come in when crimes cross borders."

"Oh." She smiled. "I see. Sure."

"The sheriff here just let it ride for a while, keeping his eyes open. That was the smart thing to do. Then one day, about a year-and-a-half ago when he still felt decent, he was at a law enforcement conference in Phoenix and heard about a supply of drugs missing from a veterinary clinic with no sign of a break-in and no employees they could clearly suspect. Now the sheriff had something to look into. Turns out the vets from that same clinic were up here at that same time for a week of fishing. Their outfitter? The guy who had access to their wallets, keys, all that?" Investigator Collins raised an eyebrow for Aretha. "Hilarious Sorgensen."

Crowe's eyes were skimming Aretha too, neither of those scavengers imagining that she had dressed for the Dog. She wore a white silk top, short-sleeved, tightish, and v-necked. She crossed her legs in pale orange capris and she very faintly clapped a thin leather sandal against a foot tipped with freshly painted, pale orange toenails.

My face was getting hot. I suggested a shortcut: "So Lyndzee Peterson explained how they did it?"

I hardly got a glance from the FBI guy. But I had cut Collins to the chase.

"Yes," he said. "Sheriff Chubbuck contacted us with part of the picture, and our involvement produced several more of these mysterious, unsolved thefts. But Ms. Peterson filled in the blanks. Sorgensen advertised heavily in medical and veterinary publications. And his business here, the fishing thing . . ."

He faltered and Russell jumped in. "You know how shuttle drivers have the keys to the guides' vehicles. You know how clients show up in their pants, with wallets, keys, hotel passcards." He spoke rapidly, as if he feared Collins would cut him off. "All that stuff ends up in a guide's vehicle, which sits at a boat ramp all day. Sorgensen knew where everybody was floating every day, knew where they were taking out, knew where the drivers left the keys."

When Aretha declined to nod or smile for him, Crowe shut up, letting Collins tell us that according to Lyndzee, Sorgensen used the internet and made phone calls around the country, probing, looking for business hours, vacation closures, one or two-man operations. He liked to pick places that had young employees or someone else who might be easy to blame. Sometimes, based on his research, he sent Lyndzee out to go through certain vehicles. He trained her to recognize the kinds of keys that might open clinics and pharmacies and so on. He trained her to swap out hotel passcards for dummies, and sometimes he sent her to raid hotel rooms. She brought the keys back to Sorgensen, he made copies on his own key cutter, and then Lyndzee put everything back the way it was. When Sorgensen thought he had a go, thought everything was right, he sent his girl, immediately, with copied keys, to the location in question—usually a smallish operation in a logistically feasible location. Lyndzee arrived in town, located the clinic, entered, filled suitcases, locked back up, and flew straight home.

"Flew back home with suitcases full of drugs?" I interrupted. "Through airport security?"

"No." Once more Collins spoke to Aretha instead of me. "She would ship boxes. UPS. FedEx, so on. She would find the clearances and manifests that those people have for shipping controlled substances. She was trained how to fill them out. The boxes came to Sorgensen's shop, which used to be a dental clinic years ago and remains on the federal list. And because these crimes occurred in an apparently random fashion, in completely unrelated parts of the country, nobody caught on. Unlike a lot of criminals, Sorgensen was a smart man. But, of course . . . not smart enough."

Collins had finished. He stood. "Are we good?" he asked Crowe with strained cheer in his voice.

"We're good. Thanks."

"If you have any more questions," Collins told Aretha warmly as he passed her his card, "just let me know."

The door closed behind him. Aretha studied the card.

"Hmm," she said. "Nice guy. Helpful."

What Real Love Feels Like

"But what about Gray?"

Acting Interim Sheriff Crowe tossed a magazine across the top of Chubbuck's desk. The familiar shape and colors spun toward me. It was that month's *National Geographic*, addressed to Chubbuck and already dog-eared from circulation. I fluttered the pages. About halfway through, Henderson Gray appeared—pictures of Gray running, pictures of pronghorn on the land that Chubbuck loved, pictures of Gray and family smiling on the new deck, all of this wrapped in lofty talk—by Gray, by poets, by biologists and anthropologists, one by the great Walt Whitman, then more verbiage by Gray—about man and nature, about spiritual quests, the Blackfoot brave and the Tarahumaran warrior, the timeless tests of manhood.

I shoved the magazine back toward Crowe. "Okay," I said. "Sure. Pride kills. Maybe I'd eat a truck grill too."

Crowe blinked at me, then nodded. "So anyway," he told us, "Sorgensen was not going to give up that shuttle business. No way, to no one."

We understood already, but Crowe went on. "If he said so, he didn't mean it. Several guides came out and said Sneed told them he was setting up his own shuttle business. They said they would have used him in a heartbeat. He would have crushed the shuttle side of Sorgensen's business. And that's why Sorgensen tried to kill Sneed."

"Wait a minute—" Because here, suddenly, was something I hadn't processed: *tried to kill Sneed?*

All along *Sneed* was the target? Sneed was not the fall guy for Jesse, the girl with a hundred reasons to die? All along I had centered everything on the *wrong victim?*

I looked at Sneed. He was glassy-eyed, appeared tuned out. "Sorgensen was really after . . ."

"Yes. He meant to kill Sneed. Jesse was mop up."

"But—" I was struggling. "Didn't Jesse get arrested? And offered a deal?"

"She fingered somebody in Bozeman. She got her deal. That was over."

Aretha said, "Then who shot Jesse?"

Crowe was liking this now, back in the driver's seat, Aretha needing his attention. He played out the moment and appeared to briefly consider putting his boots back up on the desk. At last he said, as if it were obvious, "Sorgensen shot Jesse."

"But then who set up Sneed and crawled out of the car?" I was baffled. "Not Sorgensen. Not Lyndzee because she would have tied the knot for Sorgensen, and it would have been a clinch knot—or at least something better than what it was. So who—" And then I had it. My heart surged, choked me. Crowe watched me cough out the name.

"Jesse?"

He nodded.

Aretha: "Jesse?"

"Lyndzee told us she cut a deal with Sorgensen. He told Jesse he had information that would get her father out of prison. But her friend was causing a problem and she had to kill him to get it."

We were stunned each into our own silence. Aretha's glare was aimed out the window at big sky country. Sneed mooned up at one of Chubbuck's big stuffed rainbows, tears filling his eyes. I stared into the past. Did I always have to be so wrong? Always?

It hurt to speak, to think. It hurt to overcome that awful surge of doubt. To believe was such a risk. To know was so impossible. "But she loved him," I blurted. "I saw it. I was there. I mean, I know it when I see it."

Crowe gave a jaunty little shrug. "I knew Jesse pretty well, too. I went to high school with her. After her father went in, I'm not sure Jesse had any real stable boyfriends. I'm not sure she was capable of loving somebody. More like she used people who either used her back or got out."

Now Aretha wrapped her arms around her son. He buried his face against her shoulder. I saw his gut convulse, his fingers curl to fists. When my voice returned, it was hard on Crowe.

"This kid didn't use her. I was there. He cared for her. And she cared for him."

"Yeah." Crowe gave me that shrug again.

"I mean it."

I stared him down.

"Okay, yeah," he agreed, and this time he seemed earnest. "He's a good guy. I saw them around. I never quite saw Jesse like that before. She did look different. She looked happy."

"She was happy. She was in love."

Aretha fought for control, her voice shredding. "And still that . . . that girl still tried to kill him?"

"Jesse'd do anything if she thought it would clear her father. We all knew that. That was her purpose in life, to defend her dad. I don't think she could help it." He nodded at Sneed. "She got him drunk on that sweet liquor with some animal tranquilizer in it that Sorgensen gave her, the same stuff that Henderson Gray bought from Sorgenson for those pronghorn. That junk made your son, your buddy, pass out. Sorgensen was already up the mountain in his van, a little further than that pond, waiting. He made Lyndzee hike down and watch for a signal from Jesse, but she walked right past and kept on going, which got her beat up pretty good later. Meanwhile Jesse taped the windows. She lit that little grill and she crawled out."

"She could fit?"

"It was tight. The ME found scrapes and bruises on her back and hips. So now those are explained."

Crowe's lips parted, sticky and dry. They closed again, parted once more, and he lifted an open file from Chubbuck's desk. He read for a few moments. Then, as if the whole thing had overwhelmed him suddenly, he made a troubled gulp and closed the file.

"Jesse made it out of the car, and then Sorgensen played the card she didn't know about. He never meant to give her information about her father. He didn't have any. Galen Ringer killed that guy at the boat ramp. Everybody knows that. Galen Ringer kicked the crap out of plenty of people who looked at him wrong or said the wrong thing. Jesse's dad was just kinda funny that way."

Crowe had more trouble swallowing. He looked around Chubbuck's office, at the lifetime represented. He looked at Sneed and his mother side by side in their chairs, heads down, rocking together.

"So . . . Jesse crawled out the trunk and right away Sorgensen shot her in the head. He . . . he . . . wiped the pistol, your pistol— Jesse took it from you—and threw it in through the trunk. Then he realized without Jesse, without Lyndzee either, he couldn't get the seat shut . . . and then the rod, the fly broken off in back of the seat, the knot that got your attention, all that. Just this morning I found the metal pieces of Sneed's rod in Sorgensen's burn barrel."

He shook his head. "That's about the only thing I've done right . . ."

The acting interim gave his head a woeful shake. But I bit off any sympathy for Russell Crowe. He was no relation to a lot of things, especially not to the kind of young man who ought to graduate to sheriff. But the grim truth was that blame ran wide. All of us were fools and had been fooled. All of us—even Chubbuck— had the crime turned inside-out. And my poor damaged fishing buddy was now turned inside-out and sideways, for life, by Jesse. She had done her best to murder Sneed, who at that moment stood up out of his mother's arms and told Aretha angrily, emphatically, "Because I never knew what real love feels like!"

No one spoke for a long and awful moment. Outside the window, pickup trucks rolled past, clouds floated in the big blue sky. Aretha had lost it. She was weeping.

Then I said, "No." I gripped Sneed's hand. "She loved you. I know she did."

"But she—"

"I'm sure."

"Dog—"

"I'm sure, Sneedy. She loved you. I saw it. But it's just not that easy."

Powerful Somehow

"Like you said," Aretha murmured to me after lovemaking a few days later. "It's just not that easy. Like, the fact that I'm in love with you doesn't necessarily mean that I should hook up with you, you know, for the long term."

Her head was in my lap, her eyes closed. A rain-replenished mountain creek scurried and laughed beside us. We were naked on top of my rain coat on top of a scratchy bed of moss and dead pine needles. We had been laughing at ourselves. My back was stuck in pitch against a pine trunk, and my hands flailed to keep the horseflies off my precious, precious sweetheart. Making love outside always seems like a good idea—doesn't it?—always looks good in movies and sounds good in books. But here's some advice: stand up if you can, get it done, and get dressed before the insects find you.

"Dog? Did you hear me?"

"Yes."

"Did I hurt you?"

"Yes."

"Do you understand?"

"Yes."

"Really? Ouch! You hit me! What was that for?"

"Horsefly."

I did understand. For one thing, the Sneed picture became clearer day by day as he went through a series of tests and scans and laboratory analyses. Parts of his brain would not recover. Others might. Still others certainly would come back whole, but there would always be the issue of imbalance and its effect on personality and behavior. Sneed's rapidly recovering motor skills, the specialists told Aretha, could be difficult to manage and possibly even dangerous without the full faculties of adult judgment and the restraints of accurate social awareness. His memories, they said, were valuable only so far as they came within context, which was often very sketchy. Sneed's injured brain was still somewhat in flux, to be sure, but they cautioned his mother that very soon the newness of the whole situation would be gone, the young man's status would be fixed, the doctors and therapists would step back, and Aretha would have to work very, *very* hard.

Actually, I realized, she was thinking of me. Didn't I have my own burdens, in my own life? Should I really put aside my problems to help solve hers?

No, she was telling me, I should not. More specifically, as a pro-active measure against undue density, denial, or neediness on my part, she was telling me, kindly, that she would not allow the Dog to hang around.

Okay.

Yeah.

Sure. Makes sense. Dog damn it.

The guide-shuttle idea, anyway, was wildly unrealistic. Sorgensen and Jesse had seen to that. Sneed would never drive again. Nor would he be able to keep things organized. And Aretha had somewhat warmed to the Nevada Territory, but not enough, for sure, to stake a claim.

Instead she tracked down her mother in Renton, a blue-collar suburb of Seattle. In a phone call that I was allowed to overhear because Aretha was gripping my hand as she made it, she told her mother, essentially, *You are going to help me with this. Yes, you. Me and your grandbaby will be there in a week. Get ready.*

So off we went, west, the three of us in the Cruise Master with a credit card and a week to kill. We fished the Beaverhead, the Big Hole, the Clark Fork, the Clearwater, the Spokane and the Yakima. Sneed was a handful and a delight, like a child with a Swiss cheese adult IQ and a slow left side. Perhaps most remarkable was his fishing, which improved to the extent that he regularly out-fished the Dog and made a lot of noise about it. It helps, apparently, to think less logically, to let your loop fall and your mind wander. Who knew?

"Yeah," I'd counter in my defense, "well, I have the handicap of making sure the two of you don't drown. That's why I'm always fishing downstream in your leftovers. In case you or your mother comes floating by, screaming for help."

"Excuses, Dog, excuses."

"Shall I go upstream then?"

"Hell no!" Aretha would pipe up. "I'm not fishing your back-water!"

In this manner, in a week, we achieved Seattle, where Aretha became nervous and stalled around in a fancy Sixth Street hotel for two days, getting up her courage. We visited the Space Needle and the Science Center, and we ate fresh crab—yes, *crab*—down around Pike Place Market.

After surf and turf and drinks on the third day, when Aretha stopped at the hotel desk and bought Sneed his own room for the night, I knew it was over.

In the morning, we unstuck ourselves and showered sepa-rately. I went outside with them to wait at the curb for Aretha's mother and her man to pull up. Aretha cried. I tried. Sneed banged his knuckles on a street sign pole and then punched me in the shoulder.

Finally the ride came. Aretha took a huge inhale and a last look at the Hoss-Dog, and they left.

Within an hour I was standing for some unknown reason at the edge of the ocean, a fly fisherman with wet boots and wet cheeks, against water too big to fish, under a heavy sky watching waves roll in.

It was strange, though. All that water, around me, from me, ahead of me, and yet I felt powerful somehow. I felt bigger. I felt afloat. I felt like this, at last, was my turn from the dark deep toward home.

Acknowledgments

For this book I owe Chris Miller, friend and first-class fishing guide out of Livingston, for his patience, knowlege, and generosity—and for several good days of fishing over the years. Thanks to Miya, too, for loaning me Chris and giving me a place to stay. I am also grateful to the Aserlind family for their wonderful hospitality out on Ninth Street Island over the years and to Kristy for her skills as a reader. Jerry Kustich also loaned me his time and expertise in reading an earlier version of this book. Thanks to my neighbors, Bob and Amanda, for taking care of Earl during my writing time, and most of all thanks to my family, once again, for living with a writer.

John Galligan lives and teaches in Madison, WI. He is the author of the Fly Fishing mystery series, including the award-winning *The Blood Knot*. He is also the author of *Red Sky, Red Dragonfly*, a novel set in Japan.